THE TITAN GIRLS

A NOVEL

REBECCA J KELLY

Copyright © 2022 Rebecca J. Kelly

ISBN 978-1-7356649-8-9

All rights reserved. No part of this book shall be reproduced or used in any manner without the prior written permission of the author, except for the use of brief quotations in a book review.

This is a work of fiction. Names, characters, places, and incidents are the product of the author's imagination or are used fictitiously. Any resemblance to actual persons, living or dead, events, or locales is entirely coincidental.

For my fellow space cadets.

CHAPTER 1

Failure.

It was the best word to describe the soggy romaine lettuce leaves in front of her. Delphine sighed, nudging the edges of the leaves with her gloved fingers. The heart of the vegetable, just above the hanging roots, was a perfect shade of chartreuse, bright and firm to the touch. But the leaves extending from the heart, which should have pointed straight up toward the roof of the cultivation tent, were frayed and wilted, hanging limp over the hydroponic growth chamber. In a perfect growing environment, those leaves would be a deep green. Thick, sturdy, yet pliable. Instead, they were flimsy and devoid of color.

This wouldn't do.

The new formula for the hydroponic solution was obviously not working properly and despite her best efforts to keep a positive attitude, Delphine was ready to cut the formula loose and start from scratch.

Above her, the large circulation fans shuddered to life as they began their fifteen-minute cycle, pushing warm air from the ceiling of the tent and pulling cool air from the floor. Standing, she ripped off the thick plastic gloves and planted her hands on her hips, blowing a stream of breath out the side of her mouth. It fluttered the stray strands of dark, straight hair falling out of her ponytail.

"Not what you had in mind?"

Delphine turned to see Thessa standing behind her, arms folded in front of her causing creases in the thick, black cultivation coveralls they all wore when working in the tents. Thessa was a tall woman, standing at least ten centimeters taller than Delphine, who wasn't exactly short herself. She was pulling a cart behind her piled high with sample plants plucked from the various growing tables on her way to the testing lab.

"No, it's not." Delphine shook her head and tucked the rogue strands of hair behind her ear, eyes still intent on the wilted lettuce. "I thought for sure this solution would be ace. Maybe it's the zinc…" Her voice trailed off as she mentally ran through the exact nutrient composition of the solution.

Thessa nodded, knowingly. "I can take a look at it for you if you'd like."

Delphine shook her head. She appreciated the gesture. At only nineteen in Earth years, Delphine was part of the colony's third generation of colonists, or third-gens, as they called themselves. Thessa was a second-gen and had years of experience on Delphine, but she wanted to figure this one out on her own. "Thanks, but I can handle it. I might have to start over. I feel like I've tweaked this mixture so many times, it might be time for something fresh."

"Yeah, sometimes that's the best option." Thessa patted her gently on the shoulder. "Good luck," she called as she continued down the aisle, the cart bumping noisily along the grooves in the rigid plastic that covered the entire floor of Cultivation Tent 4.

Delphine touched one of the tiny earpieces that looped over the back of each of her ears. A holographic display sprang to life in front of her eyes, transmitted from the earpieces into her field of vision. The bone conduction earpieces every colonist wore were wirelessly connected to the colony mainframe.

The bugs, as the colonists nicknamed their mandatory headgear, conducted sounds through the tiny bones at the back of the earlobe. Each apparatus was silver and shaped like a C to hug the ear from front to back. Every colonist had a set of magnetic polymer disks placed under the skin behind their ears at birth and this implant allowed the bugs to stick to the skin and provide an almost immediate response when spoken to, even in a low voice. They were also equipped with cameras and holographic projectors allowing the users to take photos and see the mainframe interface where each colonist had a private login and could keep emails, notes, texts, and pictures.

Delphine asked the bugs to display her chemistry journal. Only she could see the holo that now flashed in front of her eyes, so she had no fear of anyone coming along and snooping at her notes. She murmured some notes, detailing the effects of the new solutions on the plants and what she thought might have been the problem. When she finished, she murmured the command to close the holograph and the bugs obeyed, her vision returning to normal.

As she walked down the long tables of plants, she glanced around the cultivation tent. This tent, where she spent at least twelve hours a day, was full of edible greens. Fourteen varieties of lettuce, endive, escarole, chard, arugula, spinach, mustard greens, and bok choy, to name a few. Row upon row of plants in a hundred different shades of green lined the walkways of the tent. Each row was set up with its own light bar and watering tubes, the spray from the nutrient solutions misting out of the watering tubes at various intervals depending on the needs of the plants. Thick roots hung below the clear plastic growing tables.

The colony had eight cultivation tents in total, each identical in dimension—one hundred meters by one hundred meters, offering ten thousand square meters of growing space each, dissected into equal squares by half-meter walkways. Each tent had its own specialty. There were tents dedicated to root vegetables, gourds, beans, nuts, fruits, wheat, corn, and soy, and one tent specially designed for seed cultivation, bringing to life the tiny iterations of the plants that would keep the other tents, and, more importantly, the colonists, alive. The tent system provided all the essential nutrients for one hundred ninety-eight colonists living at Xanadu Station.

Delphine worked on rotation with six other colonists to care for the plants in Cultivation Tent 4. Thessa, the senior member, was in charge of the crew, and she had selected Delphine to be one of the two chemists who handled the hydroponic solution mixtures sprayed on the plants. The solutions gave the plants all the nutrients they would need to grow in the soil-free environment.

Her first assignment as chemist was to tweak the mixture used on several varieties of lettuce as Thessa wasn't satisfied with the output these particular species were producing. So far, the only thing Delphine had managed to do was cause a wilted mess in the sample plants she'd procured to test her new solution.

As she walked through the tent toward the lab area, she shook her head, brow furrowed. What was she missing?

She was so preoccupied, she didn't even notice Rhayn coming toward her, a stack of dry nutrient bags nestled in her arms and piled higher than her head.

"Whoa!" Rhayn said, grabbing Delphine's attention before she plowed into her.

Delphine jumped when she heard the voice, snapping out of her chemical daydream. "Sorry about that. Let me help." Delphine took the top three bags off Rhayn's pile revealing Rhayn's girly face, framed by wavy, dark blond hair cut short and falling just below her chin. Rhayn, like Delphine, was a third-gen, their birthdays only six months apart.

"Thanks. Although, I could have done it myself." Rhayn gave her a wink and a sideways smile. The two of them turned down the walkway leading to the labs.

"Yeah, sure." Delphine rolled her eyes. Rhayn was notorious for biting off more than she could chew in the cultivation tents. Six months earlier, Rhayn had nearly wiped out a whole harvest of kale by packing the storage containers too tight and piling them too high in the storage building. If Thessa hadn't happened to run a random check that day, sixteen crates of kale would have been lost. Rhayn could have faced three days of lost rations had anyone but Thessa found out about the error.

Delphine wouldn't have cared. She thought kale tasted like the cleaning solution they used on the growing tables, but food was food, and the council paid extra close attention to food inventories. If they'd gotten word that such a large volume of greens had been wasted, Rhayn would have been back in the mines for sure. Fortunately, Thessa neglected to record the error after a stern warning lecture and a promise from Rhayn to be more careful when she packaged greens for storage.

Rhayn was a third-gen, like Delphine, and she was still learning the ropes around the tent after a year of hard labor slogging methane in the mines. They were lucky to have Thessa as their lead cultivator. Many of the crews in the other tents were not so fortunate with their bosses.

When they reached the lab doors, Rhayn murmured to her bugs a command to open the door. Every colonist at Xanadu had access to approved spaces based on their job at the colony and their ranking within the gens. Without hesitation, the door beeped and slipped into the wall allowing the pair to enter the lab. They carried the nutrient bags into the dry storage room at the far end of the lab and headed down the narrow hallway to the locker room.

Once there, Delphine stripped off her coveralls and hung them up inside her locker. She checked her bugs. No new text messages. Three new emails. She motioned for the holo to bring up the tiny email icon and saw one email reminding her to take her Vitamin D supplement, one to alert her that her shift in the tent was now complete, and a third marked urgent with a message from the council. She touched the third one and spread her fingers in front of her, widening the document so she could read it.

Addressing all colonists of Xanadu,
The council requests your presence at an impromptu meeting to be held tomorrow at 0915 in the Atrium. We have news that requires input from all colonists. Please be prompt.

Sincerely,
Your trusted council members

Delphine looked up to see the other occupants of the locker room, Rhayn and two other third-gens named Talia and Maya, staring at their holos too. They all looked up at the same time.

"Meribelle," Rhayn said. Talia nodded, a solemn look on her face. Maya gulped.

"Maybe not," Delphine added.

Maya sighed and tossed her hairbrush onto the bench in front of her. She was taking over the next shift for Rhayn and she pulled her thick coveralls over the purple polyester fabric of her third-gen jumpsuit. "It might be for the best. She's been on the brink for weeks now."

Delphine waved her own bugs off and stripped her coveralls down revealing her purple jumpsuit, then stood, closing her locker door with a loud click.

Meribelle was one of the five elders who made up the Xanadu ruling council. The five council members were first-gens and direct descendants of the original twelve settlers who came to Titan and set up the colony seventy-two years prior. Being the largest moon in the Saturnian system and the second-largest moon in the entire solar system, Titan was chosen by Earth to be the first human colony in the outer regions of the system. It helped that Titan had a dense, nitrogen-rich atmosphere and a readily available supply of hydrocarbons to be used for fuel and broken down for building materials.

Two months earlier, the colonists had learned that one of the council members, Meribelle, had developed a rare form of breast cancer. The colonists working at the medical facility at Xanadu had created different types of chemotherapy using the hydrocarbons present on Titan as well as certain plant elements cultivated in the tents. They had successfully treated cancer in more than one patient over the last ten years and their experimentation and drug development processes were only getting better. It was assumed by all the colonists that Meribelle would receive treatment and ultimately be fine.

But it was far from common for the council to call an impromptu meeting like this and the girls in the locker room of Cultivation Tent 4 knew it.

"I heard they opened her up and found the cancer was all over her body," Talia said. As she spoke, she leaned forward and lowered her voice as if that small gesture would do anything to keep the council from hearing their conversation if they wanted to. Delphine shook her head, glancing at the slim camera mounted in the corner of the room.

Rhayn shrugged and unzipped her knee-high boot, slipping it off and pounding on the heel to loosen some irritant that must have been stuck inside. "Maybe they're calling us together to hold hands and sing songs," she said with a smile and a sideways glance shot in Delphine's direction.

"You should take this stuff more seriously, Rhayn," Maya said, wrapping her thick, brown ponytail into a tight bun on top of her head. "This means we'll need to elect a new elder."

"Yeah, right." Rhayn rolled her eyes. "Like that's going to happen."

"Oh yeah?" Maya said. "Why are you so sure? The law states that in the event of a council member's death…"

"…the colonists should exercise their democratic rights to elect a new member and complete the council of five," Rhayn finished. Every colonist knew the three laws by heart. They had been established by Earth before the original colonists arrived and were drilled into them as children. They even had to endure a reading of them at every monthly assembly. "Yeah, we know the law, Maya. But there hasn't been a proper 'election'"— Rhayn raised her hands and made air quotes— "in over twenty years. Ligeia will choose the next elder. You know that as well as I do."

"Lara," Delphine said, shaking her head.

"Lara," Rhayn agreed, pushing her foot back into her boot and pulling the zipper up the side in one swift movement. Ligeia was one of only ten first-gen colonists left, the head of the council of elders, and the most senior colonist at Xanadu. She had final say on all major decisions, and her eldest daughter, Lara, would soon become the only second-gen on the council. Delphine was sure of it. She was also sure that there was no colonist she'd rather see on the council *less*.

Talia was watching the conversation with wide eyes, nibbling the already-shriveled edge of her thumbnail. "Maybe Maya's right. Maybe there will be a proper election…"

Rhayn grabbed her bag and slung it over her shoulder. "Oh, there will be an election all right. But there will only be one candidate. I guarantee it." She turned to Delphine. "Want to grab some provisions? Distribution's open for the next hour. I'm starving."

Delphine shook her head. "Pala's making supper."

"Right." Rhayn nodded and bumped shoulders with Delphine as they walked through the narrow locker room door. "Come on. Walk with me anyway."

CHAPTER 2

The cultivation tents were grouped together on the northern end of Xanadu Station. The colony was set up like a giant wheel, the spokes radiating from a center node that housed the Atrium—the second most important place in the colony aside from the cultivation tents.

The girls made their way through the narrow underground tunnel leading out of Cultivation Tent 4 before joining a larger tunnel called the North Concourse. The mouth of the concourse had branches shooting off in the direction of the other cultivation tents. This was the end of the shift in all the tents so there was plenty of traffic as a dozen other girls made their way out of the smaller tent tunnels and into the concourse.

The air circulation system sent a constant breeze of warm, moist air whistling into the concourse from the tents. Delphine paused a moment and closed her eyes, breathing in the woody scent of the crops.

Rhayn rolled her eyes and grabbed Delphine's hand, pulling her out of her moment's pause. "Come on. I'll never understand you, Del. Always stopping to breathe, or whatever it is you do."

Delphine smiled and squeezed her hand before throwing her arm across Rhayn's shoulder. Only Rhayn was allowed to shorten her given name. "I just like the smell. It makes me happy." She shrugged and Rhayn laughed, a high, sweet giggle that her friend was known for.

The pair walked down the long concourse, their heavy boots thudding softly against the hard plastic flooring of the walkway, chitchat from the rest of the girls leaving the tents causing ghostly echoes to bounce along the curved walls of the concourse. The tunnel had a slight slope, leading its occupants down, down, down, gently into the soft underbelly of the moon. It was long, at least a hundred meters from mouth to mouth, and when the North Concourse eventually widened out as it met up with the Atrium, the girls found themselves one hundred meters under Titan's frigid surface.

There was a reason the Atrium had been chosen as the central hub of the colony—it was a deep, natural cave, and it presented the original colonists with the perfect place to set up shop as they built the rest of the colony around them. In fact, the West Concourse and the living quarters unit that branched off it had been part of the original cave system, a cavity of tubes and rooms they simply had to widen and fortify rather than dig from scratch.

The air in the Atrium was instantly cooler and drier than the breezes circulating in the cultivation tents. Delphine felt the difference almost immediately upon leaving the mouth of the North Concourse and removed her arm from Rhayn's shoulder, instead wrapping it around her body to ward off the chill. She preferred her surroundings warm and musty as opposed to the sharp, dry air of the Atrium that carried the faint, yet distinctly tart smells of alcohol and ammonia seeping in from the natural cave walls that surrounded the room.

Despite the chill and the bright chemical smell of the Atrium, Delphine couldn't help but gaze up and marvel at the cavernous structure. From the bottom floor, where the concourse entrances were located, to the ceiling, it was almost a hundred meters, and at the very top, a jagged oculus watched over the bustling cavern below.

The oculus was the original opening of the cave onto the Titanian surface. It was covered with a clear, polycarbonate dome shortly after the original colonists landed and started manufacturing plastics. The natural cave opening was left unchanged under the dome, with the ragged edges of the Titanian rocks jutting out in an awkward circle from the surrounding cave walls. The result, when viewed from below, was a dazzling skylight allowing a view into the hazy, peach-colored atmosphere above, filtered through the rocky fingers of the natural cave opening.

After the colonists constructed the oculus and buried its edges three meters into the dirt above, the cave could be successfully filled with breathable air, creating the open-air feel of the Atrium. The air filtration systems in the colony took care of 99 percent of the chemicals that seeped into the air from the cave walls, but there was always a hint of ammonia present when walking from the tents into the Atrium.

Delphine touched the wall of the cave next to the entrance of the North Concourse. The rock was cold under her fingers and worn smooth from many thousands of fingers doing the same thing, a casual graze while passing from one space to the next. She and Rhayn turned to the right outside the concourse onto the lowest walkway in the Atrium.

In front of them, spread out in a somewhat circular shape, was the rocky floor of the central meeting area. Ahead of them stood a stone pillar, two meters high, the place where Ligeia, head of the council, would address the colony the next morning.

The Atrium was busy at this time of day, people flooding in and out of shift changes, traversing the wide expanse of the cave floor, moving from one concourse to the next. Above the girls, six more walkways spiraled around the interior of the cave, and cut directly into the walls were the distribution rooms.

Before the colonists built the living quarters, these rooms served as their original workspaces and personal apartments. Now that the colonists didn't live in the Atrium, they'd converted these rooms into the colony distribution center where food harvested from the cultivation tents and goods made in the manufacturing center were distributed.

As they made their way through the crowd to the entrance of the West Concourse, Rhayn grabbed Delphine's hand. "Come on. Rhea needs potatoes."

"I can't," Delphine whined, dragging her feet. "Pala hates it when I make her wait."

"I know, I know. It will only take a minute. *Promise.*"

Delphine grudgingly gave up on the argument and allowed Rhayn to lead her to the nearest steps up to the first walkway above their heads. Sometimes it wasn't worth fighting with Rhayn. She had to pick and choose her battles.

Rhayn took the stairs two at a time and stopped at the first hut in the row, a tiny notch of a room cut into the cave wall where Neena stood, a first-gen with long, graying hair that hung in a thick braid down the back of her red first-gen jumpsuit. Neena looked up at them with kind, dark eyes. "Ah, Rhayn and Delphine. Let's see your accounts."

The girls dutifully pulled their account balances up on their bugs and transferred the information to Neena. There were strict rules regarding the distribution of provisions and each colonist had a ledger in their account showing what provisions they were allotted each month. Depending on the crops, these amounts changed. When the apple harvest was at its peak, the council allotted two additional bushels to each family. When there was a shortage of cucumbers, it might be weeks before they'd have cucumbers on their ledgers.

Delphine didn't really need to pick up any potatoes, but she figured if she was due some, she might as well get them since she was there. After transferring credits from the girls' accounts, Neena turned to divvy up their rations from the big plastic storage bins full of potatoes stacked against the wall behind her.

"Shame about Meribelle," Delphine said as they waited, looking intently at Neena's face to gauge her reaction to the comment. She winked at Rhayn who gave her an amused look. Neena, being a first-gen, could know more about the situation than her younger counterparts.

Neena's eyes faltered slightly as she counted potatoes into the scale. Shaking her head, she said, "Fewer and fewer of us left."

"Do you have any idea who will replace her?" Rhayn asked.

Neena's face hardened, and somehow her dark eyes grew darker in the pale light flowing out of the light strip above them. "We'll see what happens." She didn't elaborate as she finished piling up the allotted weight's worth of potatoes into two plastic bins for the girls.

When she was finished, she turned away and busied herself, rearranging several empty bins to be returned to the tents for future storage. Clearly, they were now dismissed.

Rhayn and Delphine turned to leave, taking the same steps they'd used to climb up to the first walkway. At the bottom of the stairway, they took an immediate right toward the West Concourse—the tunnel leading to the living quarters. It was almost fifty meters from the Atrium to the central living corridor where rows of apartments shot off from either side. They didn't say anything as they walked, each carrying their allotted portion of potatoes, both lost in thought.

When they reached number 113, Delphine's door, Rhayn turned to her. "What do you think Pala will say?"

Delphine shrugged but didn't reply. Rhayn nodded, pecked her on the cheek, and took off in the opposite direction toward her own living compartment. Delphine sighed and turned toward her door. "Unlock, please," she instructed the bugs. The locking mechanism made a slight click as it disengaged. The door swung open and Delphine hauled the heavy bin of potatoes into the tiny kitchen on the other side.

CHAPTER 3

Thunk.

Delphine dropped the potatoes, the sound of the bin hitting the floor reverberating through the thick flooring. Pala, who was chopping herbs at the counter, hadn't noticed her daughter's entrance into their shared apartment until the loud crack of the potato bin made her jump.

She turned to inspect Delphine and her eyes dropped to the potatoes. "You shouldn't have brought those. We hardly have room." Her eyes returned to the delicate green herbs and the thick blade of the knife on the cutting surface in front of her.

"Good to see you too." Delphine watched her mother work on the herbs, lightly chipping away at the dense green bundle of cilantro. Pala's hair was swirled into a loose bun at the base of her neck; random bits of fuzzy curls straggled out from the bun, once dark, but now streaked with gray. She wasn't all that old, but life as a colonist had not been easy on Pala and it manifested itself in her graying hair.

The two women had dark hair, but that was the end of their similarities. Delphine stood a head taller than her mother who always seemed as though she were slumping, her shoulders drooped over because of some invisible weight. She had once been strong, an athlete even, taking first prize among the second-gens in the one-hundred-meter hurdles at the annual Xanadu Games ten years before when Delphine was nine. She remembered being so proud of her mother for that accomplishment.

Now, as Pala hunched over the cutting surface, Delphine wondered how it was possible that this thin, shriveled woman once defeated a field of thirty other participants. Her green, second-gen jumpsuit hung around her bones, wrinkled and wilted, looking more like the failed lettuce leaves Delphine had engineered in the tent rather than a proper item of clothing.

As Pala continued to chop, her dull, gray eyes rested on the bright orange landscape projected on the window that hung over the small, round sink. It seemed to Delphine that she was in a daze, her hands working independently while her mind pondered the landscape. It wasn't a real landscape, of course, as they were almost thirty meters underground. The crystal LED screen was set to mimic the outside landscape based on the time of day. The colonists could choose their view of the landscape based on a series of over a hundred cameras stationed outside Xanadu. At the moment, the view showed it was the middle of the day on Titan, a day that would last almost two hundred hours before darkness set in. The colonists did not keep time based on the Titanian day and night. Rather, they kept Earth time with days lasting twenty-four hours and years lasting 365 days.

Delphine gathered a handful of potatoes and opened the door to their refrigerated pantry. Her mother had a good point—there was little room in the pantry for more produce. But she was able to push aside a bag of oranges and a carton of strawberries and make enough space to slip all of the potatoes into the pantry.

Delphine plopped down onto one of the two chairs pulled up to their little round kitchen table. They had a third chair, but it was hidden in the corner of the room. Piled on top of it were spare jumpsuits, Pala's boots, Delphine's favorite slippers, and both of their Surface Activity Suits or surf suits for short, draped over the chair back looking like someone had taken a knife to one of the colonists and removed their skin.

As she gazed on the thick, brown legs of the chair under its resident pile of clutter, she thought of Aura. An image of her sister flashed into her mind. She was sitting in that very chair, her long, dark hair pinned to the side, tongue tucked between her teeth, concentrating on her third-year homework, her fingers working the stylus on her school tablet as she completed her handwriting assignment. The thought came to her so fast, it caused Delphine to suck in her breath, as if the memory itself had punched her in the gut. She shook her head, mentally chasing the painful memory back into the recesses of her brain.

Aura.

The pain was still so close, she felt as if she might be able to reach out and physically hold it. To keep her mind from retreating again, she turned away from the third chair in the corner and toward her mother. "How was work?"

Pala shrugged but didn't respond. Delphine wasn't surprised. Her mother hated talking about work. She was a scientist in the reproductive sciences unit, meaning she was one of the people in charge of plans for the yet-to-be-born fourth- and fifth-gen colonists.

The manufacturing team had been working overtime the last few months preparing to build a new section of the colony, an expansion that could house more living quarters in preparation for the population growth planned by the council. The surface crews had been excavating the new site for almost a year and it was nearing time to start the building process.

Because of the push to increase the colony population, Pala had been working long hours preparing for a new round of fertilizations. It was for this reason she'd been so intent on her daughter attending that night's supper. They hadn't seen each other, except in brief moments of passing between shifts, in almost a week, and Pala insisted that Delphine make it back to the living quarters to share a meal before they started their next grueling seven days.

Delphine leaned her head back and allowed her shoulders to slump while rubbing her temples, willing her mind and body to relax. Pala continued to chop—she had moved on to onions.

"What are you making?" Delphine asked.

Pala pointed to the faint red glow emanating from the oven. "Roasted peppers, yams, and brussels sprouts. Corn and soy hash seasoned with onions and herbs coming up as well."

"Sounds delicious."

"Hmm." Pala finished chopping and, using the long polycarbonate blade of her knife, scooped up the pile of onions and herbs and dropped them into a pan on the cooktop over the oven that was bursting with sizzles of peanut oil. It made a loud hiss as the fresh ingredients hit the hot oil and Delphine closed her eyes to take in the smell. Her mother, despite the sadness that seemed to wrap itself around her like a wet jumpsuit, always seemed to enjoy cooking—and she was exceptional at it.

Delphine could remember when she was a child, and Pala surrounded her with delicious treats like sweet potato cookies, oatmeal fritters, and homemade cane candies, made from scratch with recipes Pala carried around only in her head. She rarely made sweet treats now, but she did muster up the strength to make a delicious supper for her daughter once a week or so. The rest of the meals, Delphine was on her own, throwing together whatever quick meal she could think of in passing. The truth was, the two women didn't have much in common, but they were both excellent at burying themselves in work.

Pala stirred the sizzling hash, adding the softened soybeans and roasted corn kernels. When the oven timer beeped, she slid out a tray of perfectly roasted vegetables, glistening with soybean oil and speckled with chopped rosemary. She lifted two plates from the shelf above the sink, leaving the third plate, as she always did, and dished up healthy portions for both of them. Delphine poured two small cups of orange juice for them and they sat down to eat.

Starving after her long shift in the tent, Delphine shoveled in a huge bite of the delicious hash, savoring the slight nutty taste left over from the peanut oil and the tart contrast of the herbs. Between bites, she asked, "Did you see the email from the council?"

Pala, who was performing her usual dinnertime ritual of pretending to lift morsels of food into her mouth while mainly pushing the food around the plate, took a gulp of juice and nodded. "Yes, I saw it."

"Is it about Meribelle?"

She shook her head. "You know I don't know that."

"Well, I thought maybe word would have gone around through the older gens. Us third-gens are usually the last to hear about anything of importance in this colony."

Pala sighed, her head tilting to the side as if she barely had the strength to hold it up. "I haven't heard. But I imagine that yes, the meeting will be about Meribelle's passing."

"And?" Delphine asked between bites of roasted yams. "What about succession? Do you think there will be an election?"

"You know the laws, Delphine. In the event of a council member's death, the colony should exercise its democratic rights…"

Delphine rolled her eyes and held up her hand. "Yeah, I know the laws. I'm asking you what you think. Do you think there will be an election?"

Pala straightened in her chair and gazed at the window again. "Of course, there will be an election. That's the way things have always been done."

Delphine scoffed and turned her attention back to her food. "Yeah, well, there hasn't been a death on the council in twenty years. Aren't you just a little concerned that Ligeia will usurp the law and appoint Lara?"

"No, I'm not. The council rules us with faith and a competent hand and I am not concerned about succession." Pala set her fork down on the table and crossed her arms over her chest. It was clear she would not provide any evidence to support Delphine's fears. It was also clear she was done with her eating charade for the evening. Her plate remained covered in food.

Delphine shook her head. "And you'll be okay with Lara being one of the council members? *Lara?*" She put extra emphasis on the last word and it came out sharp and loud.

Pala flinched at the name and turned, not looking Delphine in the eye. "If Lara is elected, there's nothing more to be done…" Her voice had grown faint, losing steam as she spoke.

"Oh please," Delphine said, and she stood suddenly from the table causing her mother to flinch again. She took her empty plate and cup to the sink and wiped them out with a damp dish towel before setting them back on the shelf.

"I'm going for a run," she said, knowing there was an edge to her voice but unable to help it. Through gritted teeth, she wondered if it would ever be possible for her mother to discuss anything with her like an adult. She grabbed her surf suit and lifepack off Aura's forgotten chair and left the living quarters, slamming the door shut behind her.

CHAPTER 4

A steep set of stairs cutting into the rock led from the floor of the Atrium up to the surface where the airlock building stood. As she entered the building, Delphine noticed that two of the six available airlocks had recently been used. The doors were closed with the orange "in use" indicator light beeping, and she could hear the faint buzz of the automatic cleaning system sucking every last bit of dust out of the capsule.

Keeping dust and foreign particles out of the colony was essential to the health of the colonists. Unlike dirt particles on Earth, the dust on Titan was produced when methane rains poured down over the landscape and wore down the rocks, which were actually water ice frozen at such a low temperature they mimicked rocks on Earth. This made the grainy dirt particles on the surface more like soot and could be toxic if inhaled in large quantities.

Colonists were allowed to come and go from the colony as they pleased using the airlocks, but they were responsible for keeping up the strict cleaning protocols necessary to get their surf suits clean before entering the airlock's main room and rejoining the colony. After each cycle, the automatic cleaning system swept every bit of dust and debris out of the airlocks to ensure there was no contamination when the door reopened after surface activity.

Delphine wrapped her surf suit and lifepack into a tight bundle under her arm. She'd taken the stairs two at a time to get to the airlock as fast as she could. The dinner discussion with Pala didn't sit well with her. It was clear Pala would stand behind the first-gens on the council tomorrow morning. This didn't surprise Delphine, but it didn't stop her from feeling true disappointment.

Since Aura, there had been almost no trace of the mother she once knew. She had withered away, mentally, physically, and spiritually, to the point where Delphine didn't even recognize the pale ghost that shared the same living space as her. The Pala of her youth would have been up and about at the news of a council member's death. She would have been calling her friends to discuss the next move, planning who she might nominate at the upcoming election, and certainly wouldn't be hastily backing Ligeia's decisions and acting as if all was well.

Delphine dropped her pack onto the nearest bench and began unrolling her surf suit. She needed to get outside, get her blood pumping. She needed to think.

The surf suit was a remarkable invention that the Xanadu colonists had created about a decade after they arrived on the moon. They originally used what Earth would call spacesuits to explore the surface and build their colony, but the suits were bulky and eventually wore out. Since they were made from elements found on Earth, it was not an option for the colonists to recreate them. Instead, they had to make a version of a spacesuit from the building materials readily available on Titan.

The answer to their problem lay, literally, on the ground around the colony in the form of substances called tholins. These tiny bits of organic hydrocarbons rained down from the Titanian sky and were responsible for the orange hue that colored the dusty surface. Tholins were primarily carbon-based and polymerlike in their composition, meaning they could be melted down and formed into a wealth of different materials. They were the basis for the plastics manufactured at the colony and used to build all colony structures. Tholins could also be worked into a highly elastic material with low thermal conductivity that the colonists used to make their surf suits.

The suits carried tiny heating wires embedded in the material all throughout which, when turned on, kept a human body at a comfortable temperature even when outside the colony in the frigid temperatures of the Titanian landscape. Because of the dense atmosphere, the surface of the moon only received about one-tenth of a percent of the sunlight humans enjoyed on the surface of Earth. This lack of warmth caused the surface to reach temperatures close to 180 degrees below zero Celsius.

Delphine unrolled her surf suit and pulled the left leg of the suit over her left boot. The material was pale gray and had the consistency of thick, rubbery skin. Once it wrapped around her leg, it sucked tight against her jumpsuit, causing an airtight seal. She pulled on the other leg and hiked the rest of the suit up around her waist, the rubbery material encasing her legs.

One at a time, she slid her arms into the suit, her fingers slipping into the gloves. The suit thinned out on the gloves and around the fingers to allow for more dexterity. Delphine found that this sometimes left her hands cold and she had to crank up the heat in this area of the suit to compensate. But it was worth it when she needed her fingers to dig for gemstones or fiddle with the tiny fittings in a malfunctioning lifepack.

The surf suit came up over Delphine's head, leaving only her face and chin exposed. She reached into her lifepack and pulled out her faceplate, a clear, polycarbonate plastic made specifically to conform to the features of her face. She placed the faceplate over her face and pressed it firmly into the grooves made for it in the surf suit.

Once snapped into place, the edges formed an airtight seal with the suit. She zipped up the triple zipper that ran along the front of the suit from her groin to her chin. The zipper had two polycarbonate plastic zippers sandwiching a zipper made from the surf suit material. When the suit was full of air, the inner zipper expanded allowing for an airtight seal.

With the suit fully encasing her body, Delphine pulled up her pugs to make sure they had connected with the suit. They would control the suit systems while she was outside. She snapped the hose from the lifepack into place, attaching it to the hose port on the back of the surf suit.

The port led to the oxygen tubing embedded in the suit, which filled the cavity around her face and head with breathable air. The lifepack held the oxygen tanks as well as the battery pack that ran the suit's life-support systems. She strapped it onto her back like a backpack and secured it around her waist with straps.

"Bring surface activity suit online, please," she said.

The suit responded immediately to her voice and she felt the fresh flow of air coming in from the oxygen tubing. The heating system started around her feet and she sensed the heat rising through the suit as it turned on in various sections before finally reaching her fingers.

"Turn up glove heat to six, please."

She quickly felt the warmth grow around her fingers. On the interior of the faceplate, the suit flashed a series of readings—

oxygen levels, carbon dioxide levels, surface temperature, and suit temperature, along with an "all clear" stamp showing that there were no issues and she could go ahead with her surface walk.

"Waive readings for now," she said.

The readings disappeared leaving only the clear faceplate in front of her. Delphine made her way to airlock number three to the left of the bench where she'd dressed. She pressed a command into the screen next to the door and it lifted, allowing her to enter the airlock. Once inside, she entered another series of commands and the door dropped down behind her. The seals emitted a clicking sound, tightening on the door as it prepared to open.

With a squeal, the system pulled the air from the lock and replaced it with the nitrogen-rich atmosphere of Titan. This took about thirty seconds and was punctuated with hissing and snarling noises coming from the air compressors in the corners of the small room. When this cycle completed, the outer door lifted revealing the pale orange world beyond.

Delphine took a few deep breaths to make sure the air in the surf suit tasted okay and asked for a final check of the suit readings. When she was satisfied that everything looked normal, she stepped out of the airlock and pressed the large, red button to her left, closing the outer door.

Titan was the only known place in the solar system that possessed a thick atmosphere similar to Earth's. The planet Venus had an atmosphere, but it was so thick, a human would be crushed to a pulp and melted shortly thereafter by the runaway greenhouse effect should they have tried to land on the surface. The planet Mars had an atmosphere as well, but it was so wispy, it represented only a fraction of a percent of that on Earth's surface.

The human body was meant to exist with the weight of an atmosphere pressing down on it. Without an atmosphere to apply pressure to the body, rapid expansion of the body's gasses would occur, possibly rupturing the lungs and causing the body fluids to boil off at a rapid pace. Astronauts going into space and walking on other planets and moons required not only a system to provide them with air to breathe, but also a pressurized suit to keep the body tissues stable in the vacuum environment. Pressurized suits could be large, bulky, and hard to navigate.

This very issue was one of the reasons Titan was chosen as the location for the first colony in the outer solar system. The atmosphere on Titan provided the pressure necessary to keep the human body intact without a bulky pressure suit.

The surf suit needed only to provide thermal regulation and a regular stream of air for Delphine to breathe. It had to be airtight because the Titanian atmosphere was toxic if it came in contact with skin, eyes, or lungs, but otherwise, the surf suit had an easy job to do considering the harsh environment for which it was made.

Delphine gazed around at the landscape. It was daylight. The hazy atmosphere on Titan allowed only a fraction of the sun's light onto the surface. But even with the minuscule amount of light, the moon seemed to emanate an orange glow from its surface: dim, but bright enough to allow Delphine to see without having to use her suit lights.

After doing a few quick stretches and some jumping jacks, she set off on a slow jog away from the airlock and toward the north where she could see the huge cultivation tents in the distance. She decided to make her way out to the construction site, just to the west of the cultivation tents. It was evening time for the colony, so she didn't think anyone would be working and she desired a nice, isolated run to unravel her thoughts from the day's events.

As she moved, the Titanian dirt rustled under her feet and she kicked up little clouds of tholin dust behind her. In front of her, she could see beyond the construction site where the dunes lay.

She had only been to the dunes once, when she was a child, and she had never been back. The older gens told stories about how the dunes looked the same as the dunes on the deserts of Earth, and how the Xanadu Plains were chosen for the colony because they offered close access to so many geological features, including the dunes.

As it turned out, studying the dunes had been a flop. The original colonists spent years searching them, taking samples, hoping to find something useful and scientifically worthy in them. All they'd found were hydrocarbons and particles of water ice.

Things were much more exciting to the east.

Baikal Lacus was a thirty-five-kilometer-long methane lake that bordered the colony. Baikal wasn't a deep lake in comparison to other lakes the colonists had studied on the surface and was only about a hundred meters at its greatest depth. But it was full of soupy, viscous liquid methane that the colonists mined to provide Xanadu Station with power. A huge methane power plant sat directly to the east of the manufacturing facilities, pumping methane through a pipe system directly from the lake. They were fortunate, so far away from the sun, that the moon itself had all the elements they needed to keep themselves in an endless supply of electrical power.

As Delphine jogged, she glanced to the eastern end of the complex and saw the shimmering shores of the lake off in the distance, surrounded by an endless expanse of flat plains.

Directly between her path and the lake was the mine, a ragged gorge cut twenty meters into the Titanian surface. The peachy color of the mine and the thick edges where the excess rock was piled reminded her of the edge of the valley where the accident occurred.

Aura.

Again, she felt the surge of pain well up inside her chest at the thought of the name. She straightened up and ran faster to beat the memory back into its respective holding compartment in the recesses of her brain. Her feet crunched on the pebbly rock as her pace quickened.

Mining at the colony consisted of breaking the ground up with huge, methane-powered excavators and hauling the broken rock to the smelting plant south of the mine. There, the colonists melted the rock down and put it through a rigorous filtration and desalination system until only the hydrogen, oxygen, and by-products remained, separated into neat storage tanks. It would have been difficult for an Earth-dweller to believe, but the gorge in front of Delphine supplied the colony with all the potable water they needed and all the oxygen they could breathe.

Mining by-products served as fertilizer in the cultivation tents and were melted down into the polymers used to make a variety of plastics the colonists needed to build infrastructure, equipment, and even the surf suit Delphine wore on her body. As she ran, looking out over the lake and the mine, she thought about the brilliant chemical makeup of the land and how, without it, the Xanadu colony simply would not exist.

There was no way Earth could have understood how perfect the moon would be for colonization. True, it had been chosen for a reason. Their space agencies had sent many probes to the moon and had several satellites dedicated to studying it before the colonists first arrived. But the amount of knowledge the scientists at Xanadu had garnered in the generations since that first landing was leaps and bounds ahead of what they had brought with them from Earth.

As Delphine ran, she began to feel the warmth of her muscles overpowering the surf suit.

"Turn body heat down to four, please," she instructed and the suit obeyed.

In an instant, Titan's chill pressed in on her from all directions and the cooling effect gave her skin a fresh tingle. She pressed forward. The huge black bubbles of the eight cultivation tents stood out in stark contrast to the pale glow of the hazy atmosphere behind them. The construction site came into view not far in the distance.

The plan was to build a new set of apartments here that would connect through an underground tunnel to the current apartment block, although only the excavation had been done so far. Three large excavators sat unused inside the deep hole of the site where the new living quarters would soon be built. Rough piles of excavated rock stood behind the site, cutting a sharp contrast to the smooth, rolling dunes beyond.

As she neared the site, she noticed something moving on the east side of the excavated hole.

CHAPTER 5

Delphine tilted her head to one side, trying to get a better view of the source of the movement. Closing in, she soon saw two figures wearing surf suits, obviously the pair that had used the other two airlocks before Delphine had entered the airlock room.

The other two colonists were hunched over a mound of debris pulled up from the hole. They appeared to be picking through it, digging with their hands into the icy soil. As she ran closer, Delphine could see immediately that one of the suits had a bright dye pattern swirled all around it in striking blues and purples.

Rhayn.

She would know her best friend's surf suit anywhere. Rhayn had gotten the suit only a few years earlier for her birthday and her mother had been pissed when Rhayn took it upon herself to break into the materials shop and steal pigments so she could dye the gift. The act hadn't surprised Delphine at all. It was exactly the sort of thing Rhayn had been doing her whole life. But the deed earned her two weeks of lost rations, not to mention a disappointed sigh from her mother every time Rhayn donned the swirly patterned surf suit.

When Delphine asked Rhayn why she'd chosen blue and purple to adorn the light gray suit, she'd shrugged, saying, "I needed something more."

Delphine approached the pair. As she walked up behind them, Rhayn turned, flashing Delphine a smile through her faceplate. The voice comms in the surf suits were automatically programmed to hook up with other suits in range to allow the occupants to speak to one another freely. This comm link could be turned off, but it had to be done manually.

"Well, well. What are you up to?" Rhayn asked, standing and brushing dust from the legs of her suit. "Just a little midnight jog?"

"It's not midnight," Delphine said, although she had no idea what time it was. She prompted her suit to display the current time on her faceplate and saw that it was after 2230 hours. She was genuinely surprised it had been that long, before she remembered she'd gotten off work late that night and had a late supper with Pala.

Rhayn shrugged. "Close enough. Past your bedtime anyway. Did you have another skirmish with Pala?"

Delphine flinched. She and her mother didn't fight that much... did they? "No skirmish," she said. "Just a light disagreement."

Rhayn shrugged, the slight smile curling on her lips indicating she knew better. "About the succession, huh?"

Delphine only nodded and glanced down at Rhayn's partner, still bent over the pile of rubble, not paying much attention to them. She could see through the faceplate that this was Rho, Rhayn's twin sister.

Rho stood taller than Delphine and Rhayn. Although the two of them looked similar in the face, they couldn't have been more different. Rhayn was silly, charming, the kind of girl who kept your secrets and told you she loved you. Rho was quiet, witty, and never let anyone get too close. She and Delphine were friends, of course, but didn't share the same kind of friendship Delphine and Rhayn shared: unbreakable since they were young children. Rho had always been on the outskirts of their relationship, peering in from time to time, but never coming too near the two of them.

Rhayn and Rho were close too, but in a different kind of way. In a twin kind of way. There were times when Delphine watched them whisper to each other in tones only the two of them could understand. She'd watched them cuddle against each other when they were sad, press their foreheads together while they laughed, and she'd swear she'd even seen them read each other's minds.

Twins were uncommon on Titan. In fact, Rhayn and Rho were the only pair to have been born in all of the third-gen and only the fifth pair to have ever been born in the colony. All of the colonists at Xanadu were female and they used in vitro fertilization for reproduction. Medics harvested eggs from motherhood applicants and fertilized them using thousands of male DNA samples that had been frozen on Earth and made the trip to Titan along with the original twelve colonists seven decades earlier. The samples now resided in the cryogenic freezing chamber in the medical wing, which was part of the science and medical complex located south of the Atrium.

Every colonist learned the history of Xanadu as a young child during their school years and all colony records were kept in the colony library for reference. According to the official logs, Earth chose a team of twelve women to be the first colonists on Titan. Women were chosen for a practical reason: they were necessary to give birth to offspring. The idea was that instead of sending men, frozen male DNA could be sent instead. This would free up space and resources on the journey to Titan and would allow for a deeper genetic pool. Once there, the women established the Xanadu colony, created and expanded infrastructure, and started the colonization process by using the frozen samples to reproduce. All embryos were to be engineered as female until Earth deemed it time to start breeding male colonists, again, in an effort to deepen the genetic pool for the longer term of the colony. So far, that command had never come and, as directed by Earth, all offspring continued to be engineered as female.

Twins were very uncommon considering the fact that the embryos were fertilized in the lab. But it did happen from time to time that an embryo would split after implantation, causing the birth of identical twins.

Rhayn and Rho, however, were not identical, that much was clear simply by looking at them. Rho was tall and slender, with sleek brown hair cropped short to her head. Rhayn was curvier with similarly short-cropped hair, but it was lighter, more of a sandy blond, and thick with waves. They even had different colored eyes—Rho's were an amber hazel while Rhayn's were deep brown. But they were unmistakably siblings, sharing the same high cheekbones and oval face.

They were fraternal, meaning they came from two separate embryos—an even rarer occurrence at the colony. In fact, the twins standing before Delphine now were the only example of fraternal twins in the history of the colony. The scientists at Xanadu had mastered the in vitro process to such an art, it was rare to have even a single pregnancy fail. So, when the twins were born nineteen years earlier, it was considered a strange quirk in the process that somehow, two fertilized embryos happened to be implanted into their mother, Rhea.

Delphine knew how strange it had been because her mother, Pala, was with Rhea during their birth. When Delphine and Aura were children, Pala often told them the story of the night the twins were born.

Rhea went into labor just as a hull breach alarm went off in the hospital wing of the science and medical complex. All colonists had to rush to ensure the breach didn't compromise the air quality of the entire colony. Any colonist with a surf suit handy was put to work fortifying the outside walls, while the rest of the colonists moved important scientific experiments and medical patients out of the wing.

It was a terrifying night, Delphine remembered her mother saying, and Rhea couldn't have picked a worse time to start feeling the contractions. So, Pala stayed in Rhea's apartment with her until the babies were born. She was shocked at how easily they came into the world—not a single complication. Pala, who worked in the reproductive sciences unit, had the medical training necessary to perform the basic functions necessary to deliver a baby and ensure the safety of the mother after delivery. Together, they bathed and swaddled Rhayn and Rho, and while Rhea fed them, Pala cleaned up the living quarters.

The next day, after the hull breach was successfully fixed, the colonists met in the Atrium so the council could give their blessing to the new twins. It was considered a good omen by the colonists whenever twins were born. Pala always mentioned how proud Ligeia was of Rhea for carrying and birthing the babies, and she even kissed the two infants on the top of their heads in front of the entire colony. They wouldn't learn until later in their lives that they were, in fact, fraternal and that their birth had been caused by an error in the in vitro process.

 Delphine remembered a time as a young girl when the medical staff at the colony took a great interest in the twins, trying to understand the error that would lead two embryos implanted in one woman. Rhea was always very protective of the twins, never allowing the medics to study them too closely. She didn't want them to feel different from the other colonists simply because they had been born under a strange circumstance.

 Rhayn knelt back down to the pile of rubble they had been examining before Delphine interrupted them. Rho continued to stand, her amber eyes studying Delphine as if she'd caught them in the middle of something secret and important.

 Delphine turned her attention to the pile of rock and asked, "What are you looking at in there?"

 Rhayn continued to sort through the rock with her fingers, picking up small piles of it and allowing them to fall through her gloved fingers. "My detector said there was Tanite here. Must have been dragged up with the excavation. But we can't seem to find it."

Tanite was a clear mineral found on Titan and used by the colonists to make jewelry, beads, and other decorative elements for their clothes and living quarters. Neither Rhayn nor Rho were all that good at making anything with it, but several of the colonists were talented at that type of thing and would pay good credits for sizable chunks of Tanite to make little odds and ends to sell to others.

"Well, the detector said there *might* be Tanite here. It's probably microscopic," Rho said, shaking her head and dusting her surf suit off with her hands.

"Yeah, well, even so, I wanted to check it out," Rhayn said.

"So, you're out scrapping at ten thirty at night?" Delphine asked, puzzled by this.

Rhayn gave the rock pile one final flick with her hand before standing and brushing the dust from her fingers. She shrugged. "Yeah, why not? There's always so many people out here during the day. We figured we'd check out some of these readings. Rho tweaked the detectors on our surf suits to see if we could pick up bigger stashes, so we figured we'd come out here tonight and give them a try."

Rho worked as a mechanic in the engineering lab located next to the library. She was also great with computers and programming. Delphine wouldn't put it past her to soup up a surf suit so it could more easily detect valuable minerals on the surface.

"Care to join us, running girl?" Rhayn asked. "We're planning to check out all the rock piles they've pulled up on this side of the dig. When we ran a preliminary scan earlier, the stuff was showing up everywhere. Could mean some serious credits! We'll split 'em with you."

Delphine glanced at Rho to make sure she was okay with this arrangement. Rho simply shrugged, not one for words, but Delphine did notice a slight smile cross the corner of her mouth.

"Why not," Delphine said. "Nothing else to do in this place." She gestured around at the desolate landscape. Despite her previous desire to be alone on her run, she was actually glad she'd run into the twins. A bit of treasure hunting at the excavation site sounded like a good way to take her mind off her mother and the morning assembly meeting.

The three girls spent the next hour using Rho's surf suit scanners to analyze piles of rock and debris. When they got a hit, they'd all get down and dig through the icy soil, even making a game of it with Rhayn offering a kiss on the cheek to the first person who struck loot.

Rho had been right. Much of what they were detecting was microscopic, but after a few bouts of digging, they found six Tanite crystals buried about a half meter down in the rubble. The Tanite wasn't huge, each chunk about two centimeters in diameter, but it was something and would net them about ten credits for each piece.

While Rhayn and Delphine dug after one particularly strong hit by the detector, Rho walked ahead to scout out more potential dig sites. Delphine was getting closer to the base of a particularly big chunk of rock, sweat beading up on her forehead from the effort, when she heard a transmission from Rho about thirty meters ahead of where they were digging.

"Hey guys," Rho said, her voice its usual calm, but with a hint of curiosity underlying her words. "I think you need to come see this."

CHAPTER 6

"What do you think it is?" Rhayn asked, tapping the surface of the object with the tip of her boot.

"Your guess is as good as mine," Delphine said, squatting to get a better look at it.

The threesome stood in a small valley on the northern end of the construction site, a good half kilometer from the colony. Before them lay a smooth, dark object partially buried in the dusty orange Titanian surface.

The part they could see was about a meter square and seemed part of a larger, disk-shaped object. Touching the smooth surface, Delphine wiped away a thin layer of dust and peered at the object. She glimpsed something familiar and continued to smooth dust away from the surface. Soon, her entire faceplate reflected back at her.

"Is this metal?" she asked, turning toward Rho and Rhayn who stood behind her.

Rho bent down. "Could be. What else would reflect like that?"

Metal was rare on Titan. Although different forms of metal did exist within the surface layers of the moon, they were rare and difficult to find. The colonists used other resources from the planet to craft most of their building materials, tools, and machinery. The only real metal Delphine had ever seen was in the relics that still existed from the original colonists. They had metal in their spacesuits and in their tools, but anything made on Titan since that time would have been forged out of industrial plastics.

"How'd you find it?" Rhayn asked, tapping her sister on the shoulder.

"My detector picked it up. It looked like a huge deposit of Tanite at first, but the makeup didn't match." Rho asked her bugs to project the detector's findings on her faceplate. She paused as she read through them. "It says the makeup is unknown. But that's just the programming. I have it specifically set up to search for Titanian minerals, not metals. I could change the search parameters and rescan this, but I can't do it out here."

"What should we do with it?" Rhayn asked, her hands planted on her hips, head cocked to the side, studying the object from a distance. It looked like Rhayn didn't want to get too close to it.

Delphine glanced at Rho who was still reading through her detector findings, then back to Rhayn. "Well," she said, "I don't think it's going to hurt us. Let's dig it out and see how big it really is."

"You don't think this is from..." Rhayn said, biting her lower lip, her voice drifting off before she completed the thought.

"Earth," Rho finished for her. "It's gotta be. This wasn't made here."

"Yeah, well, we'll never know if we don't dig it out," Delphine said. She planted her knees in the dust next to the object and started to dig around the edges.

Rho followed her lead, walking around to the other side. Rhayn hung back, her face twisted in a worried grimace.

"It'll be a lot easier if you help us," Delphine called back to her.

With a sigh, Rhayn gave in and dropped to her knees in front of the object. With the three of them all digging at the same time, it didn't take them long to completely uncover it.

The object was saucer-shaped, three meters in diameter, perfectly round, its surface made from gray, polished metal. It was thickest in the center, about a meter thick, tapering to the edges. Underneath it were six legs, evenly spaced to allow it to settle on the surface of the moon. Other than the legs, nothing protruded from it.

Delphine glanced around the area and noticed they were standing inside a small circular valley surrounding the object. "This is a landing crater. It must be some sort of space probe."

Rho nodded and pointed at the pile of dust that had once covered the object. "I'll bet it got covered up during the last storm. When was that, two, maybe three months ago?"

Rhayn nodded, peering down to inspect the legs of the vehicle. "More like three. I remember, we were coming off shift during the last harvest when it hit."

Delphine remembered the storm well. It had lasted three full days with winds topping 130 kph. The entire colony had been forced to hunker down in their apartments and they'd closed off the West Concourse in case there was a breach in any of the aboveground areas. Fortunately, the tents and all the manufacturing facilities were built to withstand 150 kph winds, so there hadn't been much damage, just a few busted tiles on the outer layers of plastic that surrounded the cultivation tents.

Delphine ran her hand over the top of the probe, examining the surface closely.

"What are you doing?" Rhayn asked.

"I'm trying to see if there's any sort of hatch or opening. I mean, this thing has to have something inside of it. They wouldn't send an empty flying saucer all the way to Titan for no reason."

Rho and Rhayn both nodded and followed suit, running their gloved hands over the top of the probe to find a way to open it. Delphine felt around on the underside and her finger caught a tiny ridge in the metal. When she pushed it on, a panel popped open and she knelt down to take a closer look.

"Hey, come look at this," she called to the twins who moved to her side and peered at the panel over her shoulder.

Delphine lifted the panel to reveal a screen about ten centimeters square and nothing else. When she touched the screen, she jumped back as the probe emitted a loud noise, loud enough that they could hear it through their surf suits.

"Shit!" Rhayn yelped, grabbing her chest, her heavy breathing rattling over the comm links.

Rho laughed at her. "Gave you a bit of a scare, did it?" She gently pushed Delphine to the side and touched the screen again to reveal what looked like a menu of options. With the hazy light and the awkward placement of the probe, it was difficult to read what was on the screen. Rho turned to Delphine. "We should take this into the colony. Then we can look it over properly."

Rhayn grabbed her sister's arm. "There's no way we can bring this thing in without Ligeia confiscating it," she said. "If she even catches wind that we know it's here and didn't tell her, we'll be in for hard labor for sure."

"What if we take it to the maintenance shed north of the cultivation tents?" Delphine said. "It really only gets used during the big harvests and we aren't due for one of those for a few more weeks. Plus, it has an airlock."

The shed was used to house some of the larger pieces of cultivation equipment as well as all the excavation machinery. Because of the construction, the excavation machinery was in use and wouldn't be back in the shed until the build site was complete. The shed sat fairly dormant and would stay that way until the tent crews needed to get in there before harvest. It had its own airlock along with an access tunnel to Cultivation Tent 4 where Rhayn and Delphine worked.

Rho nodded. "Sounds like a plan to me."

"What if we get caught with it?" Rhayn asked. "I don't know about you, but I'm not excited about the idea of having to explain this to the council."

Delphine thought about it for a moment and put her hands on her hips. "Well, we'll just take it in there for now so we can get a better look at it. It's probably old, you know, predates the colony. Earth sent lots of probes here before the original twelve got here. After we get a good look at it, we can always bring it back here and act as if nothing happened."

This seemed to placate Rhayn who nodded. Rho seemed unsure. She gazed at the probe, her amber eyes hard, her mouth drawn in a tight line. After a moment, she nodded too but didn't say anything.

The three of them surrounded the probe and Delphine counted down as they lifted it up off the surface. It was heavy but not unmanageable. The worst part was getting it over the lip of the impact crater. After that, it wasn't too difficult to carry it over the even terrain between the landing site and the machinery shed located at the north end of the colony complex.

It took about thirty minutes to traverse the distance and all three girls were gasping for breath by the time they approached the extra-wide airlock to the shed. With machinery coming in and out of it, it needed to be much larger than the airlock Delphine had used to get out on the surface hours earlier. They opened the outer door and carried the probe inside before Rho pressed the big red button that closed the door and started the decontamination process. Two minutes later, they'd been blasted by bursts of air and the entire space had been vacuumed clean.

Cool air flooded into the space and the inner door opened automatically, allowing the girls to drag the probe into the open area in the center of the storage shed. To call the room a simple storage shed would be an understatement as it stood ten meters tall at its center and covered five hundred square meters of floor space. With the absence of the excavating machinery, the shed was largely empty save for a few pieces of harvesting equipment lining the northern wall. Eerie orange light filtered through from the translucent plastic panels that made up most of the ceiling.

They nudged the probe through the inner airlock door and closed it behind them. Delphine carefully placed her end of the probe on the thick plastic flooring and walked to the control panel next to the airlock door, lightly touching the display panel to bring it to life. She pulled up the program for the lights and the soft glow of the overhead light panels came to life, illuminating the object in front of them.

In the light of the storage shed, the girls stared wide-eyed at the probe's surface. It shone the reflection of the lights almost perfectly, making it look like it had light emanating from itself.

Rho pulled her faceplate off and quickly stripped off her surf suit, stepping out to show her purple third-gen jumpsuit and lace-up calf-high boots. She reached under the probe to find the hidden panel they'd discovered before and touched it, watching it open before their eyes. When she touched the screen on the inside, the probe made the same noise it had out on the moon's surface: a high, piercing noise that reverberated over the empty space of the storage shed causing the girls to quickly cover their ears.

"That's strange…" Rho muttered, examining the inside screen closely.

"What's strange?" Rhayn asked, pulling her own surf suit free from her legs and tossing it to the ground.

Rho was silent for a moment while she examined the inner part of the probe. "I don't really understand any of these commands. There are numbers here, but there are also symbols that I've never seen before."

She touched the screen in several places and without warning, a cap on the top of the probe gently shifted and began to lift up, revealing more of the probe's inner workings. Delphine, having shed her own suit, walked over to the machine and knelt over it, looking into the one-meter-diameter opening that had just presented itself at the top of the probe.

Inside were a host of different instruments. They appeared to be scientific instruments used for atmospheric study, but the technology was nothing she recognized. The probe obviously still had power because several lights flashed on the delicate machines inside.

"It almost looks like this is the outer casing to hold these scientific instruments," Delphine said, pointing into the opening.

Rho was still busy punching in commands on the screen. She seemed to be figuring her way around the system. She pressed another set of commands and a similar cap on the bottom of the probe opened up and gently fell to the floor. Underneath, there were more scientific instruments. They looked more like soil- and rock-testing equipment.

"I think you're right," Rho said. "But this isn't the kind of technology I've ever seen before. I think I'm figuring out these symbols though. It appears to be a sort of shorthand. This is obviously a control panel."

"Wait," Rhayn piped up, crossing her arms over her chest. "Why would there be a control panel on a space probe? If this thing was sent from Earth decades before the colony was here, it would need to be totally self-sufficient, right? I mean, it's not like there were people running around before Xanadu who could operate it and open it up. So, why have a control panel?"

Rho and Delphine looked at each other, neither offering up an answer to the question. The three girls stood silent for a moment before Rho cleared her throat. "Maybe it's not from before. Maybe it was sent here recently."

Rhayn shook her head. "No way. There's a war going on there. Ligeia says they have no way to send anything here until the war is settled."

Delphine watched as Rhayn continued to shake her head. She turned to Rho who glanced at Rhayn before dropping her eyes to the floor. An alert pinged from her bugs. She pulled up the holo to see a message from Pala.

Where are you??

Delphine sighed, clearing the bugs from her vision. "I need to go. Pala's asking where I am and it is past midnight. We have to be at the meeting at 0915 and then we have a full day of work in the tents."

Rho nodded and closed the access panel to the control screen on the probe. Instantly, the two open caps slid back into place and the probe became a solid saucer once again. "Yeah, I have work tomorrow too. We'd better head out."

"What about this thing?" Rhayn asked, thumping the underside of it with her foot.

Delphine pointed to the northwest corner of the machine shed. "Let's take it over there. We can pull one of those tarps over it and hide it behind that big harvester. Nobody will find it there. Then we can come back tomorrow after work and take a better look at it." She gestured toward Rho. "Maybe you can work out the computing and figure out that shorthand. There could be some communications built into the code."

Rho nodded. "I'll do a bit of research while I'm at work tomorrow and see if I can find anything in the mainframe archives to figure out what the symbols might mean."

They lifted the probe and moved it to the corner of the shed before pulling a dark gray tarp over it. When they were finished, they inspected their work and amazingly, it blended right in with the wall and the machinery around it.

After they were satisfied that nobody would mess with their find, they suited up and made their way through the airlock and back out to the surface.

CHAPTER 7

The alarm sounded in Delphine's ear, a light, airy ping coming through her bugs. She had been slogging through that space between dreaming and waking, her feet leaden as she tried to push forward through a dream where it seemed as though she was walking through thick sludge. She was carrying something in her arms, a white bundle, but she had no idea what it was. All her dreaming mind knew was that it was very important and she needed to move quicker. But the substance around her feet wouldn't allow it and she became more tired and frustrated the longer the dream went on.

When at last she realized the pinging noise was there to rouse her from her dream, her eyes flew open and a gasp escaped her throat. She sat up in her bed, panting and damp all over. Her bugs displayed the time, 0856. They were due at the meeting in less than twenty minutes.

Pala floated through the small hallway between their rooms and gazed inside Delphine's door. "Bad dreams?" She clasped a cup of tea in her hand, her long, thin fingers creating a web around the white, plastic mug. She was already dressed in her green jumpsuit, her hair pulled back in a tight bun at the back of her head.

Delphine shook her head, running her fingers through her hair. "Not bad, just strange."

Pala nodded and looked into her tea as if she knew exactly what Delphine was talking about. "You shouldn't stay out so late. It's not good for your sleep rhythms."

Rolling her eyes, Delphine flung her legs off the side of the bed and stood, ignoring her mother's comments. When she'd come in last night after finding the space probe, she'd been so tired, she nearly collapsed into Aura's chair as she took off her gear and left it in a pile on the kitchen floor. She knew her mother had been awake, but not a word came from Pala's bedroom while Delphine brushed her teeth and washed her face.

As she'd lain in bed, she remembered hearing Pala walk to the kitchen and sit with a loud sigh. Pala didn't sleep much anymore.

Now, as she watched Delphine rummage through a drawer for a fresh jumpsuit, Pala said lightly, "We'd better not be late for the meeting this morning. What were you doing out so late anyway? You can't have been out on the surface all that time."

"We won't be late," Delphine replied as she pushed past Pala on her way to the bathroom. She opted to ignore her mother's second question.

In the shower, Delphine set the water temperature the coldest it would go, allowing the low-flow showerhead to spray her body with a frigid mist. The icy water droplets warmed on her skin and slithered down her body, taking some of her heat with them. She stood in the cold shower as long as she could bear it before jumping free from the icy blast and wrapping herself in a thick robe.

After she dressed and ran a comb through her hair, she pulled it back in a ponytail and went to the kitchen to grab some fruit and a soy bar. Pala was waiting for her there.

"Ready?" Pala asked.

Delphine nodded, her mouth full of blackberries. The two women left apartment 113 with exactly five minutes to spare before the meeting started. Other colonists straggled along with them down the concourse that led to the Atrium, but it was apparent once they neared the end of the long tunnel that most of the colony had already gathered at the meeting spot.

The air grew cooler, crisper, the closer they came to the Atrium's open space. Delphine picked up that familiar, tart ammonia scent and curled her nose at it. As the West Concourse opened up into the Atrium, she looked around—almost all of the 193 colonists of Xanadu were already there. It had been nearly thirty days since they'd had a colony-wide meeting, so she hadn't seen some of the women in weeks. She noticed several of her fellow third-gens were in various stages of pregnancy, their bellies prominent under their purple jumpsuits.

The fourth-gen was well on its way from the looks of it. Delphine shivered thinking about it. She knew her time would eventually come, but she honestly wasn't sure she wanted to have children. The thought of it made the berries and soy rumble about in her stomach and she had to turn away from her pregnant counterparts to keep her breakfast from coming back up.

She wasn't sure what her issue was. She knew procreation was important to the genetic health of the colony and that every woman here would need to at least try to have a child at some point in her life. But she often wondered if perhaps the child-rearing gene hadn't imprinted on her when she was still a frozen embryo in the vast backlogs of the cryostorage facilities.

At the far north end of the Atrium, standing two meters above the cave floor, stood a stone pillar. It had steps cut into it leading to the top where Ligeia, the leader of the council of elders, now stood. The hazy light from the oculus, high overhead, bathed the room in an orange glow. Delphine could tell that they would soon be into the Titanian night. The light was dimmer now than it had been the day before when she and the twins found the probe. Still, it offered plenty of light for the meeting as Delphine noticed that the large, overhead light banks were not turned on.

Ligeia wore the traditional red first-gen jumpsuit. Her hair was almost as red as her jumpsuit and it hung in long, thick cords down her shoulders and back. The rest of the council—the ones who remained alive—wore matching jumpsuits and sat on large stone seats flanking the speaking pillar.

Sheva, the second-in-command, sat to Ligeia's left, her sleek black hair wrapped in an intricate braid around her head, framing her pearl-white skin. Nerine sat to the left of Sheva. She was the youngest of the council members, in fact, the last of the first-gen births. She had deep brown skin and matching eyes, her black hair creating a curly halo around her head.

To Ligeia's right sat Diomare, the most beautiful of the council members, in Delphine's opinion. She had olive skin and black eyes with high cheekbones. Her brown hair was cut short, just under the jaw, and her arms crossed at the chest. And to Diomare's right, the fourth council chair sat empty.

Meribelle's chair.

Delphine and Pala wandered into the room and took a spot on the ground next to Rhayn, Rho, and Rhea. There were no chairs in the Atrium so everyone had to sit on the floor or stand against the outer wall of the cave. The floor of the cave was solid rock, rusty orange in color, and cold to the touch. Delphine shivered as cold seeped up from the rock right through her jumpsuit as she sat cross-legged on the floor.

As they settled in, Ligeia made a deep, throaty noise, and the hum of chatter around the room gently died down to silence.

"Welcome, Xanadu colonists," Ligeia said, her hands clasped in front of her torso, her cheeks pink as she smiled a greeting to the group. "Welcome, my friends." She spread her arms to her sides as if giving the entire room a hug. This was how she began every meeting, with a greeting to her friends. Delphine fought the urge to roll her eyes. Ligeia was many things, but Delphine would certainly not consider her a friend.

"As you have probably already seen, we are down one member," she said, again clasping her hands in front of her chest before turning to face the empty chair next to Diomare. "Meribelle has passed away."

A low gasp escaped the crowd. The noise surprised Delphine because she was relatively certain everyone in the colony knew the meaning of the impromptu meeting at which they were now gathered. But, she imagined, it was still a shock to many of the colonists to hear the words spoken out loud, and from their leader, rather than through the gossip chain.

Ligeia nodded, a look of sad understanding on her face. "Yes," she continued, "it is a sad time for those of us close to Meribelle. She fought a hard battle and our amazing medics did such a good job caring for her in her final days. Let's give them our blessings."

She pointed to the group of medics standing in a circle near the edge of the Atrium. They were set apart from the rest of the colonists by the stark, white med coats they wore over their jumpsuits. This wasn't all of them, but Delphine could tell Ligeia was singling out this group to make a point. They stared at each other blankly, not knowing what to say or do. In unison, the colony members raised their right hands in the direction of the group of medics, holding them there for a few seconds before dropping them back to their sides—the traditional blessing given on Xanadu.

Ligeia did the same and said, "Thank you. Without medics, life would take us much quicker here in this harsh landscape. Let's all say a blessing for them before we sleep tonight, shall we?"

This time, Delphine did roll her eyes. She had never understood Ligeia's obsession with blessings before, especially now when her own gen mate was gone. Meribelle's passing left only ten first-gen colonists alive. Delphine did a quick glance around the room counting the remaining six red jumpsuits in the crowd, minus the four council members.

"As is tradition," Ligeia's voice continued to boom and dance around the walls of the Atrium, "we shall start our meeting with reading of the minutes, old and new business, followed by the recitation of the laws, and a communications update. Once the formalities are complete, we will tackle the problem of succession."

Delphine sighed and allowed her shoulders to slump. The council held one of these meetings every forty days and they were always the same format. Since this one had been an impromptu meeting, she'd hoped it would not have to follow the same rules. But it did not seem she would get her wish.

Ligeia gestured for Sheva to begin her portion of the meeting before taking her own seat on a stone bench at the back of the speaking pillar. Only Ligeia stood on that pillar; the other council members spoke from below while Ligeia presided over all.

Not only was Sheva second-in-command, she was also the recordkeeper. She was in charge of keeping minutes from every colony meeting, including the ones where not all colonists were present. Everything she documented about the happenings at the colony was uploaded to the colony mainframe and saved in triplicate to ensure the full record of the colony would never be lost because of disaster.

She stood from her chair next to the pillar and tapped her left bug, pulling up a holograph of the minutes from the last meeting. The holograph was only visible to Sheva, but Delphine could see the faint silvery outline of it surrounding Sheva's face.

"Hear, hear, colonists of Xanadu!" Her voice was loud and clear, much deeper than Ligeia's thin, tight voice.

"Hear, hear!" replied every colonist followed by a swift slap of their open palms on the front of their legs. Even though she knew it was coming, the loud snap of this gesture echoing through the walls of the Atrium always made Delphine jump. Rho noticed the reaction and gave Delphine a sly, sweet smile.

"Our last meeting was held here, in the Atrium, at 0915 on the morning of Friday, colony date two six four in the seventy-second year of Xanadu. The record shows that the following topics were discussed…"

As Sheva read the minutes, Delphine did her best to zone out her voice, and she was partially successful in diminishing it to a dull hum in the background of her thoughts. It was strictly prohibited to engage ear bugs during a colony meeting, so she spent her time mulling over her thoughts on the space probe.

It had been so late the night before when they had returned, and she'd slept in longer than she intended to, so she hadn't gotten the opportunity to really think about the discovery they'd made. Glancing at Rho and Rhayn, she noticed they both had the same expressions on their faces, both with their foreheads crinkled, eyes glazed, lost in thought. Apparently, the twins were doing the same.

The object was definitely from Earth. It wasn't the sort of thing anyone from Xanadu could have made. The numbers and symbols on the control panel were so strange. Rho thought they were some sort of shorthand. Perhaps a scientific code that the colony wasn't aware of. But Delphine couldn't get Rho's final words out of her head... *Maybe it's not from before. Maybe it was sent here recently.*

Was that possible?

Before yesterday, Delphine would have answered absolutely not—there was no way Earth could send something to Titan with the great war waging. The great war was always part of the communications update Ligeia gave at every all-colonist meeting. The colony records were clear on the great war. It had started nearly three decades prior when the colony was still in its first-gen, only a few years after the twelve original colonists landed and set up the bones of the great colony that now surrounded them.

The International Space Exploration Federation or ISEF, was in charge of all communications with the colony, and during the first few years of the war, the colonists got almost no updates from the home planet. The ISEF officials told the council of elders that they had to move their base of operations underground to protect them from the radiation that now scoured Earth's surface because of nuclear fallout.

According to their history lessons, the great war was the reason nobody from Earth ever came back to Titan. There had been plans at one point to bring a fresh set of new colonists to the moon after the bulk of the colony infrastructure was put into place, but because of the fighting, this was never to be. As it was, ISEF barely had the resources to keep up with a random communications check from time to time.

And if they had sent a probe or a ship to Titan, why wouldn't they have mentioned it?

Only Ligeia and the council of elders were allowed access to the communications array on the south end of the complex. Communications picked up from Earth were sporadic at best. And with the eighty-three-minute turnaround time between Titan and Earth, it made two-way communication impossible.

Ligeia would relay any messages received to the colonists at the regular meetings and let them know how she responded. At times, there were no communications updates to give, and more often than not, they were simple messages referencing the ongoing war and the lack of resources along with requests for status updates on the colony. Many of the colonists held out hope that one day, Earth would return with new ships, new technology, and new colonists, giving those colonists who wished to leave Titan a way to return to Earth and those who wished to stay, new blood to mix with. Sadly, they were always let down when Ligeia gave them communications updates, for no ship was on the way to Titan, and from the sounds of it, there would be no ship coming anytime soon.

Sheva continued to drone on in the background of Delphine's thoughts. She had moved on now to the old and new business portion of the meeting. Delphine caught little snippets here and there of what they had discussed during the last meeting—mostly regarding the building project and the design of the new living quarters units.

"Discussion" was actually a strong word to describe what went on at the regular colony meetings. There were people slated to speak on certain topics. The engineering team had been in charge of putting together plans for the new building project and their leader, a large woman named Delma, had been the only one to speak on the subject. Nobody dared to speak outside their turn and it was almost unheard of for anyone who wasn't slated to speak at the meetings to ask questions or bring up any sort of rebuttal to the proceedings. It was simply the way it was. The council of elders determined what they would work on and the rest of the colonists were put to the task of figuring out how to achieve it, no questions asked.

"And now for the recitation of the laws. Please stand," Sheva said, clearing her bugs and turning to point at the cave wall behind Ligeia's perch on the pillar. There was a loud bustle as everyone stood from their seats on the cold floor and momentarily stretched their legs.

The wall was a sheer cliff face running seamlessly from floor to ceiling in the cavernous space. It was the flattest portion of the room. Inscribed on the wall, in giant lettering placed there many years before when the original twelve first took over the cave as their home, were the three laws of Xanadu, carved directly into the rock surface for all to see. They read:

> 1. *Xanadu shall be ruled by a council of five elected elders. Once elected, elders shall remain on the council for the entirety of their natural lives.*
>
> 2. *The council of elders shall hold sole responsibility for the creation of regulations that serve the best interests of all colonists. Only the elders may create or nullify regulations and any colonist caught breaking those regulations shall be punished in a manner seen fit by the council.*
>
> 3. *In the event of a council member's death, the colonists shall exercise their democratic rights to elect a new member and complete the council of five.*

Everyone's gaze fell on the wall with one exception—Ligeia continued to stare forward, watching the crowd with her pale, green eyes. On cue, every colonist began to recite the three laws. When they were finished, everyone raised their right hand in blessing over the wall. When the ritual was complete, they all sat once again and waited for the next part of the meeting, the communications update. Delphine sat but kept her back straight and her eyes right on the pillar. For the first time in an hour, she was interested in hearing what would be said at the meeting.

Sheva took her seat as her portion of the meeting was now complete and Ligeia rose to address the crowd. She took a moment to straighten her jumpsuit, smoothing it with her hands before clasping them in front of her chest. Ligeia always did this show before she began a speech, closing her eyes and bowing her head to her fingertips as if praying over her words. The sight of it normally didn't bother Delphine. She didn't even pay much attention to it most of the time, but today, she felt like gagging watching Ligeia prepare herself for speaking. Delphine let out a loud sigh and crossed her arms over her chest. Pala heard this and gave Delphine a swift nudge with her elbow and a side-eye that read *knock it off*. Rhayn suppressed a giggle.

After several long moments with her head bent and eyes closed, Ligeia's face emerged and she planted a big smile on it, opening her eyes and dropping her hands to her sides.

"I'm pleased to say that after eighty-two long days, we finally have an update from Earth." As she said this, she held her hands out toward the crowd, waiting for the desired reaction.

As if on cue, the colonists let out a collective sound that mixed relief, surprise, and joy. This was clearly the reaction Ligeia was hoping for. Her smile grew larger and she nodded as if in agreement with herself.

"Yes, I knew you would be happy to hear about this development. But," she paused, her smile dropping into an overdrawn frown, the same kind a child would draw on an unhappy stick figure, "the news is not good. The great war wages on. According to ISEF, they continue to suffer regular bombing strikes from the enemy and the radiation levels on the surface of the planet are at dangerously high levels. In fact, they are having a difficult time keeping the communications equipment maintained. There are no plans to send new colonists or a new spaceship to Titan at this time."

Now the sound released from the crowd was a groan of sadness and disappointment. Ligeia nodded again, happy with this reaction as well.

"I radioed back to them and gave them a full status update on the colony. I let them know the fourth-gen is progressing beautifully." As she said this, the smile returned to her face and she gestured around to several of the pregnant third-gens standing near the front of the crowd. Delphine watched them blush and reach down to cup their bellies protectively.

Ligeia continued, "And I let them know that we have gone forward with the plans to build the new living compartment section of the colony, the largest project taken on in the last thirty years here at Xanadu. They wish you to know that we have their full support in taking this big step to grow the colony population and perhaps double the number of colonists by the time the war ends and they can once again return to Titan." As she finished, she clasped her hands together and tilted her head to the side as if to show how proud she was to be their leader.

There was a murmur from the crowd and a brief moment of applause as each colonist gave Ligeia two loud claps, again, the customary response to the communications updates.

Delphine wasn't surprised to hear that there was no real news from Earth, but, for the first time in her life, she began to wonder how true these updates were. If that probe was really sent to Titan recently, then it threw out everything Delphine and the rest of the colony had always believed about Earth and its relationship with Xanadu. If it was true, then Ligeia was lying—either about what the communications from Earth said or if there actually were any communications coming from the home world.

She had never cared for Ligeia with all her theatrics and blessings and prepared speeches, but Delphine had never imagined their leader might be lying to them. Now, as she watched Ligeia soak up the response from the crowd, she couldn't help but feel the tingle of doubt spread through her gut, licking at the base of her throat. She swallowed hard in an effort to quell the unease but it was no use.

Rhayn reached over and placed her hand on Delphine's knee. Delphine turned and saw the worry and fear present behind Rhayn's eyes. She was having similar thoughts. Delphine glanced at Rho who simply had her head bowed, her long fingers clasped in her lap.

"Now," Ligeia continued, taking a few steps forward on the pillar, "let's move on to the final order of business for today's meeting—the succession plan." The crowd fell silent, for this was what they all truly came here today to find out.

Council members enjoyed special privileges that allowed them to live longer than the rest of the colonists. They were not assigned a regular job and they rarely went outside the colony to keep the wear and tear of normal colony life from cutting their life expectancy. They were housed in a separate group of apartments at the very back of the living quarters wing, safest from radiation, and with their own air and water filtration systems. Delphine had never seen a council member apartment, but she'd heard they were at least three times the size of the regular apartments that most families shared.

They had access to their own private growing tent where they could set up their own gardens full of the foods they enjoyed eating the most, never having to wait on rations like the rest of the colonists. The council also had first access to the manufacturing facility and anything made therein. They could order special clothing, bedding, and even have special furniture made without having to work extra hours as regular colonists would. They had first access to any new medical and technological advancements that came out of the research and development departments.

Which was why it had come as such a shock to the rest of the colonists when Meribelle was diagnosed with cancer. Council members rarely got sick and when they did, the medics were there with every medical resource in the colony to cure them of their ailments. It was very rare for an elder to die. So rare, that the last one to pass away had been over twenty years earlier, before Delphine was even born.

Ligeia turned slightly to ensure she was facing the entire crowd. "Arrangements have been made for Meribelle's departure. Those who wish to visit her and give her a final blessing are encouraged to do so. She will be cremated tonight and her ashes will be laid in the burial grounds immediately after."

The mention of the burial grounds made Delphine's back straighten and she reached up to her throat, suddenly unable to swallow.

Aura.

She closed her eyes and took in a deep drag of the cool cavern air, trying to clear her sister's memory from her mind. Rhayn, seeing the reaction, moved closer and put her arm around Delphine's shoulders.

"Are you okay?" she whispered into Delphine's ear so only she could hear it. Delphine nodded in reply and took another deep breath, settling her nerves. Rhayn gave her a squeeze and did not let go of her shoulder.

"Of course," Ligeia continued, "this means we now have to elect a new elder to take Meribelle's place. The law is very specific. The council must be a group of five and we now only have four." She gestured to her left and right at the remaining council members seated below her. "The election will be held tomorrow morning at 0915 here in the Atrium. I now open the floor for nominations."

As soon as the words left her mouth, a fierce look came over Ligeia's face and her green eyes grew piercing as she examined the crowd beneath her. She no longer wore the overexaggerated smile she had pasted on her face earlier. Her smile now leaned to the side, slight and sly, as she swiveled her head looking around the room, daring someone to come forward.

Delphine watched Ligeia's reaction and shook her head, pursing her lips. She knew as well as every other colonist that this was no time to stand up and volunteer a nomination. The look on Ligeia's face said it all—speak and suffer the consequences. Rhayn shot Rho a look that said *I told you so*. Rho simply shrugged.

The crowd murmured as each woman turned to their neighbor, curious as to what they might do. After a few awkward moments, Ligeia seemed satisfied enough to move on, the smile growing large again on her face.

"Since there are no other nominations, I would like to make one." She looked down into the crowd and gestured with her fingertips at the front row. Ligeia's daughter, Lara, stood from her crouch and walked forward.

Lara, a second-gen, looked almost identical to her mother with long, red hair hanging to her waist. They had the same high cheekbones and tight jawlines. But Lara was shorter and slighter than Ligeia, making her look like a shrunken version of the head elder. As she took her place next to her mother, Lara grinned, a big, sweet, sickening grin.

Ligeia placed her hand on Lara's shoulder and whispered something into her daughter's ear. When she turned to address the crowd, she too was smiling, no doubt beaming with pride. "I would like to nominate my daughter, Lara, as the next member of the council of elders. She is the head of our reproductive sciences laboratory and it's because of her pioneering work in the field that we have grown our colony to its current size. Her knowledge of medical and scientific research is second to none and it would be an honor to us all if she would join the council."

Lara pressed her hands to her heart and her eyes welled with tears. Delphine was fairly sure this was meant to be a humbling gesture, but she knew Lara better than most and humble wasn't something Lara related to in any way. As the head of the reproductive sciences lab, she was Pala's superior and Delphine had heard many things from Pala over the years. Unsettling things.

According to Pala, Lara was accustomed to getting her way and she wouldn't accept anything that wasn't 100 percent her idea. She was gossipy and played favorites. She was often late to work or never showed, yet nobody said anything because she was Ligeia's daughter, and nobody dared to cross Ligeia. In short, Lara acted like a child—a spoiled one—even though she was nearly forty years old and had two daughters of her own.

Lara used the back of her hand to wipe her eyes before turning to her mother. "I accept your nomination, Ligeia." Then she turned to face the crowd. "I would be proud to serve you, my fellow colonists, as one of your elder members."

There was a wave of whispers as the crowd took in this news. Ligeia gave Lara a slight nod, signaling that her turn on the pillar was done. Lara nodded back and left the pillar, taking her seat again in the front row.

"Since there are no further nominations, we will have an election tomorrow morning to formally elect Lara as an elder on the council of five. Please be prompt as you join us tomorrow so we can take care of this business and go on to celebrate our newest council member. This meeting is adjourned." Ligeia held up her hand and said her usual farewell. "To my fellow Titan girls, have a blessed day."

CHAPTER 8

Rhayn held Delphine's hand as they headed down the concourse leading to the cultivation tents. They had waited until the Atrium was almost empty before departing for their work duties, in an effort to speak privately about the events of the meeting. Unfortunately, other colonists had had the same idea and there were quite a few stragglers on their way to the tents along with the two. They had to walk close and speak in hushed whispers.

"Okay, I can tell you're pissed," Rhayn said, squeezing Delphine's hand tighter. "But really, are you surprised? This is pretty much what we expected would happen."

Delphine shook her head, unsure about what exactly was bothering her. She understood what was happening, and yes, Rhayn was right, she'd expected it. But she couldn't shake the idea that everything was wrong. "I just don't get it. Why must we carry on with this election charade? It seems so pointless."

Rhayn nodded and cracked a slight smile. "Because Ligeia needs to get her kicks while she can still get 'em, right? She loves all this attention. Eats it right up."

"I guess..." Delphine paused, searching for the right words. "I guess I'm just starting to question all this. For the first time in our lives, something about the colonies is about to change. And it seems wrong *not* to question it. Does that make sense?"

"Sure it does. But the question is, what good is it going to do to question Ligeia? She's in charge here and there's really nothing that's going to change that, right? So, why bother?" Rhayn shrugged as she said this.

The gesture made Delphine angry. She let go of Rhayn's hand and stopped in the middle of the concourse, turning to face her. "Why bother? Because if nobody bothers, nothing is going to change around here! I'm sick of having these five old women ruling over us. They were all elected to the council decades ago and they haven't worked a proper job in all that time. They have no idea what life is like in this colony."

"Oh?" Rhayn crossed her arms in front of her chest, eyebrow raised. "And what *is* life like in this colony? We have the food we need. We have our friends, our families. It's the only life we know, Del. And it's decent."

Delphine sighed and turned to keep walking down the concourse. Rhayn followed. "I'm not saying life here is bad. It's just that... well, it doesn't seem fair that the council members get to make all the decisions but they don't have to do any of the actual work. I mean, this fourth-gen they're planning is going to put a huge strain on the colony resources."

Rhayn shrugged. "That's why they're building the expansion."

"I know, but none of us got a say in whether or not we were going to expand. It was just decreed upon us and we went to work. Wouldn't it be nice if we actually got to participate in some of the decision-making around here?"

"Sure, that would be nice. But what do you propose we do? I mean, in a way, it's easier to leave the heavy decisions to them. That's what leadership is all about after all—making choices that can't be made by the masses."

"It's not that I'm against leadership. I understand that the laws are in place for a reason. We can't live without any rules around here. But, why do these elected leaders of ours get a free ride for the rest of their lives? Why do they get to continue making decisions twenty, thirty, even forty years after they're elected?"

Rhayn threw her hands up. "You got me."

"And why does it have to be Lara? She's one of the nastiest of the bunch when it comes to department leads."

"Yeah, well that's a power play. If Ligeia can get her daughter on council, it will make it easier for her to control what happens around here."

Delphine wrinkled her nose and shook her head. "And what happens next? Those elders aren't getting any younger—they're all, what? Like in their sixties? What if Ligeia can get all her daughters elected?"

She shivered at the thought of it. Ligeia was one of only a handful of colonists who had been granted more than two children. She had four daughters—Lara, Lexa, Lisa, and Lina. What would happen if Ligeia was able to take over the council through her daughters?

"Don't say that," Rhayn said in a whisper, looking around them to make sure nobody heard. "That can't happen. It just can't. Surely someone will say something…" Her voice trailed off. She wasn't so sure.

"Right, that would be a nightmare." Delphine shivered again at the thought. "And why can't someone from the third-gen be part of the council too?"

"Are you volunteering for the job?" Rhayn smirked as she said this, giving Delphine the side-eye and gently poking an elbow into her ribs for good measure.

"No," Delphine said, wincing and rubbing the sore spot where Rhayn elbowed her. "No, I'm not saying *I* should be the one on the council. I'm just saying, why aren't there more people on the council? Why don't we put some limits on how long council members can be in charge? And why don't we have a proper election?"

"We *are* having a proper election," Rhayn said, rolling her eyes. "Weren't you listening? Ligeia asked for nominations. Why didn't you speak up?"

Delphine stopped walking and turned to Rhayn, giving her a frustrated sigh. "You know as well as I do why I didn't speak up. It's not allowed. And even though it's not written in the rules, we all know it *is* a rule. I could end up losing rations for a week or doing surface labor out in the mines if I were to say anything."

Rhayn shuddered at the mention of surface labor. She'd been on the wrong side of the council several times in the past and it had earned her time in the mines. Mining and excavation were necessary parts of life at Xanadu, but it was the work nobody wanted, which was what made it the perfect punishment. Anyone who misbehaved ran the risk of getting reassigned at any time. And dismissal of rations was a common occurrence that was used to punish those who committed small infractions like theft or vandalism. But really, you didn't have to do anything wrong to get a harsh punishment handed down from the council. Simple things, like disagreeing with your boss, gossiping about the wrong person, or making detrimental errors in your job could earn you any punishment the council deemed worthy at the time. There were no rules when it came to job assignments. It all depended on how well the council liked you and who was on your side.

Delphine immediately felt bad for mentioning the mines. She knew how much Rhayn despised the fourteen-hour days she'd had to put in for over a year outfitting piping on the methane pipeline and hauling rock to the smelter. She remembered the day Rhayn was reassigned from the terrible job to the cultivation tents. Rhayn had actually cried, something Delphine had never seen before or since in all her nineteen years with her best friend. She knew Rhayn would do anything—anything—to stay clear of hard labor.

"I'm sorry," she said, hanging her head and pulling Rhayn in for a hug. "I shouldn't be complaining about this. I don't know what else to do."

The two embraced for a few moments and Rhayn whispered, "It's okay," before pulling away and giving her a sideways smile. Delphine kissed Rhayn's cheek and grabbed her hand before they headed off again down the concourse. She tapped her bugs to display the time and realized they were going to be late if they didn't book it down the remaining fifty meters of the tunnel. Any late clock-in would go in their files and, although Thessa was good about letting that type of thing go, they never wanted to have too many of those small infractions on their record.

"Come on," she said, pulling Rhayn along as she picked up the pace. "We don't want to be late."

CHAPTER 9

After her ten-hour work shift, Delphine returned to her apartment to find Pala there, picking at the remnants of a late meal. She could tell her mother hadn't eaten much of the soy patties on the plate, but it was obvious she'd put forth an effort. The patties appeared to have been freshly made, and of the two on the plate, perhaps one-quarter of one had been consumed.

At least she tried, Delphine thought.

"I didn't expect you to be home yet," she said as she dropped her backpack onto Aura's chair and gestured at the plate in front of Pala. "Got any more of that?"

Pala nodded and pointed at the countertop where three more soy patties were resting after their peanut oil bath. Delphine could smell the nutty scent from across the room and she walked over to the plate, grabbing one of the patties and taking a huge bite. She hadn't realized how hungry she was until she'd walked into the kitchen.

"Thanks," she said, the word muffled under the mouthful of soy patty. They were still warm on the inside and crunchy on the outside. It appeared Pala had just fried them. They had a drizzling of green herbs over the top to accent the deep brown color of the patties.

The taste and smell of this simple meal reminded her of her childhood when Pala would make a big batch of them every fourth day. Aura had been a picky eater and fried soy patties were one of the only things she would tolerate. Delphine had never been hard to please when it came to food, but these were a particular favorite of hers.

As Delphine munched on the remaining patties, Pala stared at the window, oblivious to her daughter's presence. She continued to push the food around her plate with a fork, an unconscious action, Delphine had no doubt. Her mother had been avoiding food for six years—it wasn't surprising that she would mindlessly go through the motions.

Delphine had learned not to mention it anymore. When she first noticed the fact that her mother wouldn't eat, she had been worried, asking her regularly what was wrong. Was the food too spicy? Did she not like the meal? Perhaps she'd like something different? And eventually, she would come right out and say something: You need to get help. This isn't healthy. You have to eat something.

None of it ever worked and eventually, Delphine gave up. She had to pick her battles with Pala. The moodiness and depression that followed Aura's death had only served to make her more fragile. Delphine worried that too much pushing on her part would send her mother over the edge. So, she didn't mention it anymore and simply resigned herself to the fact that she would probably watch her mother push food around her plate until the day one of them died—and at this rate, Pala would certainly go first.

"I didn't expect you to be home," Delphine repeated. "Why aren't you at work?"

When Pala still didn't answer, Delphine stomped her boot on the floor, causing a *thwack* that echoed throughout the room. Pala jumped and sucked in a deep breath as if she hadn't even been breathing.

"Sorry, I'm distracted." Standing, she took her plate to the sink and dumped the unfinished soy patty crumbles into the designated compost sack. As she started washing her plate, she didn't look at Delphine. "I... I had an episode."

Delphine swallowed hard. That was the third time in the last few months this had happened. "Was it bad?"

Pala shook her head. "No, not so bad. Just got a bit dizzy. Lara let me off early so I could rest."

"Uh-huh," Delphine said, unconvinced that she was getting the full story. "Did you see the medics?"

"No. I didn't think it was necessary. I came home and had a rest and some tea and now I feel okay."

Delphine dropped her head and rubbed her temples. "This isn't healthy. You have to see the medics about these episodes. What triggered it? Was it the meeting?"

Pala turned to face her, wiping her wet hands on the front of her jumpsuit. "I don't know. It could have been. All that talk of death and succession. It's a lot for me. Besides, who would I talk to? Who's going to help me with some sickness that can't be seen or inspected?"

Delphine sighed. She didn't know the answer. She understood her mother's pain, but it aggravated her that after this many years, Pala still hadn't dealt with her grief. The eating, the depression, the fainting episodes—it was going to catch up to her soon. Delphine could see her getting frailer by the day and, as much as she hated to admit it, it worried her.

This type of health issue wasn't something the women of Titan discussed openly. Suffering over the loss of a loved one was supposed to be short—grieve their loss, take your time away for a bit, then get yourself together and move on. There was work to be done and everyone had to pitch in. Nobody seemed to understand it when someone took things harder and suffered longer than they were "supposed" to. Nobody liked it when someone wasn't pulling their weight, especially someone as young as Pala. And Delphine knew that soon, people would start to notice.

Pala turned away from Delphine without a response and filled a glass of water at the sink. "I'm going to lie down now. It's been a long day and we have the election first thing in the morning."

Delphine nodded and watched her mother shuffle lightly down the hallway and disappear into her bedroom. When she'd gotten off work, she'd been so tired, she thought she might fall asleep on the walk to the apartment. But after her discussion with Pala, she was unsettled, restless.

Everything about the day hadn't sat right with her and she knew she'd never be able to sleep if she tried now. Pushing the empty plate into the sink, she took a big swig of water from her cup and grabbed her surf suit and lifepack from Aura's chair before heading to the airlocks.

CHAPTER 10

Outside, Delphine purposely turned the heating down in her surf suit to let some of the chill of Titan's atmosphere cool her bones. She found that she ran better when her body was cool, almost like she was trying to outrun the chill.

It wasn't too long before she was in the full swing of the run and so distracted by her thoughts that she didn't realize she'd unconsciously run right to the machine shed.

The space probe.

In all the hustle and bustle of the day, she'd totally forgotten about it. She veered off her path and jogged around to the back of the building where she could enter through the airlock.

Once inside, she stripped off her suit and left it in a crumpled pile on the floor. As she approached the far corner of the room where they'd hidden the probe, the sound of something moving caught her attention. She stopped and swiveled her head, listening, her eyes sharp as she peered into the darkened corners of the shed. It was nighttime on Titan so there was no light coming in from the windows, only the light banks hanging in the middle of the room, leaving the corners of the shed in darkness.

She jumped when, out of the corner of her eye, she saw something—*someone*—move in the shadows. Her body went rigid until she realized it was Rho standing from a seated position on the floor, brushing off her jumpsuit.

"You scared me," Delphine said, holding her chest.

"Sorry," Rho said, walking up to her. "But you kinda scared me too. I wasn't expecting anyone to come in here. When I heard the airlock cycling, I threw the tarp back over it and ran to hide."

"What are you doing out here this late?"

"I wanted to have a better look at this thing. After the meeting this morning and all… well, I couldn't sleep. So, I figured I'd come out here and tinker with it, see if I can't figure out who sent it. What about you?"

Delphine nodded. "I couldn't sleep either. Pala's having… problems. Anyway"—she gestured toward the space probe— "let's bring it out here so we can see it better. I'll grab the far side."

They threw the tarp off the probe and carried it gently out of the shadows and into the better lit section of the shed. Once there, Rho located the access panel they'd found before and flipped it open. It made the same loud beep as it had the first time they'd looked at it. She examined the interior. It was definitely a control panel. It had a touchscreen display and it was lit up, casting a strange, blue light on Rho's face.

Although Delphine pored over the panel too, it didn't mean anything to her. There were a bunch of numbers. Some appeared to be readings, others looked like they displayed times, and still others looked like altitude measurements. Bars and lines and circles indicated graphs of some sort. At the bottom, there were long, horizontal bars with buttons on them. Rho touched one of the buttons and slid it along the bar. The light on the interior of the craft brightened the farther she moved it.

She pressed a button at the top of the display and the top panel of the probe opened up, same as it had when they'd brought the probe to the shed. After she pressed another button, the bottom panel opened. Then she flicked her wrist to the side and the panel configuration changed, displaying a whole new set of buttons and displays. She did this again and again, finding there were a total of twelve display panels that could be accessed by swiping the screen left or right. On the very last one, a picture emerged.

They both jumped back, a gasp escaping Rho as she realized what they were looking at. It was a picture of the two of them, staring at the probe. Rho waved her hand in front of her face and the picture mimicked the movement.

Delphine swallowed hard and moved closer, her eyes squinting at the display. "It's a camera," she said, her voice full of disbelief. Rho looked at Delphine and nodded. Delphine frowned at the image. "Can you change it back? I don't know... I don't like the idea of it catching us on camera."

Rho swiped the display panel to the right and the original screen they had seen when they first opened the probe returned. "Well, I can change the view on this panel, but it's probably still filming us."

"Why would there be a camera on it?"

Rho sighed and crossed her arms over her chest. "Well, they obviously expected to catch something worth looking at. I mean, probes have always had cameras, right?"

Delphine slowly walked around the probe, running her fingers over the smooth, reflective surface. "I think you're right."

Rho looked confused. "Right about what?"

"I think this thing is new. There's no way this predates the colony. I mean"—she waved her hands toward the probe—"look at it. It *looks* brand new. Something a hundred years old would be incredibly corroded by now after being on the surface that long."

Rho nodded. "And it would have been buried. I guess there's always the possibility that it was buried and now it's been uncovered by the latest windstorm. But I think you're right, there's no way one of the old Earth probes would have been so close to the surface and in such good shape."

Rho reached into the cavity of the probe and touched one of the instruments inside. It was a metal box with holes in it revealing the complex wiring within. There was a set of antennae at the top of it that looked like they could retract when not in use. "This looks like something that would measure atmospheric elements. Those antennae might be taking samples and testing the readings inside. But that's just a guess."

The rest of the probe was full of similar types of instruments. The ones near the bottom had scoops and drills and little shovels that seemed intended for taking rocks and samples.

"Why would they send a probe to Titan with all this experimentation equipment?" Rho asked, crouched so she could see the bottom of the probe. "If they needed experiments done, they could have just asked us. Right?"

Delphine sighed. "Maybe it's because they don't know we're here."

Rho stood, a look of disbelief on her face. "What do you mean by that? Of course they know we're here."

Delphine crossed her arms at her chest. "But what if they don't? I mean, think about it, Rho. Why send something like this when there's a colony full of people who can run all the experiments you like?"

"Yeah, but that logic is flawed." Rho pointed at the control panel. "If they didn't know we were here, they wouldn't have put a control panel on it. Something we could access and use."

"Good point." Delphine nodded. "Let's think about this. We know it came from Earth. That much is clear from the numbers and symbols in the controls. We know it came here recently and it's not a precolonization probe. It's in too good a shape to be that old. We know it carries scientific instruments, and likely, the instructions on how to use them." She paused, mulling it over in her mind. "What if they sent this for *us* to use for some reason?"

"Us?" Rho didn't look convinced.

"Yeah, us. What if this is a new scientific package and we're meant to use it to take readings and send back our findings?"

Rho cocked her head to the side, considering this. "Okay, so they want us to use this. Why wouldn't they have said anything? Ligeia relays all messages from Earth to us at our meetings. Surely she would have mentioned that they were sending something... right?"

Delphine shrugged. "Maybe not. Maybe those communications updates she gives are all bullshit." She expected Rho to argue with this, but Rho didn't. Instead, she gave

Delphine a quizzical look before returning her attention to the control panel on the probe.

"Well, if we want to find out why they sent it, we need to make sense of this control panel. If they really wanted us to use this, it shouldn't be too difficult to figure out." Rho started tapping the touchscreen. As she did, little lights turned on throughout the device as the small instruments activated and turned off. Rho's eyebrows were knitted tight down the center of her forehead as she concentrated on the screen in front of her.

"Here." She pointed at a group of buttons. "These appear to be the individual controls for the instruments. There are twelve of them shown here. And when you click on this, like this"—she demonstrated by clicking on the button and another screen popped up on the panel—"they pull up the actual navigation systems for each of them."

Rho continued to tap the screen and the small, square boxy machine they'd looked at earlier buzzed to life. The antennae at the top extended to various heights and stopped, took readings, and extended farther until they were sticking up a meter above the probe. Rho pointed at the control panel. "Here are the atmospheric readings coming in from those antennae. They are testing for eight different measures. Look at this one here." Rho pointed at a particularly tall bar graph on the left side of the screen. "It's reading atmospheric pressure, while this one"—she pointed at a pie chart next to the pressure graph—"is dissecting the air and measuring the various elements. Each pie represents certain elements. The blue pie is oxygen, this one is nitrogen, and these smaller slivers are trace gasses, like Argon, CO_2, and so on. This actually matches exactly with the breathable air mixture of the colony. So, it does appear to be pretty accurate."

Delphine nodded and touched the control panel herself, exiting from the screen that controlled the atmospheric tester and going back to the main screen. "I feel like there should be something on this first screen that tells us more about this probe. If they were going to put something like that in here, it would be at the first screen. Don't you think?"

Rho nodded and peered down at the panel. "I wish they'd labeled these things so we could understand them." She shook her head.

Suddenly, a holographic image jumped to life in front of them. The girls jerked away from the image in unison, backing up a few steps from the probe.

The holograph was projecting from the same camera that filmed them earlier. Apparently, it had the ability to both take video and project video. It stood about a half meter tall in front of them and it was flawless, much more technologically advanced than the holographs used at Xanadu. There were no glitchy springs as the picture stabilized. It was clear as a bell.

"Is that a..." Rho's voice trailed off as she and Delphine started cautiously moving closer to the image.

"I think so," Delphine said, her mouth hanging open in wonder.

It was a man. The 3D image standing before them was a holograph of a man. He wore a blue jumpsuit, similar to the Xanadu jumpsuits, although his had more pockets and had a noticeable ISEF patch on the left breast. He had short dark hair and dark skin. Delphine had never seen a man before, but she was relatively sure this was one. He had big, muscular shoulders and a wide neck.

The holographic man stood still for a moment, his arms at his sides, before he began to speak. Unfortunately, they could hear no words. The man continued to speak, his mouth moving without sound for over a minute before the holograph abruptly cut off and was replaced again by the glow of the control panel.

"Can you play it again?" Delphine asked.

Rho nodded and tapped the same command she'd done before. As before, the holograph jumped to life, clear and without any pixilation. The man stood with his arms crossed and began to speak. But they still couldn't hear what he said.

"Hmm." Rho bent down to the control panel, studying it up close. "The sound isn't working. But maybe it's turned down or something. Let me see if I can find the control for it." She bit her tongue between her teeth as she touched the screen trying to find controls for the sound.

Delphine crossed her arms over her chest and started pacing behind Rho. "So they obviously are sending us a message, right? That's the only reason they would include a holograph in the software of this thing." She scratched her neck and then unconsciously touched her ear bug, moving it back and forth behind her ear as she paced. "Earth sends a probe to Titan. Either Ligeia didn't know they were planning to do that, or she's lying to us. The probe is obviously meant to react with us in some way. There's a *man* in the holographic image. I mean really, that's crazy! They would know there are no men here. So, what does all this mean?"

Rho looked up from the control panel and Delphine stopped pacing. "It means," Rho said calmly, "that something strange is going on." She looked at the space probe, then back at Delphine. "We weren't meant to see this. If Ligeia finds out we have it, it won't be good for us."

Delphine swallowed hard. Yes, that much was true and she knew it. "What do we do?"

Rho took a deep breath. "Well, we need to figure out how to get the sound working so we can hear what the holographic message is. I can come back tomorrow after my shift and tinker with it. There must be a setting somewhere that's not configured correctly."

"What should I do?"

"I can't shake the idea that there's a big disconnect between what we're being told about Earth and what's really going on." Rho stood back and scratched her head. "What about the colony logs? Maybe there's something in there that can shed some light on this."

"Yes." Delphine began pacing again, staring intently at the floor. "Yes, that's a good idea. That's where everything is saved."

Rho walked over to Delphine and put her hand on her shoulder. "Do you think you can access them?"

Delphine nodded. "I think so. I'd have to go to the library."

The library was part of the science and medical complex. There weren't books there, as a library on Earth would have, but the colonists referred to it as the library because it was where all the servers containing the colony records were kept. Everything that had ever happened at Xanadu, starting with the original colonists' arrival on the space freighter Sirena, was recorded there.

"Yeah, you can go there," Rho said, "but do you think that's a good idea?"

Delphine shrugged. "Every colonist has the right to see the records, right? They have to allow me in."

Rho's face was tense. "I'm worried you'll bring unnecessary attention to yourself if you go there. I'm sure they're watching that place. If there is something strange going on here, they won't want anyone looking through the records."

Delphine had to agree. It was an unwritten rule that you didn't ask too many questions at Xanadu. Nobody poked around in the colony records. It wasn't something anyone had the time or desire to do. They took Ligeia and the council for their word.

"What if I say I'm going there to do some research about Aura?" Delphine said. "I can tell them I'm writing something about her life and need her records for it."

"That could work, but will that be too hard for you?"

Delphine thought about this a moment. "No, it will be fine. I'll take a few notes on Aura, enough to make it look like what I'm doing is legit. And then I'll snoop around the records. I won't be able to stay there long. Maybe there's a way I can copy over some of the earlier logs to my bugs and read through them later?"

Rho nodded. "Yeah, that's a good idea. You won't be able to download anything directly, but you could take screenshots with your bugs as you scroll through the logs."

"Okay, it's a plan. What should I focus on while I'm there?"

"Well, I'd say recent Earth communications are important. See if you can find the exact dialogues. You'd think they kept recordings of the radio communications—at least, they're supposed to. Start there and see how far back you can get."

Rho tapped the control panel and folded it back into place, shutting the probe down. They carried it back to its original hiding spot and covered it with the tarp before heading to the airlock to put on their surf suits.

"What about Rhayn?" Delphine asked. "Should we tell her about all this?"

Rho nodded. "I'll fill her in."

They suited up and turned the lights off in the shed before heading out the airlock and into the frigid Titanian night.

CHAPTER 11

The next morning in the Atrium, the meeting started much the same way it had started the day before. Ligeia stood on the pillar, her hair coiled into a thick braid hanging from the base of her neck and down her back.

Sheva read the minutes from the meeting the day before. The only business to discuss was the business of the election which would be handled at the end of the meeting. The entire congregation recited the three laws, and Ligeia blessed everyone and reported no new communications update.

With the formalities completed, Ligeia clasped her hands in front of her chest and bowed her head as if in prayer. When she emerged several long moments later, her eyes were cloudy with tears and a huge smile spread across her face.

"I want to thank each of you, my fellow colonists, for taking part in this historic process: the election of a new council member. As you know, we abide by the three laws set forth by

Earth many years ago, and in choosing to elect our councilmembers, we show our support for Earth and those laws." She paused and gestured for Lara to stand and join her on the pillar. Lara was wearing her green jumpsuit and Delphine noticed that tiny gold flowers had been embroidered along the seams of the jumpsuit—an embellishment most colonists couldn't afford. Her copper hair had been braided as well but was piled on top of her head as if she were wearing an extravagant headpiece.

Lara stood and walked up the steps to join her mother on the top of the speaking pillar. Ligeia took her daughter's hand and raised it to her mouth, kissing the back of it before turning to address the crowd.

"I present to you Lara, our newest candidate for the council of elders."

The crowd gave the customary single clap of the hands in unison before falling silent.

"Are there any further nominations from the colonists?" Ligeia asked, her spine straightened and her eyebrow raised ever so slightly.

Delphine swallowed hard. She didn't understand all this. She didn't know if what was going on here was right. But she had the gut feeling that it wasn't. She thought about Pala, struggling daily to cope with the loss of her daughter. She thought of Aura—what would she have done in this situation? She was much more vocal than Delphine. She would have said something…

"Ahem." Delphine cleared her throat and stood. She felt her mother's body go rigid next to her and Pala gently touched the back of her hand as if deciding whether or not she needed to tug Delphine's arm to get her to sit back down.

Ligeia hadn't noticed Delphine's muttered noise, but her eyes shot over to Delphine as soon as she realized someone in the crowd had stood. The rest of the colony turned to stare at Delphine, their eyes wide and curious. Rhayn and Rho were seated a few rows ahead of Delphine with their mother, Rhea, and the look on Rhayn's face could have melted rock when she realized what Delphine was doing.

For a split second, Ligeia's eyes were wide and sparks of anger seemed to fly from them. Delphine could see the heat rising from her throat in a pink flush of the skin. But it only lasted a second. Ligeia apparently had excellent self-control and she immediately softened her eyes and resumed the smile she'd worn before Delphine's interruption.

"Yes?" Ligeia said, addressing the crowd rather than speaking directly to Delphine. "You have something to say, Delphine? A question, perhaps?"

"Well..." Delphine cleared her throat again. She suddenly felt like her voice might flee her body altogether and abandon her. But she took a breath and straightened her shoulders, holding her head up high and looking Ligeia straight on. "Yes, actually, I do have a question."

Ligeia perked a single eyebrow. "Ah, yes, of course. Questions are welcome here." She gave a big sweeping gesture with her arms indicating the Atrium was a safe place for free speech—even though everyone knew it most certainly was not. "What question would you like to ask?"

Delphine glanced around her and panic immediately crawled up her spine as she watched the glowing faces of the colonists stare at her. She tugged on the hem of her jumpsuit sleeve to help calm her nerves. "I'm curious as to why there needs to be only five women on the council of elders?" A gasp escaped from the crowd as if she had said something utterly blasphemous. "What I mean is," she paused to clear her throat, "why can't there be representatives on the council from all of the generations? It seems as though it would be fairer to all if there were more members on the council." She wasn't sure what she was doing, and she wished she'd thought this out better. But she was in it up to her neck now and might as well keep going. "It also seems strange that council members would hold their council seat for a lifetime. Wouldn't it make sense to hold elections more often? To get new people involved in the governing of our colony?" She bit down hard on her lip and glanced around her. Nobody spoke, but they were all staring at her.

Ligeia stared at her blankly for several moments. It felt like an eternity to Delphine as she watched Ligeia mull this over in her head. The room was eerily silent, the only noise coming from the faint blast of wind rolling across the surface above. The longer Ligeia stared at her, the more antsy her fingers got and she crushed them into a hard fist to keep them still. Finally, Ligeia spoke. "Do you believe the council has been unfair about something?"

Delphine raised her hands in apology. "No, no, certainly not. It's just that—"

"You think things can be done better than they have been for the last seventy-two years. Is that correct?"

"I-I-I only suggest it because, perhaps this is a good time to make some changes—"

"And what about the laws, Delphine? What about the laws sent to us from Earth?" She calmly crossed her arms in front of her chest. She said the word "Earth" with extra emphasis as if referring to some superior being.

Delphine nodded vigorously, feeling the panic continue to climb up her spine, one vertebra at a time. "Yes, I know the laws are important. I understand they came from Earth. But maybe we've outgrown the laws. Maybe it's time to update them—"

"Ah," Ligeia cut her off again. "*You* think the laws are inferior to our current colonial state." She drew out the word "you" giving it more than a single syllable. "*You* think the council is inadequate to sufficiently service the needs of Xanadu. *You* want to see change. Am I understanding that correctly?"

Delphine shrugged. "Well, I don't think it would hurt to have a few more people on the council. A few more elected officials that can truly represent the needs of the colonists." She cleared her throat and steeled herself knowing the retribution she would get for her next words. "It also seems unfair to have two colonists from the same family on the council of five."

She expected Ligeia to attack this last comment. To fly into a rage over the implication that there might be something dishonest going on. She'd seen Ligeia do it before and physically braced herself for the onslaught of words.

But they never came. Instead, a wide, sweet smile grew on Ligeia's face. "Ah, I see. So, you would like to put your own name into consideration. Is that it?"

This caught Delphine off guard and she winced, blinking rapidly. "N-n-no. No. That's not what I'm saying." Delphine paused, took a deep breath, trying desperately to find the right words. "I'm only saying that perhaps it's time to expand the council—"

"So, let me make sure I have this straight—you are not willing to put your name into the vote?" Ligeia's smile turned into an exaggerated frown and she tilted her head to the side as if speaking to a child. A stupid child. "Do you not believe you would be a good candidate to represent your generation?"

"Well, no, it's not that. That's really not the point." She squeezed her hands into tighter fists, her fingernails cutting into the skin of her palm. She was slowly but surely losing her grip on her stance. "That's not the point," she repeated, this time with more force. "I just think that the laws set forth by Earth so many generations ago are out—"

Suddenly, Pala stood from her seated position and grasped Delphine's upper arm. "May I address the council, Ligeia?" Pala's face was rigid, her mouth a thin, tight line. But her gray eyes bored into Ligeia with a ferocity Delphine had not seen from her mother in a very long time.

"Pala," Ligeia said, a smile again returning to her face. Delphine hated the way her mother's name fell out of Ligeia's mouth. Again, it sounded as if she were addressing a misbehaving child. "Please, if you have further insight into what your daughter is trying to say, we are all ears." She made a sweeping motion with her hands indicating the entire room. Lara stood behind her mother, her dark eyes glowering, chin lifted, and spine as straight as a rod.

Pala cleared her throat. "I apologize, Ligeia, for my daughter's impromptu declaration. Please"—she bowed her head slightly—"forgive her for this disruption." Then, she straightened, pulling her shoulders back and giving Delphine a slight sideways glance. "I think what Delphine is trying to say is that perhaps this might be a good time to entertain some changes. Small changes certainly never hurt when done in a smart way. And you, Ligeia, are one of the smartest people here at the colony. We have no doubt that, if we choose, as a colony, to implement a larger ruling council, you would execute the updated laws with absolute grace."

Delphine stared at her mother, dumbfounded. Not only had Pala stood in front of the council—in front of the *entire* colony—and delivered an elegant address, she had managed in a few smooth sentences to stroke Ligeia's ego in just the right way.

Ligeia whispered something into Lara's ear and Lara gave a small nod before moving to the back of the pillar allowing Ligeia room to move forward and address the entire crowd. "It seems we have some unsatisfied colonists in our midst." She gave a slight nod in the direction of Pala and Delphine, who still stood, Pala gripping Delphine's arm, Delphine wrapping her fingers in fists so tight, her knuckles were turning white. "This has not been the first time in the history of Xanadu where we have had unsatisfied colonists. And I am sure it won't be the last." As she spoke, she began to slowly pace from one side of the large stone pillar to the other. Clearly, this was why she'd asked Lara to step back—to give her more room to work the crowd.

She went on, her voice sweet as sugarcane. "But let us not forget, it is not *us* who have created the three laws of Xanadu. *We* are not the ones who put the framework of our organization into place. No, no, no." Still pacing, she wagged her index finger to accentuate her point. "The laws have been around longer than Xanadu itself. They were put into place for a very specific reason—to keep law and order within the colony walls. To allow us the freedom to grow and prosper in a civil…" Stopping on the word *civil,* she paused for dramatic effect before continuing, "society. No, the laws are not a product of the colonies. They are a product of Earth."

Nodding with a self-satisfied smile, she kept going. "Earth sent specific instructions to the twelve original colonists—our foresisters, our mothers, our grandmothers. These instructions were complete and clear with no interpretation necessary. The council of five is to rule over this colony. And it is our duty to respect our mothers and grandmothers and the mother planet they called home."

Ligeia clasped her hands together and took a moment to pause, her eyes moving throughout the room before she continued, "Earth sent us these laws and it is our duty to respect them!" As she said the word *duty,* she curled her hand into a fist and raised it up in the air as a show of solidarity with a planet she had never seen and probably never would. "Earth may not have the ability to come back to us just yet. But someday, they will. Someday, they will return to Titan and they'll want to see how we did. Do you think they would like it if we neglected to follow the very laws—the very *simple* laws—they set forward for us from the beginning?"

A hushed murmur trickled through the crowd as people straightened their backs, listening intently to their fearless leader.

Several people nodded their agreement. One woman in the front row mimicked Ligeia by holding her fist up and turning to the crowd before saying, "We respect Earth!"

Ligeia, pleased with the reaction, turned her attention back to Pala and Delphine, who remained standing, frozen. "I think not. And Delphine..." She frowned and shook her head as if disgusted. "I certainly hope that you wouldn't consider yourself a candidate for nomination to the council, dear. We all know what a difficult time you had after the... incident." Her voice trailed off and she shot the crowd a knowing look, her eyes dripping with pity. "Someone of your," she paused, twirling her finger in the air, trying to come up with the right word, "*unstable* mental state would most certainly *not* be an asset to our colonists."

Shame washed over Delphine the same way the cold, Titanian atmosphere did when she would first emerge from the airlock for a run. But this time, she had no surf suit to keep the unwanted sensation away. No, this cold shame sank bone deep and caused a shiver to pass up and down her body. She dropped her eyes, unable to look at Ligeia. Unable to bear the eyes of her fellow colonists resting on her, fueled by pity.

To her surprise, Pala, who was still holding tight to her arm, cleared her throat and spoke. "Ligeia, I understand your concern. Delphine *has* had a difficult time... as have we all. She does not wish to be a council member. She is simply making a suggestion for a way in which our colony might run"—she looked around at the uneasy faces of the crowd—"smoother. And we hope that you, our erudite leader, might take the suggestion into consideration. That is her only wish."

Ligeia considered Pala for a moment, her arms crossed at her chest, green eyes sharp. Eventually, she said, "Ah, I see. The council members and I can certainly discuss this at our next scheduled meeting. But until that time, we will continue with the election as *our laws* specify." She gave Pala and Delphine one final hard look before turning away. They shakily took their seats.

"Sheva," Ligeia said, snapping a finger toward her second-in-command. "Please begin the election process. Since we have no additional nominations, Lara will be the sole name on the ballot."

Sheva nodded and stepped forward to address the crowd and give instructions on how they were to proceed with the vote. But Delphine was not listening. She sat, slumped over, the shame of the experience still cold inside her body. After a few moments of hearing Sheva drone on in the background of her thoughts, Delphine started to feel the coldness ebb, replaced by a searing heat, and white-hot anger boiled up from within her. It spread through her gut, her chest, her face. Before she knew it, she was flushed with it, her teeth clenched and her hands dug into fists at her sides.

Suddenly, she didn't want to be here. She *couldn't* be there for fear she might actually explode. How *dare* Ligeia use her sister's death against her like that? How *dare* she drag up Delphine's private hell and parade it around in front of the entire colony?

Delphine stood, stopping Sheva midspeech, and turned to leave the Atrium. Pala grabbed her hand and said in a low voice, "Delphine, please…" but Delphine was having none of it. She ripped her fingers away from Pala as a snarl escaped her lips and pushed past the colonists standing between her and the exit.

Not a second too soon, she reached the concourse and took off at a run toward the living quarters, tears stinging her eyes. When she was far enough away, she stopped and allowed the sobs to take her.

CHAPTER 12
FIVE YEARS EARLIER

"Would you hurry up?" Delphine stopped, digging the toe of her boot into the dusty surface. She turned to see Aura lagging about ten meters behind her. She could hear the deep push-pull of Aura's breath sounding over the communication link as she struggled to keep up with her older sister.

They were almost to the top of the crest that led into Sol Canyon. The canyon, a good kilometer's walk away from the colony, was the best place in the vicinity of Xanadu to hunt for gems. Aura, who had just turned eleven, hadn't been to the canyon before and Delphine promised to take her there after her birthday. But when she'd offered to make a trip out to the canyon that day, she hadn't taken into account how slow Aura was moving around in her surf suit.

Colonists weren't allowed to use surf suits until the age of ten, and even then, they had to undergo a rigorous training protocol to get them ready for surface work. Technically, Aura shouldn't have even been out on the surface without the supervision of someone over the age of sixteen, but this was a rule that hardly anyone followed. Delphine had been out on the surface many times in the four years since she had turned ten and she wasn't worried.

The problem was, moving around in the surf suits took some time to get used to. It normally took Delphine only fifteen minutes or so to jog to Sol Canyon on her own, but with Aura in tow, they were quickly coming up on the thirty-minute mark and they weren't even over the crest yet. She commanded her ear bugs to pull up the time on the faceplate of her suit and sighed when she realized how late it was getting. She still had afternoon lessons to finish and Pala would have a fit if they were late for supper.

"Really though, is that as fast as you can go?" Delphine asked, her hands on her hips.

"Well, *excuse* me!" Aura said, breathless, drawing out the long *u*. "I don't have four years of experience running around out here. My legs are tired!" After a few more huffs, she trudged the final few meters and hauled herself upright where Delphine stood. Aura was a head shorter than her older sister and Delphine hadn't realized how much smaller she looked outside on the vast, open plains of the surface. Even with the added bulk of the surf suit, she looked so tiny and fragile in the dusty, inhospitable landscape.

Delphine rolled her eyes and gently bumped a fist into Aura's shoulder. "Even if you had the same experience, you'd still never be able to keep up. You're like a mini person."

"Hey!" Aura gave Delphine a shove. "I'm not mini. I'm just smaller than average. Besides, I can't help it that you're a giant with long legs!"

Delphine laughed. She loved her sister and had to admit, the kid had some fight in her. "Well, mini—I bet you can't beat me to the top of the ridge." She turned and pointed at the crest about fifty meters ahead of them. It was a bit of a steep climb, but it was the last major hurdle before they could descend into the canyon on the other side.

"I bet I can!" Aura shouted so loud that Delphine flinched when the voice hit her communications link. With one quick movement, she shoved Delphine so hard, she fell back, her butt slamming into the surface and causing a plume of dust to rise around her. Aura took off toward the crest, her short legs pumping at full speed.

Delphine muttered an obscenity under her breath but couldn't hold back a laugh as she hauled herself up and started off after her sister. The two raced the remaining distance with Delphine purposely keeping a meter behind Aura to give her an advantage. After Aura beat her to the top, she collapsed onto her knees, wheezing inside her mask with fists raised in victory.

"I beat you!" she yelled at the top of her lungs.

Delphine, who was also out of breath from the sprint, sat next to her. "You sure did, kiddo. Fair and square."

They looked out over the canyon laid out in front of them. Delphine didn't come here often. But when she did, she always stopped to take in the beautiful view. The gorge of Sol Canyon dropped three hundred meters from where they stood to the canyon floor and continued north over two kilometers from where they stood at the southern end. It was a bright afternoon with the hazy Titanian atmosphere almost glowing around them. Delphine could easily make out the lip of the east rim, which wasn't always possible, especially when the Titanian night was close. The sides of the canyon were steep, but there was a worn path cut into the rock in a switchback pattern that the colonists used to descend to the bottom.

Before they began their descent, Delphine warned Aura to stick close behind her as they navigated the switchbacks. The path was less than a meter wide at its widest point and the edges fell away sharply onto the steep, rocky walls. Falling over the side wouldn't necessarily be deadly, but a slide down the sheer rock face would hurt like hell. Delphine knew this from personal experience when she and Rhayn got a little carried away horsing around on the path and took a wicked tumble the last fifty yards into the bottom. They'd emerged with more bruises than she cared to count and they had been lucky that neither of them had been forced to endure the walk back with a broken ankle.

They made their way through the first few sets of switchbacks without incident and Delphine turned to Aura. "How are you holding up?" She knew Aura didn't handle heights very well, so she was somewhat nervous about the descent.

Aura nodded and gave her a thumbs-up. "Good," was all she said, her face twisted into a nervous smile.

"You sure? We can turn around if it's too steep for you. I promise, I won't tell all of third-gen that you're a wimp."

"I'm not a wimp! I'm fine."

"Promise?"

"Promise."

They continued on their way, taking each step carefully and running their gloves along the canyon wall to help keep them steady on the trickier sections of the path. After about fifteen minutes, they had made their way to the bottom and Delphine heard Aura sigh with relief.

"You know, the climb out is a lot harder," Delphine said, smiling.

"I know that!" Aura said defensively. She straightened, brushing dust from her gloves and started to pick her way around the big boulder field littering the bottom of the gorge.

"We'll find the best gems this way." Delphine gestured for Aura to follow her to a small hollow carved into the canyon wall where she and Rhayn had found a treasure trove of red and pink beryl once before. Aura squealed when she began digging in the loose dirt around the mouth of the hollow and pulled out a piece of dark red beryl that could have easily weighed five grams. The look of awe on her face made Delphine smile wide as she patted her sister on the shoulder. "That's a good one!"

Aura nodded in agreement. "It will make a beautiful pendant! Maybe I can learn to cut them myself. I could get some serious credits from these!"

Delphine laughed. "Absolutely. Rhea can teach you how to polish them. She makes the best pieces."

The pair continued searching the loose rock of the canyon for the next fifty minutes, gathering a surprisingly full sack of gems. Mostly red beryl, but a few small pieces of diaspore and ametrine as well. Overall, it was an excellent haul. Delphine imagined bragging to Rhayn about it when they got back. Then she remembered she still had afternoon lessons to attend to. She checked the time on her faceplate. "Ugh, we have to get going, kid. I've got chemistry and math this afternoon and Pala will *not* be pleased if we're late for supper again."

Aura's shoulders slumped. "Ahhh," she whined, "but we've only just gotten here. And we've found so many!"

Delphine shrugged. "Sorry, but that's how it goes. It's going to take us a good thirty minutes to climb out of here and another twenty to walk back. We can come back again next week."

"Promise?"

"Promise." Delphine held out her hand and Aura shook it, a sign that Delphine meant to keep her word and bring her sister back to the gem spot.

They made their way back to the switchbacks and began the climb. About halfway up the canyon wall, Delphine could feel her limbs burning under the weight of hauling her body and her surf suit up the steep path. She turned and saw Aura was trudging along but keeping up surprisingly well, stamping one boot in front of the other in step behind Delphine. As she watched her sister, she couldn't help but smile with pride at how well Aura had handled her first long outing on the surface.

They were almost to the lip of the canyon when Delphine heard it—a long, slow beep. It wasn't uncommon for a suit to beep and buzz from time to time alerting the occupant to the status of suit vitals or weather patterns. Most of the time, Delphine simply ignored them as she was so used to the sounds. But this beep was not a normal suit alert. This sounded more like an alarm.

She immediately pulled up her vitals and scanned the readings on the faceplate. Everything looked normal. Oxygen level was about 50 percent, well within normal limits for the walk back. Nitrogen, trace gasses, temperature, atmospheric pressure. Nothing seemed out of place.

It was then that she realized—the beeping wasn't coming from her suit, it was coming from Aura's and she could hear it through the communications link. She called for her bugs to pull up vitals on Aura's surf suit. It took only a moment for her eyes to find the source of the alarm:

Oxygen Level Critical: 1.04% Remaining

"Aura," she said, trying to keep her voice calm. "Has your suit been making that noise for long?"

Aura looked up, her face red and sweaty from the exertion. "That beeping noise? Yeah, I guess. It's been a little while. I figured I'd take a look at it after we got to the top. Why?"

Delphine took in a long pull of air and closed her eyes. She commanded her ear bugs to double check the readings on Aura's suit. The flash came back a moment later with the same notification.

"Oh my God…" Delphine's voice lost power and she felt as though her blood were draining out of her body.

"What?" Aura asked.

Delphine grabbed her by the shoulders and tapped her faceplate against her sister's. "Aura! Your oxygen's almost out! Why didn't you say something earlier??"

"I... I... I..." Aura stammered. "I don't know! I didn't realize it was so low!"

"We've got to get moving! Now!" She grabbed Aura's hand and they began running up the final leg of the switchbacks. They ran over the crest and down the other side, moving at full speed. After a few minutes, Aura stopped and put her hands on her knees.

"Delphine! I can't run all the way back! I can't... I can't seem to... catch my breath!"

Delphine pulled up her own oxygen reading. She was at 46 percent. She forced herself to calm down and think. She needed to call for help.

"Mayday, Mayday! Xanadu station, do you read? This is Delphine and Aura on the surface. Do you read me?" she shouted into her ear bugs, ordering them to send a blast broadcast to anyone who might be within transmission distance from the colony.

"Xanadu here. What's the problem?" came a response almost immediately. It was Thessa, a second-gen Delphine knew worked in the cultivation tents. She must have been the closest colonist to them. Delphine could see the top of the cultivation tents just beyond a ridge, but they were far—too far. They would never make it that far without help.

"Thessa! This is Delphine. We're on the surface, me and Aura, and she's almost out of oxygen." Tears began to stream down Delphine's face as she spoke. Her surf suit responded by blowing a steady stream of air on her face to keep her eyes clear and dry. She could hear her voice breaking. "I... I don't know how it happened! We were distracted. We didn't realize she was so low. We need help now!"

The communication link clicked and Thessa's voice came back, crackling a bit through the distance. "How much oxygen does she have left?"

"Less than half a percent! Send someone in a rover now! We're still almost a kilometer away from the colony!"

"Roger, Delphine. I'm getting in the rover myself. Give me a few minutes to suit up. Keep moving toward me if you can. Turn on your beacon so I can track you."

Delphine instructed her bugs to send out a beacon and turned to Aura whose face was pale. Her lips were a strange shade of purple and she was struggling to suck in as much air as she could with each gulp. She could see from Aura's suit readings that the suit had plenty of the other gasses necessary to create breathable air. Aura could fill her lungs as much as she wanted but without oxygen, she would pass out.

Maybe there was a way she could share her oxygen supply with her sister. Delphine posed the question to her ear bugs but got no useful answers. She turned Aura around and examined the lifepack on her back. If she could work quickly, maybe she could switch her lifepack with Aura's. Delphine mentally ran through the possible problems with this plan.

First, if she disconnected either of their lifepacks, the Titanian atmosphere would rush into the surf suit from the exposed hoses. Mostly made up of nitrogen, the atmosphere wouldn't kill them immediately, but the foul air surrounding them had trace amounts of extremely deadly gasses such as methane, propane, and hydrogen cyanide. Once the packs were switched and turned back on, these poisonous gasses would need to be flushed out of the suit before the occupant could breathe the air coming from the lifepacks. If Delphine really hustled, she would have Aura's pack switched to hers in a matter of thirty seconds—but it would take the suit at least another minute to clear out the existing atmosphere and replace it with breathable air.

Then there was the problem of temperature. She took a quick glance at the outside temperature gauge on her ear bugs. The number made her shudder: −172.6 degrees Celsius. If she unhooked her lifepack, the deep cold from the surrounding atmosphere would take care of her much quicker than the deadly gasses. It would take only moments for her skin to freeze solid.

But as she watched Aura kneeling before her, struggling to catch her breath, she realized she was out of options. There was no way she could save her at this moment. Their only chance was to keep moving toward the colony, where hopefully, Thessa would be on the way with the rover.

"Aura." Delphine grabbed her sister's shoulders and forced her to look into her eyes. Her mother's gray eyes stared back at her, wide and terrified. "I'm going to put your arm on my shoulder and we're going to run. Do you hear me? I need you to run as hard as you can!"

Aura nodded and, still gasping, she made an effort to straighten up. Delphine threw her sister's arm over her shoulder and grabbed her around the torso. "Let's go!" she shouted, urging her exhausted legs forward. Aura followed suit and they began to run.

After a few meters, Delphine could feel Aura's legs start to give way. She willed herself to move forward. *Push!* she shouted to herself as she wrapped her other arm around Aura and tugged her forward with all her might.

Time seemed to slow down. Delphine couldn't hear anything except her own ragged breath and the light wheeze of her sister as she struggled by her side. She pushed forward, counting each step as she dug her boots into the soft, rocky soil of the surface.

Ten steps.

Twenty steps.

Twenty-five steps.

Keep going! she screamed inside her head. When she hit thirty steps, she called up her ear bugs and said, "Thessa! How far away are you? Do you hear me?"

The communication link crackled and Thessa's voice came through, clearer now. "Delphine, I picked up your beacon. I'm in the rover now, just leaving the cultivation tent. ETA is three minutes to your location."

Tears flowed freely from Delphine's eyes and she cursed as her surf suit continued to try to keep her face dry with a blast of cool air. Three minutes was too long.

Forty steps.

Forty-five steps.

Fifty steps.

She *had* to keep moving. "Aura," she sobbed, "we're almost to the rover. Please! Please hang on until we're there! I've got you. I won't let you go. I'm going to save you!"

There was no response. But Delphine kept pushing forward.

Fifty-five steps.

Sixty steps.

Sixty-five steps.

Her legs burned and the constant swoosh of her breath inside her helmet was deafening. With all the exertion, the suit was having a hard time keeping her faceplate clear of condensation. She could hear the tiny fans inside the helmet whirring along with her breathing, but beads of water formed on the cloudy faceplate and dripped down into her neck.

She fell into a rhythm, counting steps and counting breaths. Her arms gripped Aura's body tighter and tighter the farther she went. She could see the tops of the cultivation tents better now. They were a little over a half a kilometer away now, she guessed by their size. They were doing it! She was getting closer!

After what felt like an eternity of counting her steps and her breaths, Delphine finally saw what she sought most—the lights from a rover speeding toward her over the ridge of a dune. It was thirty meters away. She kept pushing. Kept counting. Squeezed her sister tighter.

When Thessa pulled up to the pair, she already had the cargo door of the rover open, her own body shielded from the atmosphere with a surf suit. She jumped out of the rover and helped Delphine haul Aura into the main pressure compartment of the rover. As soon as they were inside, Thessa slammed her fist into the round, red button next to the pressure door. Once the door was sealed, Thessa pressed commands into the control panel next to the door and the harsh Titan atmosphere began to flow out of the vehicle, replaced by blessed, breathable air.

Delphine watched the atmosphere readings on her ear bugs and as soon as the levels inside the rover were clear, she ripped off her faceplate while Thessa did the same for Aura. She was so exhausted from the last few minutes, the strength immediately left her body and she felt her back go slack as she slumped onto the floor. The rush of change in atmosphere made her head spin and she felt almost like she had water in her ears. She couldn't focus. She could hear Thessa working on Aura next to her, but it didn't seem real, almost like they were very far away and she could barely make out what was going on.

Before she passed out on the floor of the rover, a final thought rolled through her head. I did it. I saved my sister. I got her to the rover. She's going to be okay.

CHAPTER 13
PRESENT

But, of course, Aura wasn't okay.

Delphine couldn't remember much about what happened next. But she knew she woke up in the colony medical wing, screaming for her sister. The medics had to sedate her and it was a full three days before she finally learned the truth—Aura did not make it to the rover. She had run out of oxygen and passed out well before that. When Thessa got to her, Aura was already gone. Despite her best CPR efforts, Thessa was unable to bring Aura back.

Delphine had failed.

She had failed to protect her sister from the dangers of using the surf suits. She had failed to properly check Aura's gauges before they left the colony that day. She had failed to get her sister back to the colony fast enough to save her life.

She thought about that day often. Not because she wanted to remember it, but because she felt it was her penance. Her weight to bear. To remember Aura's wheezing breath and the desperate, scared look in her eyes. Delphine had analyzed every movement they made that day and catalogued all her mistakes. They had spent way too long in the canyon. She hadn't checked Aura's suit vitals at all until she heard the alarm. She shouldn't have had Aura out that far from the colony to begin with. It was against the rules—and obviously for good reason.

It had all been her fault. Her failure. When she'd stood there on the surface, wasting precious seconds, trying to decide whether she should take off her own lifepack and strap it to her sister, she had failed to act. Failed to do what was necessary to save Aura. Delphine would have died if she'd removed her lifepack, she knew that. But she could have saved Aura. She could have acted quickly enough to get the pack transferred to her sister before she herself froze to death.

She *knew* it deep in her bones, though Rhayn had tried to convince her it wouldn't have worked. She would never have gotten it switched in time and then they both would have died on the surface. No, Delphine still believed it with all her heart. She could have done it. It was her fault that Aura died that day.

That night, after the meeting in the Atrium, Delphine lay in bed, hopelessly awake, staring at the ceiling of her room. She thought about what Ligeia had said at the meeting. Referred to her *unstable mental state*. Was she unstable? She couldn't decide if this made her angry, or if Ligeia had her full agreement.

In the months that followed the accident at the canyon, Delphine had sunk into the deepest recesses of her mind. She couldn't finish her annual studies with the rest of the third-gen and hadn't eaten, slept, or even moved for days at a time. She remembered Pala drifting in and out of her room—the room she had shared with Aura—occasionally bringing her herbal tea or baked goods. But Pala never spoke to her, only hovered in front of her before leaving as quickly as she could.

Delphine could see the hurt in Pala's face. No, it went further than hurt. Delphine knew it from the tight line of her mouth, her hard gray eyes, the clench of her jaw—her mother was *angry*. At her. And Delphine didn't blame her one bit. She felt as though her mother's anger fueled her depression. Gave her more reason to sink into the oblivion of her own mind.

It was Rhayn who saved Delphine's life.

She and the twins had always been friends, of course. The third-gen was the largest of the generations at Xanadu, but despite its size, the third-gens were tight. The group spanned in age from late twenties to early teens, but they all knew each other and shared their signature purple jumpsuits. The group of third-gens in the same age range as Delphine and the twins was the largest of any age group, with thirty-two girls between the ages of nineteen and twenty-one. Their group was particularly close since they did their schooling at the same time.

Even though they were close, Rhayn and Delphine weren't *that* close. Not until Aura died. They had only been part of the same circle before. Two people floating around in a group, trying to make their way through adolescence without losing their minds. When Aura passed away, it had a profound effect on the third-gens. She was a friendly, outgoing member of the group, and they all mourned her loss.

It was eleven months after the tragedy when Delphine found Rhayn standing outside her living quarters knocking on the door with a slow, deliberate rap of her fist. At the time, Delphine wasn't interested in consolation. She'd entered her depressive state and had had so much consolation she could practically bathe in it. So, when she opened the door to see Rhayn standing there, her sister Rho hanging back, staring out from under her long, dark eyelashes as she always did, Delphine didn't expect anything new or extraordinary from the pair. She remembered letting out a long sigh, rolling her eyes, and bracing herself for another wash of consolation by hugging her arms to her body—a means of protection from everyone else and their need to help.

The consolation never came. Instead Rhayn tilted her head to the side and planted her hand on her hip saying, "Get dressed. We're going outside."

Delphine had flinched at the command, as if the words had been accompanied by flying daggers. "Excuse me? What do you mean 'we're going outside'?"

"Exactly that. Get your surf suit on because we're going outside." As she said this, Rhayn looked back at her sister who simply gave a curt nod in agreement.

"I'm not going outside." The thought of putting on a surf suit after what she'd experienced wasn't just off-putting, it was an impossibility. There was no *way* she was going back outside.

No way.

But apparently, Rhayn did not share this opinion, and if Delphine had learned anything about Rhayn in the time since, she knew that when Rhayn wanted something to happen, she found a way to make it happen.

"Nope. Not the right answer," Rhayn replied, suddenly reaching for Delphine's shoulder and whirling her around to face the empty living quarters. With a gentle push, Rhayn led her into the kitchen.

Delphine hadn't had the strength to move much at all before that, but that one push by Rhayn had made her angry. Whipping back around to face Rhayn, Delphine pushed her friend's hand off her shoulder. "I don't know what you're getting at Rhayn, but I am *not* going outside. That's the end of it." There was an unexpected bite in her voice she didn't know she could still summon.

Instead of arguing further with her, Rhayn smiled and glanced back at Rho, winking. "Now that's the spirit." She grasped Delphine's shoulders in her hands and came close to her so they were almost nose to nose. Looking deep into her eyes, Rhayn gave it to her straight. "You are not dead. I hate to be the one to break it to you, Del. But *you* are not dead."

"I'm well aware of my current state—"

"No!" Rhayn interrupted, with more force than Delphine had ever heard come out of her mouth. "Listen to me. You. Are. Not. Dead!" Her words were sharp, each one packing a punch at Delphine's ego. "I'm only going to repeat this one more time: put on your surf suit because we're going outside. It will be awfully cold out there without it." She ended her speech with a chuckle that Rho mirrored from the open doorway behind her.

Something in Rhayn's words got through to Delphine in that moment. She wasn't sure what it was, but this was the first time since the accident that anyone had actually stood up to her. Forced her to listen. Forced her to do anything. With a skeptical side-eye, Delphine had said, "Okay."

Delphine remembered moving in a daze of disbelief as Rhayn helped her secure her surf suit. Rho had checked Delphine's lifepack and gauges and had tethered the suit readings to her ear bugs to ensure that she could monitor Delphine's vitals during her first surface walk in nearly a year. Delphine remembered actively trying to push fear and panic out of her mind as Rhayn secured the faceplate on her surf suit, tapping her own faceplate to Delphine's to show she was with her all the way.

That first trip outside the colony had been surreal. She wasn't sure exactly what she expected when the overhead door to the airlock had lifted that day and the sharp prick of the chilled Titanian atmosphere spiked at the edges of her suit, but what she got was a strange feeling of triumph. Not that she really did anything on that first excursion—it amounted to an easy walk around the perimeter of the Atrium with Rhayn holding tight to Delphine's hand and Rho keeping a steady pace behind the two of them. They had stayed outside for less than thirty minutes, yet the experience changed Delphine from the inside.

Relief and a sense of normalcy returned. Walking and jogging and working outside the colony were part of Delphine's life. She had loved the sensation of her surf suit melding to her skin as the tiny heating elements in it charged to life under the immense cold of the frosty atmosphere. She had loved the feel of the sandy soil crunching under her boots every time she went for a late-night run. Without regular access to the surface, Delphine had been a passenger lost, trying desperately to find her way without her sister or her normal routine.

Rhayn had given her back a piece of that routine. She had forced Delphine to move out of the dark cloud of fear and depression and back into the dim light of Titan's surface. Without Rhayn and Rho, Delphine was certain she would have slipped even further into her own mind and perhaps, wasted away like her mother.

When the trio had returned that day after her first trip to the surface since Aura's death, Pala had watched from her room as Delphine stripped off her suit and hugged the twins. Her hard eyes had followed Delphine, scrutinized her movements, and Delphine could feel the weight of them as she put away her gear and stood in front of her mother, waiting for the reaction. It didn't come. Pala simply stared at her.

"I had to go back out," Delphine had said, her eyes clouding. "I can't stay here in this tiny compartment thinking about Aura for the rest of my life." She gestured around her. "You understand, right?" She desperately needed Pala to forgive her. To replace the anger in her eyes with love again.

But still, no reaction came. Pala sighed and turned into her room, closing the door behind her with a soft thud. That was the last time the two had spoken Aura's name to each other. The last time they had discussed the incident at all.

From that day through the next few years, Delphine stuck close to Rhayn. She showed up at Delphine's door every time they had a mandatory meeting, before every class lesson, and for every meal. Somehow, and Delphine was never sure how, Rhayn got herself assigned to every work assignment put on Delphine's schedule during those first few years after the accident so they could be together if Delphine needed her. Rhayn walked with

Delphine, ate with Delphine, listened when Delphine needed to scream or cry or laugh. She would spend nights in Pala and Delphine's living quarters, holding Delphine when she couldn't sleep or stroking her tears away when the nightmares took over.

While Pala sank further into herself—refusing to eat, refusing to talk, refusing to get help—Delphine began to heal under Rhayn's care. She caught up on her studies by doing double workloads and finished the next year with the rest of her third-gen age group. She got back into her routine of going on regular runs outside, first with Rhayn and Rho always in tow, and eventually, on her own again. She successfully applied for work in the cultivation tents. She managed to get her life back on track.

Occasionally the pain would return, sometimes with greater force than the original blow of losing Aura, causing Delphine to have breakdowns—the dark days, she called them. Days where she couldn't move or speak or even think without pain and guilt ripping through her body. But Rhayn was always there to hold her and talk her through, even if it took a week to pass. And the other colonists, including Thessa, Delphine's boss in the tents, were understanding with her, giving her as much time as she needed to get herself back in working order.

As the years passed, Delphine had fewer and fewer dark days. She learned to cope with her feelings rather than allow them to overcome her. Yet, it was still there, the guilt, like a dark smudge at the back of her mind, waiting for its chance to overtake her and blot out the light forever. This was what Ligeia had referred to at that meeting—the breakdowns, the dark days when she couldn't leave her room and others had to carry out her work duties for her.

Delphine stared at the thin strip of light piercing her darkened room from the hallway and wondered if perhaps Ligeia was right in her jarring assessment of Delphine's mental state. Her first reaction had been anger, intense anger at the gall Ligeia had to bring up her problems in front of the crowd. But maybe she was right to do it. Maybe it was Ligeia's way to protect the rest of the colonists. To protect them from Delphine, someone hurting and angry and unstable.

With sleep nowhere near her, Delphine sighed and sat up in bed, taking a long, slow sip from her water glass before standing. She tapped her ear bug to see that it was half past midnight. There was only one thing she could think to do. She headed into the kitchen and grabbed her gear before heading to the airlock for a run.

CHAPTER 14

"Ouch! Damn..." Delphine murmured under her breath as a trayful of pruning tools fell from the shelf in front of her and landed square on the toe of her boot. The tools made a loud and prolonged clatter as they scattered around the supply room in all directions. Delphine sighed, bent to rub her sore toe through the boot with her fingertips, and righted the heavy tray so she could start collecting the tools and putting them back.

"Here. Let me help." Rhayn bent down next to her and picked up several sets of shears that had landed underneath the shelving unit. She grunted as she reached for a pruning knife wedged in the very back, where the shelving unit met the wall. After pulling the knife loose, she dropped it into the tray and smiled. "Heck of a way to start the day, huh?"

"Yeah, no kidding," Delphine replied, collecting the last of the scattered tools and depositing them back into their tray.

It was the morning after the election in the Atrium and Delphine had reported to her shift in the cultivation tent as if nothing had happened the day before. As if she hadn't been called out and humiliated in front of the entire colony. Rhayn had met her at her door that morning, arms crossed, a slight smile on her lips. "Didn't think you'd get out of work this morning, did ya?" she had asked.

Actually, Delphine had considered messaging Thessa and asking for a late start. After her middle-of-the-night run, she'd showered and fallen into bed, exhausted but still unable to find sleep. It had been a fitful night of tossing and turning before the alarm finally pinged on her ear bugs to get up for work. Although the idea of skipping out on the morning shift appealed to her, she knew it wouldn't fly. Not with Thessa and certainly not with Rhayn. Keeping to her schedule was the key to keeping her mind healthy, and if she cut out, it could spiral her into a series of dark days. So, it didn't surprise her one bit that Rhayn had dropped by her living quarters to ensure she was making the trek to work. Rhayn knew as well as anyone else that Delphine didn't do well when she wallowed.

Plus, Delphine didn't want to give Ligeia the satisfaction of knowing how much her words the day prior had affected her. Not showing for a shift was a serious offense—one that would surely have made its way up the ranks to Ligeia. They'd been lenient with her in the past, but Delphine was sure this generosity wouldn't extend to her now that she'd stood up to Ligeia in a public meeting. She could lose three days' worth of rations if she didn't show for work and that wasn't a risk she was willing to take. It was better to push the mental haze aside and go to work, blend in, keep from drawing more attention to herself.

But she was already paying a price for her sleepless night. In a daze, she'd gone to the utility shed with Rhayn in search of pruning shears and ended up dropping the entire tray on her foot because she wasn't paying attention to the task at hand.

Delphine grabbed the set of shears she'd meant to pull from the tray and tucked them into her utility belt. Rhayn helped her hoist the tray back onto the shelf before elbowing her with a gentle nudge.

"Chin up," Rhayn said, flashing her a smile, "tonight will be better."

"Is it that obvious?"

"Well, your eyes are as wide as avocado pits and it's clear you haven't brushed your hair. So yes, it's obvious."

Delphine sighed and ran her fingers through her tangled ponytail. Rhayn could always tell when she'd had a bad night. This both comforted and infuriated her. She shrugged and followed Rhayn out the door and into the tent where the dense, warm air hit them like an invisible fist.

Outside the supply room door, they ran into Maya, a fellow third-gen talking to Thessa. They were speaking in low voices. Delphine couldn't help but catch the tail end of their conversation as Maya said, "…can't believe the nerve. Who does she think she is?"

Thessa cleared her throat loudly and both women fell silent as they appraised their workmates. "Good morning," Thessa said, nodding first at Delphine, then at Rhayn. She tucked a loop of blond hair behind her ear before looking away, down the walkway behind them.

"Morning," Rhayn repeated, pretending not to notice the strange discomfort that had settled on the group. "What's up?" She shot Delphine a sidelong glance and the corner of her mouth ticked up.

Maya cleared her throat and shoved her hands deep inside the pockets of her coveralls. Her thick, brown hair was pulled tight in her signature topknot, perched on top of her head. "Oh, we were just discussing the election yesterday." As she said this, she straightened up and looked Delphine square in the eyes.

"Maya," Thessa said, almost under her breath, "let's get back to those sweet peas before the solution…"

Maya interrupted her and continued, "Specifically, we were talking about the three laws and how generous Earth was to leave them as a guideline for our governance." She stepped forward, hardening her glare and crossing her arms at her chest. "And how well our council has worked to uphold the three laws throughout the colony's history and has managed to ensure a peaceful existence for all colonists through those three laws. Don't you agree, Delphine?" As she finished, a sweet smile spread over Maya's lips and she gave a quick glance to the camera sitting just behind them over the door to the storage room. A fine performance, no doubt.

Delphine furrowed her brow, a wave of discomfort settling over her. Before she could speak, Thessa grabbed Maya's arm from behind and tugged it toward the walkway. "Come on, Maya, we need to get back to work."

Maya wasn't having it. She wrenched her arm loose from Thessa's fingers and resumed her stance, arms crossed, eyes piercing as she waited for Delphine to answer. "Don't you agree, Delphine?" she repeated.

Delphine took a step toward Maya, heat rising in her face. "Excuse me? What is that supposed to mean?"

"Exactly what it implies. You seem to think you're above the three laws for some reason and that's *not* okay. Our council is wise and just and they are directly responsible for the success of this colony. I think you owe them some respect."

"Look! It's really none of your business what my thoughts are on the three laws or the council, is it?"

Rhayn put a hand on Delphine's shoulder and said, slowly, "Easy, Del."

Delphine didn't realize it but her hands were balled into fists at her sides and she had inched closer to Maya. "And what of it if I do disagree with them? It's not against any regulation to disagree, is it? Last I checked, we could still have our own opinions about things around here."

"Your own opinion is one thing," Maya said, moving another step closer, her breath hot on Delphine's face. "But blatantly showing disrespect for Ligeia is another. It's not something that should be tolerated, in my opinion."

A laugh escaped Delphine's lips. "In your opinion? That's a joke! So, you can have an opinion but I can't?"

"Not about this, you can't. The laws are there for a reason. Respect them or pay the penalty!"

"Respect?" Delphine spat the word out and Maya flinched slightly at the sharpness of it. "What does it say about our *fearless leader* that she would call me out in front of the entire colony? What kind of leader does that??"

"The kind of leader who's not going to take shit from some lowly third-gen who's looking for a bit of glory. That's what you want, isn't it? You want to be on the council yourself? Admit it!"

"That's not true and you know it," Delphine said through gritted teeth.

"Oh?" Maya raised an eyebrow. "Well, seeing as how you're a half a click away from crazy, I wouldn't put it past you. And what about that? I think Ligeia was perfectly within her rights to call you out for what happened."

"What is that supposed to mean?"

"The way I see it, there's nobody to point any blame at but you. *You* are responsible for your sister's death and you know it."

As soon as she moved, Delphine new it was a mistake.

Before she could even process what Maya had said, her eyes filled with red and her fist, as if moving on its own, separate from her body, caught the edge of Maya's jaw with stunning precision. A stream of blood shot from Maya's mouth as one of her teeth landed on the floor with a soft clink. In an instant, Delphine had pushed Maya to the ground and was straddling her, pounding a fist into Maya's face over and over again. Guttural screams escaped from Delphine as she hit Maya, forcing her anger and frustration to push itself out in the form of quick jabs. Maya's finger scratched at Delphine, leaving long, jagged welts on her cheeks and neck. It seemed to go on in slow motion like that for what felt like an eternity before Delphine felt Rhayn's strong arms wrap around her, pulling her to her feet.

Thessa pulled Maya upright at the same time and was holding her back in a similar fashion. The look on Thessa's face was pure disbelief as she struggled to keep Maya from pouncing back at Delphine.

"You bitch!" Maya screamed, holding her jaw with one hand, the other flailing toward Delphine. Her right eye was already swelling and a purple bruise had started to form across her cheekbone.

The commotion caused three others, another third-gen and two second-gens, to come running down the walkways from the tent's interior. The women stared in disbelief at the scene before them. Rhayn held Delphine who was sobbing through screams of "Take it back! Take it back *now*!" Thessa continued to hold Maya who was now cursing at the top of her lungs about how her jaw was probably broken.

Before anyone could make another move, Thessa let go of Maya and grabbed Delphine by the arm. "That's it! This is unacceptable. Come with me."

Delphine managed to calm her sobs and looked back toward Rhayn who simply shrugged, her eyes wide and her mouth hanging open. She turned back to Thessa and said, "Where are we going?"

Thessa responded in a cool voice. "To see Ligeia."

CHAPTER 15

Their footsteps made an eerie *thump, thump, thump* that echoed through the empty concourse beyond the exits of the cultivation tents. It was rare for Delphine to be in the concourse in the middle of a shift. Usually, she was exiting the cultivation tents with all the other tent workers, providing enough noise to block out the sound of her footsteps. But now, as she and Thessa headed toward Ligeia's living quarters, she could hear every sharp thud.

She walked a short distance behind Thessa with her head hung slightly, not wanting to speak to her or look her in the eye after what she'd done. Violence was *not* something tolerated at Xanadu and Delphine knew that. It was rare for anyone to even raise their voice to a fellow colonist. Causing scar tissue was something almost unheard of.

It was almost a half-kilometer walk from Tent 4 to Ligeia's quarters at the far eastern end of the colony complex.

Delphine took this time to mentally run through the ridiculousness of her actions and the possible repercussions.

Okay, so Maya had been a bitch for saying what she had... but she was also kind of an idiot. Delphine remembered a time during their secondary-level courses when Maya dunked her fingers into a vat of acid during a chemistry experiment despite repeated warnings from the instructor about the dangers of the chemical, because one of the other girls had dared her to do so. She had said afterward that she didn't believe the instructor's warnings and that she'd never backed down from a dare. The incident had almost cost her a hand and she'd spent three months in the medical ward receiving regular skin grafts and stem cell injections to get her hand back in working order. Delphine could still see the pale scars from the incident on the tips of Maya's fingers where the damage had been the worst.

So attacking her simply because she had no foresight to question the leadership of the colony wasn't the best decision. Why would Maya question things? She barely had the sense to keep her fingers out of a chemistry experiment. Just thinking about the incident made Delphine's face flush and she shook her head in disgust at herself.

They exited the concourse and entered the Atrium, Thessa holding a quick, steady pace while Delphine followed. Unlike the concourse, the Atrium buzzed with activity as off-duty colonists sat in groups chatting, stood in lines to collect provisions, and headed in and out of the concourses.

She could tell by the weakening light filtering through from the oculus that the Titan night was approaching. Xanadu was on the leading face of the moon, meaning it was the first area to encounter the sun when emerging from behind Saturn. It was also the first area to plunge into darkness when the moon swung around in its orbit. The bright glow of the atmosphere in sunlight was waning and Delphine could tell they were on their way to the seven and a half days of darkness the moon experienced every fifteen days. Something about the darkening sank into Delphine's mind, chilling her. It was as if her home world understood that she was headed toward an unpleasant future.

The pair rounded the outer wall of the Atrium and entered the West Concourse leading to the living quarters. Delphine had never actually been inside Ligeia's home before, but she, like all the colonists, knew where it was. There was a block of apartments at the farthest end of the colony living quarters section reserved for council members and their families. From time to time, Delphine would go for a run inside the colony when she didn't feel like suiting up for the surface and this was the best place to do it among rows and rows of hallways lined with doors leading to the apartments where the colonists lived.

She'd run past the council apartments many times before and always wondered what it was like on the other side of those doors. There were a few critical differences between the council apartments and those doors relegated to the regular colonists. First, the council doors and those of their families were much farther apart. Where six doors lay on either side of the hallway outside Delphine's apartment, this hallway butted up to the back wall of the cavern where the living quarters wing was built and only had doors on one side. Ten doors spanned the entire length of it—meaning each apartment was at least three times the size of the one Delphine shared with her mother.

Another notable difference in the council members' wing were the doors themselves. Regular living quarters apartment doors consisted of a standard one-and-a-half-meter composite door, gray, with a single access panel allowing the colonists to scan their bugs and gain entry to the apartment. The doors to the council apartments were twice the size of the standard doors: taller and made from a rich purple composite. They had the traditional access panel like all other doors, but they also had special locking panels that required a special code to enter.

As she and Thessa made their way down the corridor, Delphine took note of each of these special doors and wondered, what was so important in there that they needed special code locks? She furrowed her brow. And then it occurred to her—the standard access panels could be opened by the occupant of the room, but they could also be opened by anyone with a heightened security clearance. This included department heads, medics, and council members. The extra locking panel was a way for the council members to safeguard their living quarters further by setting their own entry code that only they could know.

They had access to everyone, and nobody had access to them. Delphine had never thought about it before. She'd seen the doors many times but never looked too far past the vibrant color. Yet now, she realized how clever this setup really was.

"Hmm," she said, not realizing the sound had escaped her lips until Thessa stopped walking and turned to look at her.

"Yes?" Thessa asked, her face stone and a hint of annoyance at the edge of her voice.

"Oh, nothing. Just nervous, that's all." Delphine shrugged and Thessa turned around and resumed her stride.

After another minute of walking, they reached the door at the very end of the hall, the apartment cut the deepest into Titan's underbelly. Ligeia's living quarters.

Thessa signaled her bugs to wave her security badge to the access panel, which beeped in response.

A moment later, a deep voice resonated from the panel. "Yes?"

Delphine recognized the voice as Ligeia's.

Thessa cleared her throat. "Hello, Ligeia. Apologies for this intrusion but we've had"—she looked back at Delphine for a moment—"an incident in Tent 4 and I believe it's important that you know about it."

There was a long pause and sweat crept down the back of Delphine's neck as she waited for Ligeia to speak again.

"I see," she finally said, her voice through the panel as clear as if she were standing right in front of them. "And you feel this is something that requires council intervention?"

There was no doubt in Delphine's mind that Ligeia could see them standing in front of her door and knew exactly who she was talking too. In fact, it wouldn't surprise her at all if Ligeia hadn't pulled up footage from the security cameras in Tent 4 and knew exactly what the incident was. According to rumors, Ligeia had access to footage from every camera at Xanadu, over four thousand of them, even those placed inside the apartments of the colonists.

"Yes, I believe council intervention is necessary. There was violence involved in the interaction."

"I see." There was a faint click and the screen on the access panel turned green. "Please send Delphine in. You may go back to the tent, Thessa. Thank you for your willingness to bring this important matter to my attention immediately."

Thessa stared at the door and nodded before turning to leave. She gave Delphine one last look as she walked back down the hallway they'd come through. Delphine sighed and pushed on the door, now unlocked, before entering Ligeia's apartment.

CHAPTER 16

For a short moment, Delphine couldn't believe what she was seeing. She blinked rapidly to make sure her eyes weren't deceiving her. After a moment, she realized, no, she wasn't seeing things, and her mouth dropped open while she slowly swiveled her head to take it all in.

All the apartments Delphine had been in were compact, modular, and exactly the same from one to the next. The only difference she'd ever seen in them was that one side of the hallway was a mirror image of the other. Since the colonists, aside from council members, were never allowed to produce more than two children, all apartments had three bedrooms, a small bathroom, and a common room where the kitchen and eating area were located.

The room that now spread out in front of Delphine was enormous. She gaped at the sheer size of it. The ceiling was at least six meters above her head and made of the interior of the cave wall itself. Like the walls in the Atrium, the ceiling of Ligeia's apartment ascended upward to an oculus, this one much smaller than the one in the Atrium but just as impressive.

The same weakening, orange light filtered through the oculus in this room and cast hazy shadows all around the cavern. This was obviously part of the natural cave system that the original colonists had used to make the living quarters wing. But Delphine had no idea that there was *another* oculus at the colony. How did she not know about this?

She stared up at the thick plastic dome that poked up through the surface above. It was much more symmetrical than the one in the Atrium which was made to cover the natural cave opening. The opening that led to the surface appeared to have been cut through the cave ceiling by colonists. There was nothing natural about this shape.

Delphine was so transfixed by the opening above her head, she didn't notice that Ligeia had appeared and was now standing next to her.

"Do you like it?" Ligeia asked, causing Delphine to jump. Her voice did not sound as deep or menacing as it had through the access panel outside the door. In fact, it didn't even sound like it did at the regular colony meetings in the Atrium. It was calm and smooth and seemed to float through the air that separated the two.

"I... I had no idea it was here," Delphine said, looking back up at the oculus and shaking her head in disbelief.

Ligeia smiled and nodded, looking up to admire the oculus herself. She was wearing a flowing red robe that crossed at the front and tied with a pink sash at the waist. Her red hair was pulled into a loose bun at the back of her neck with wisps escaping around her face. Delphine had rarely seen colonists wear anything but their standard-issue jumpsuits, color coordinated according to generation. Ligeia, being a first-gen, always wore her own red jumpsuit to match the rest of the first-gens when she was out and about in the colony.

Colonists were allowed to have other items of clothing, but they were not easy to come by. Fabric was made in the manufacturing facilities for practical purposes—jumpsuits, bedding, baby diapers, cleaning supplies. It was difficult to get extra fabric and nearly impossible to get anything that wasn't the dull polyester that composed their jumpsuits. Delphine touched her own jumpsuit, feeling the stiff fabric between her fingertips. Whatever this was that Ligeia was wearing, it was flowy and appeared much thinner and softer than her own garment. It had, no doubt, been specially made for Ligeia—a feat only council members could pull off.

Ligeia didn't seem to notice, or care, that Delphine was eyeing her luxurious robe. She threw Delphine a wide, sweet smile and walked across the cavernous room toward what appeared to be the kitchen.

"This oculus was built during the original construction of the living quarters wing. They wanted this room to be the meeting space for the colony but decided against it when they found the Atrium later in their excavation." She reached the kitchen and murmured something into her ear bugs. In an instant, carefully placed lights sprang to life, illuminating the raw cave walls around them. "I normally don't care for artificial light. Titan's atmosphere has the most magical coloring. But it is getting dark out there and I like to be able to see my guests."

In the kitchen, Ligeia pulled a large pitcher from the refrigerator and set it on the countertop along with two small glasses made from absolutely clear plastic. The kitchen was a separate room cut into the wall of the cavern but facing the enormous living space. It had bright, white cabinetry lining the walls and an onyx countertop running around the perimeter of the space. Between the kitchen and living room was a large island with a light bar suspended over it and several jars of canned goods artfully arranged in the center. They appeared to be canned fruits, from what Delphine could tell—peaches, pears, raspberries, green apples, and plums. The jars were obviously meant to be decorative as they were made from various shades of plastic blown into strange shapes. Nothing like the utilitarian, reusable ration jars that lined the cupboards in Delphine's kitchen.

The floor of the cavern had been leveled and covered in the same black flooring that covered her own apartment floor. There was a difference though. Ligeia's floor was covered with a huge, pale gray rug centered in the room, which reached almost to the perimeter walls.

Delphine, who stood inside the doorway, looked down at the rug and took a tentative step onto it. It was soft underneath her boot. She noticed that Ligeia was barefoot—a perk of having the luxury of a rug, apparently. It appeared to have been handwoven and was at least four meters square. In all her life, Delphine had never seen such a magnificent rug. The only rugs she and her mother had were two small rag rugs made from recycled cleaning cloths they used as a bathmat and doormat.

"Lemonade?" Ligeia asked, pouring the cloudy, yellow liquid from the pitcher into the small glasses. One for her and one for Delphine.

Juice was not an uncommon beverage in the colony. They had a room set aside in the canning and preserving section of the cultivation tent where they could extract juices. Each colonist was allowed one jar of juice in their weekly rations: not much, but enough to satisfy a sweet tooth from time to time. For the most part, everyone at Xanadu drank water as they knew the importance of keeping hydrated, especially in their closed-air circulation system where humidity was kept purposefully low.

Lemonade, on the other hand, was *very* rare. It required lemons, which were not grown in any of the main cultivation tents. And cane sugar, also not a big portion of their food harvest. Cane sugar was allotted to food rations only when there was an abundance and was mostly used for creating protein packs and ration bars, foods that could give a colonist plenty of calories during long work schedules on the surface. Nobody had a spare jar of the stuff lying around their kitchen—especially not enough to make an entire pitcher of lemonade.

"Sure," Delphine said, accepting the small cup from Ligeia.

She brought the cup to her lips and paused a moment to smell the fragrant liquid. It was tart and surprisingly strong, reminding her of the industrial soap they used to clean equipment in the cultivation tents. The soap was made from a combination of chemicals mixed with oil squeezed from orange rinds. Oranges were hardier than lemons, especially the variety cultivated at Xanadu. They were soft and meaty, extra sweet, and easy to peel. They had adapted the fruit to grow from a bush rather than a tree, making it much easier to grow in the hydroponic environment of the cultivation tents. Because oranges were a favorite among the colonists, a large grove of them was kept in Cultivation Tent 2 and every bit of the fruit was used in some capacity or another.

But lemons—there were no lemons growing in the cultivation tents that Delphine knew of. Delphine took this to mean that Ligeia cultivated her own lemons and probably her own sugar cane in her personal garden—another perk of being a council member.

She took a sip and as soon as the juice hit her tongue, her whole face puckered in surprise. Sipping the lemonade felt like getting slapped on the cheek. She was so taken aback by the sweet-and-sour mixture that she immediately began coughing up the drink, her eyes watering.

Ligeia, who had been watching Delphine from behind the kitchen island gave a hearty laugh and said, "Are you okay, dear? I suppose you've never had lemonade before."

Delphine, who was finally recovering from her coughing fit, pounded her chest with her fist to get the last uncomfortable rasps out of her throat. "It's okay. I was just surprised, that's all."

"Well, I do enjoy my lemonade strong. For me, the best ratio is two parts lemon juice to one part syrup. It gives it a real punch." As she said this, she punched her fist in the air to emphasize the word.

Delphine gathered herself and took another sip of the lemonade, this time, ready for its strength. As the liquid slid down her throat, it almost burned it was so strong, and she couldn't help but pucker her lips again at the sour taste.

"Actually," she said, "I have had lemonade before, but not in a long time."

Ligeia's eyebrow lifted as she inserted a tiny spoon into her cup and tinkled it around the edge, stirring the drink. "Oh? And when was that?"

Delphine stared into her cup, wondering if she'd offered too much information. "Meribelle once brought lemonade to one of our classes. I was very young, but I do remember her pouring each of us a cup to try." Meribelle's lemonade had been much less tart than the concoction she now held in her hand, pale, mild, with a slight hint of sweetness. She remembered it tasting good and she gulped down the entire cup while the rest of her third-gen classmates had squealed with delight at the new drink. She kept this part of the story to herself and forced another gulp of Ligeia's lemonade.

"Ah yes, Meribelle was a dear, sweet soul, wasn't she? I remember she used to make class visits quite often when she was younger." As she spoke, Ligeia drifted from the kitchen to the living room, her red robe fluttering in her wake. She gestured for Delphine to follow her to two long sofas that sat facing each other in the center of the room. They were gray, like the rug, and made from another type of soft, luxurious fabric Delphine had never felt before.

As she sat, she allowed her fingers to graze the top of the cushion and wondered, again, where this came from. She'd never seen a sofa like it. The sofa she shared with her mother was half the size, only large enough for the two of them to sit on and made from a thick, scratchy, orange polyester. Delphine had learned at an early age not to sit on it without something to cover her legs or else she would spend the next day itching. But this fabric felt smooth and silky under her fingers. It made her want to remove her clothes and let the fabric touch her entire body all at once.

"So, Delphine. What brings you here today? It appears Thessa wasn't happy with your behavior in the tents. Tell me what happened." Ligeia crossed one long leg over the other and bent down to set her cup on the clear plastic table that occupied the space between the two sofas.

Delphine cleared her throat, unsure of how to begin, but Ligeia cut her off before she could speak. "Actually, don't tell me. I know what happened. I watched the camera footage of the incident."

Delphine remembered that Ligeia had instant access to any camera within the walls of Xanadu—and, for that matter, those outside the walls as well. Of course she had seen the fight between Delphine and Maya.

Ligeia continued, "I'd like to say, Delphine, that I don't entirely disagree with your actions."

"Really?" The word escaped Delphine's lips before she could think about it but she couldn't help herself. The confirmation surprised her.

"Yes, really." Ligeia picked up her cup and drained the contents. A tiny drop of lemonade seeped out the corner of her mouth and Ligeia used her slim fingers to wipe it clean before it could fall on her beautiful robe. "I watched the entire confrontation and I don't blame you for being upset. Maya shouldn't have come after you like that, especially after your embarrassing incident at the election the day before."

"I wasn't embarrassed…" Delphine took offense at the insinuation that she *should* be embarrassed for standing up to the council.

But Ligeia ignored Delphine's comment and continued, "And bringing up your sister's unfortunate death in such a harsh, methodical way? That was inexcusable."

Delphine raised an eyebrow upon realizing the irony of those words. Here Ligeia was admonishing Maya's comments when she herself had done the same thing in front of the entire colony a few hours before. But, for the moment, she kept her tongue still and continued to listen.

"However, despite the malicious nature of Maya's accusations, it's never okay to resort to violence, Delphine. I hope you understand this." She glanced at Delphine looking for reassurance that her words had sunk in. Delphine simply nodded.

"Good. I'm glad we have an understanding." Ligeia stood from the sofa and collected the two lemonade cups, taking them with her to the kitchen and depositing them in the sink. "You remind me a lot of myself when I was your age. Has your mother told you what the colony was like back then? Back when there were but two generations?"

Delphine shrugged. "Not really. I guess she's told me stories about her mother. But never much about the colony or other colonists."

Ligeia nodded, resting her hands on the shiny, black countertop. "No, I imagine she hasn't. Well, she was very young when I was finishing up my studies along with the rest of the first-gens. That was back when the original colonists were still alive. My mother was one of them as was your great-grandmother."

"Yes, she has mentioned the original colonists before. I guess, they were the council before the new council was appointed?"

"That's right. There were twelve of them." Delphine knew this, of course. It was one of the first things they learned in their colony history courses as small children. Ligeia took her seat back on the sofa and continued. "Twelve brave women made the long journey on the Sirena to start anew. And yet, our laws specify that only five elders shall sit on the council." Ligeia paused and raised an eyebrow, waiting for Delphine to respond to this.

Delphine furrowed her brow and mentally recited the first sentence of the first law in her mind: *Xanadu shall be ruled by a council of five elected elders.* It was true—she'd never thought about how that was possible when the original colonists numbered twelve. They had learned in their lessons that the early colonists shared responsibility over ruling the colony. But nobody had ever questioned how this contradicted the first law. As it dawned on her, she couldn't believe she'd never asked the question before. So, she asked it now. "Why did they not follow the first law?"

Ligeia smiled. She had driven the conversation in this direction on purpose, no doubt about that. And Delphine had done her duty in asking the question Ligeia had hoped she would ask. "Because, dear, they were the original twelve. The first law, in all its brilliance, was not meant to be served by the original colonists. No. They were simply the messengers for generations to come. And because they were not bound by the laws of Earth, they were able to construct the colony as they saw fit." She waved her hand around, gesturing toward the lavish apartment they now sat in. "This beautiful space belonged to my mother, one of those twelve. She used to tell me stories about her journey here on the Sirena. Tell me, what do you know about the ship that brought the original twelve to Titan?"

Delphine cleared her throat and searched her mind for what she had learned as a child about Xanadu's history. "The Sirena was a freighter, the largest and fastest ship that had ever been built by humans. Although humans had been exploring and colonizing the inner solar system for many decades, they had never ventured to the outer reaches with crewed flights until they built the Sirena."

Ligeia nodded and gestured for Delphine to continue.

"It took three Earth years for the crew to reach Titan's orbit—eight months of loading and preparing the Sirena to leave Earth and another twenty-eight months of flight time. They wanted the colony on Titan to serve as a stopover on future interstellar flights."

"What else? What else do you remember from your history lessons?" Ligeia asked.

Delphine wasn't sure what the point of this conversation was, but she figured she might be in for a softer punishment if she played along. "They made the trip as planned and arrived on time at Titan. From there, it took them three more months to shuttle their equipment and supplies down to the surface before they left the Sirena for good. That's when they started Xanadu—building in this cave system which had already been scouted out for the colonists by Earth space probes."

"Tell me." Ligeia leaned forward in her seat, her green eyes sparkling under the soft lights overhead. "What happened to the Sirena after the colonists left it?"

"It went back to Earth, guided by the onboard computer system. They were planning to use it as an interstellar vehicle, so they didn't want to leave it stranded out here."

Ligeia nodded and smiled. "Precisely. It went back to Earth. And do you know what that meant for the colonists? For their offspring? For us?"

"No…" Delphine said, biting her lip and drawing the word out, hesitant.

"It meant that unless Earth sent a ship back to us, we were here permanently. All of this…" She gestured around the room again. "It was built after the Sirena left. After the colonists were left alone on their new world. You see, Delphine, this is our home. It was *their* new home. And they knew that there would be no return ship for at least several decades. They opted to make this place their own."

Delphine scrunched up her face. "But I thought it was because of the war on Earth that no spacecraft has returned to Titan. I mean, we've always been taught that the plan all along was to bring more colonists here. To grow the colony."

A strange look came over Ligeia, a look of uncertainty Delphine was sure she'd never seen on their leader's face. But she recovered quickly, a wide, confident smile spreading across her lips. "Ah, yes. The war. The war has been a problem. But no, those original colonists knew that no matter the situation on Earth, they would not be seeing a rescue ship during their lifetime. They knew they were here to stay."

Delphine shook her head, exasperated by this strange conversation. "I'm sorry, but what does all this have to do with my punishment or the incident in the tent?"

Ligeia chuckled and stood, straightening the front of her robe and smoothing her hair. "I'm not concerned with punishment, Delphine. I don't really care what happened today in the cultivation tent. I care about what you said at the election. I want to get to the root of why you have doubts about the council's leadership. And this, our history, has plenty to do with it."

She walked across the room and retrieved a holographic monitor from a large desk that was pushed up against the far wall. After setting the holograph down on the table in front of Delphine, Ligeia took the seat across from her on the opposite sofa and switched on the device. When Ligeia pulled up a picture, the image projected from the monitor jumped and sputtered before stabilizing. For the first time in two days, Delphine was reminded of the holograph on the space probe she, Rho, and Rhayn had found. That holographic image had been instantly clear, no jumping or vibrating, no static. It was evidently more advanced technology than what she now looked at.

The image was of a group of women. Like the man in that perfect holographic image from the space probe, these women wore dark blue jumpsuits with the ISEF logo stitched on the left breast pockets. They had their arms slung around each other and they were standing in front of what looked like a kitchen. It had a high ceiling with light bars running across it and the entire room was stark white. Delphine could make out row upon row of cabinets behind the women along with countertops and strangely shaped utensils hanging from hooks on the walls. In the middle of the room, a long, white table surrounded with chairs stretched out behind the women.

The camera must have been mounted higher than the group because they were all looking up to make eye contact with it. And they were smiling. Some of them even appeared to be laughing. Twelve women in total.

Delphine took in the holographic image, her brow furrowed as she tried to make sense of what she saw. "This is them?" she asked, pointing at the group, her mouth dropping open.

Ligeia nodded and pointed to the tallest member of the group, a woman standing in the middle of the picture, her red hair cropped close to her head. She was the only one of the women not smiling. She was also the only one not looking directly at the camera. She was staring off to the right, and she didn't look happy or sad or angry. If anything, the woman's expression was neutral.

"That is my mother," Ligeia said. She looked proud as she gazed at the holographic image of her mother's face. "Her name was Leah."

"I had no idea there were pictures of them."

"Yes, there are pictures of them, but not many. Some of us first-gens still have them. They took many pictures and video logs during that time, which can be found in the library archives, mostly for the purposes of documenting the development of the colony. It was very rare to find a picture of all twelve of them in the same shot. This picture is one of my most prized possessions. It shows the original twelve on board the Sirena shortly before it arrived at Titan. They were so happy." A nostalgic look passed over her face and for a moment, Delphine wondered if Ligeia might cry. But she took a deep breath and continued without tears. "They loved each other, Delphine. They loved their mission. They knew that the colony they would build on Titan would be the most advanced human colony in the solar system. And they knew it was their destiny to ensure its success."

Pausing, she shifted in her seat and crossed one leg over the other. She clasped her hands together in front of her as she always did when she addressed the colonists in their monthly meetings and her eyes met Delphine's. "*That* is why they passed the laws down to us. The laws came directly from Earth and each one of these women gave their lives to ensure those laws reached the next generations of Xanadu. Do you understand now why it's so important for us to abide by the laws?" She didn't wait for Delphine to answer before continuing, "Those laws are the bedrock on which this colony was founded. Removing them—or even modifying them—is out of the question if we plan to grow our population."

Ligeia stood from her seat on the opposite sofa and walked around the table to sit right next to Delphine. Grasping Delphine's hands, Ligeia looked directly into her eyes. "*This* is why it's so important for the colonists to uphold the laws, Delphine. Without them, we would devolve into chaos. They were structured the way they are for a reason. We don't need to know that reason. The people of Earth who sent the original twelve knew what they were doing. And questioning the laws in front of the entire colony is something I cannot tolerate. Do you understand? I need to know that you understand this. Because if you continue to question the authority of the council, then I really will have to enact a punishment."

The words were cold and threatening, but spoken with a passion that made Delphine understand. Ligeia was pleading with her to avoid making waves. Not to raise questions. When she spoke up at the election, she had done more than humiliate herself in front of the entire colony; she had planted seeds of doubt in the fertile minds of the colonists. And Ligeia was determined to pull those doubts before they could take root. To do that, she needed Delphine and every other colonist on board. Questioning their history would do nobody any good in the long run. Delphine saw that clearly now. With a single, deliberate head nod, she showed Ligeia that she understood.

"Good," Ligeia said, releasing a long breath, a smile returning to her lips. She stood, her red robe brushing against Delphine's pant leg as she moved. "Now, would you like another glass of lemonade before you go?"

Delphine nodded again and Ligeia turned toward the kitchen. She focused her attention back on the holographic image that still stood on the table before her. As she looked at the image, something jumped out at her as odd. She narrowed her eyes and leaned in to get a better look.

"Ligeia?"

"Yes, dear?"

"Why are there so many chairs in this picture?"

Ligeia stood still and silence took the place of her bustling around the kitchen. After a moment's pause, she walked back to the sofa where Delphine sat staring at the holograph.

"What do you mean?"

"In the background of this picture, there are fifteen chairs around that table. See? Eight on each side and seven on the other." Delphine pointed at each chair, counting them aloud.

Ligeia drew in a sharp breath, then paused, obviously counting the visible chairs in the background of the picture. "Well," she said, her voice shaking ever so slightly. "I'm sure they had many chairs on that ship. They had probably just gathered them all in one place so they would be able to find them when they needed them."

Delphine began to speak, but before she could utter a word, Ligeia swiped her hand over the image and the holograph disappeared, replaced by a blank blue screen. She picked up the monitor and switched it off before returning it to the desk. Turning to Delphine, she touched the back of her hand to her forehead. "You know, it might be better if you leave now without another glass of lemonade. I apologize, but I feel a headache coming on. Don't worry about returning to the tents today. Feel free to take the rest of the day off."

Ligeia flashed Delphine a final, confident smile and left the room without another word. Delphine stood for a moment, not quite sure what to make of what had just happened to her, before letting herself out the front door.

CHAPTER 17

"Can I help you?"

The woman peering through the window of the library wore a green second-gen jumpsuit. Delphine recognized her as an older member of her mother's generation named Elyn. She had spent the majority of the half-kilometer walk to the science wing from Ligeia's apartment going over and over how she would approach this situation. Now that Elyn, the library technician, was speaking to her through the intercom below the window, she found herself overcome with a sudden case of nerves.

She wiped her sweaty palms on her thighs and cleared her throat before giving the technician a big smile. "Hi. Elyn, right?"

Elyn was a large woman with dark brown hair tied in a tight knot at the base of her skull. She sat behind a thick plastic window that faced the hallway where Delphine now stood. Behind her was a desk covered in random tools and devices used to service the computer equipment housed in the library. The job of library technician was a rather cushy affair, Delphine knew. It involved cleaning and maintaining the many racks of computers housed inside the library, as well as general upkeep in the temperature- and humidity-controlled space. Though the position was much more desirable than a job out on the surface working the mines or on the excavation crew, more importantly, Elyn served as the keeper of the keys to Xanadu's history. Anyone who wished to enter the library needed her to buzz them through the locked door to Delphine's right, and Delphine knew it wasn't going to be an easy task to get in.

Elyn stared at Delphine with one eyebrow raised before tapping her ear bug to reply. "That's right."

"May I enter the library?" Delphine pointed to the door next to Elyn's window.

"What business do you have in the library?"

Delphine knew she would have to answer this question and she delivered her prepared response. "I'm writing a story about my sister, Aura, and I'd like to do some research. It's really for my mother, a surprise for her birthday next month. I wanted to gather pictures of Aura and look up her birth information on the colony records so I can include those in my writing."

Elyn's eyebrow remained raised. "All of that information should be available on the main database. You could access it through your bugs."

"Yes, it should be, but I can't seem to find any records about Aura in the main database. That's why I've come to look here. They must have gotten erased or something." Delphine shrugged, hoping to sell the excuse. It was a lie, of course, but Elyn didn't know that.

Elyn tapped her fingernail on the desk and continued to stare at Delphine, contemplating the request. Delphine cleared her throat again and, with renewed enthusiasm, added, "I received permission from Ligeia. I was just at her apartment and she gave me her blessing. Check the cameras in the living quarters wing if you don't believe me. She thinks it's a wonderful idea and that my mother will truly love it."

"Well, I suppose if Ligeia said so." Elyn reached forward, but her fingers stopped before she hit the unlock button on the computer screen in front of her. "I wasn't given any orders though. She usually lets me know in advance for library access requests."

"Yeah, she said you might say that. She wasn't feeling well when I left—said she had a headache—but I assure you, she gave me permission. I was *just* there."

Elyn narrowed her eyes before finally relinquishing and giving a small shrug. The door buzzed as the lock released and Delphine turned the handle and entered the library, allowing the door to slowly close behind her. Now she stood facing Elyn, separated only by her desk. Elyn pointed down the hallway that ran through the center of the computer racks. "The computers to access the database are in the center of the room, between rows six and seven. You'll use your bugs to log in and, once you're inside, everything is organized by category and date. There is a thirty-minute limit for library usage. Let me know if you have any problems."

Delphine nodded and started walking down the corridor when Elyn stopped her. "Oh, and no downloading allowed. You'll have to take notes. And I'm afraid you won't be able to take any pictures of your sister with you. No data is allowed to be removed from this room, including screenshots." She pointed to the cameras mounted above the door. "Those cameras will scan your bugs on the way out." It was a clear warning.

"Got it," Delphine said and quickly made her way down the corridor, getting out of earshot before Elyn could spout off any more rules.

She had never been inside the library before and took a moment look around. The room was massive, almost as big as the Atrium. On either side of Delphine there were racks and racks of computers. Each row went on for at least twenty meters on either side. The computers were two centimeters thick and about ten centimeters wide and they were mounted horizontally on the racks rising up in columns to the ceiling. Delphine counted twenty-two computers per column with space in between where wires, wrapped in neat bundles, connected each computer to the next. They gave off a strange green light, making the entire room seem as though it were glowing.

Delphine ran her fingers along the outside of the rack to her left. It was made from the same industrial plastic that composed every piece of furniture and infrastructure at Xanadu, but this plastic was pleasantly cool. She could feel the drafts of cool air floating in from the large vents in the ceiling and the air was dry—climate controlled for the sake of the computers. A very clear buzzing noise surrounded her as she continued to walk down the center aisle. It reminded her of the noises the rovers made when they were out on the surface, their engines humming in the silent atmosphere.

The library had been named so by the original colonists. They had set up the original space to hold three hundred computers, what they had brought with them to serve as the colony's central control system. The racks, which lined the computers neatly, were reminiscent of old libraries on Earth where books lined the shelves rather than computers—at least, that was the story handed down to the colonists over the years. They considered the library the most important part of the colony because it housed the brains and memories of Xanadu. The name had stuck.

Delphine made her way to the center of the room where the computer racks opened up to reveal a small sitting area. It surprised her to see three desks and several sofas in the center, as if someone regularly used this as a sitting room. She took a seat at one of the desks and touched the computer monitor in front of her to bring it to life.

A low, soothing voice emanated from the computer. "Please allow connection to your personalized bone conduction earpieces."

"Allowed," Delphine replied, signaling her ear bugs to connect wirelessly with the computer.

"Thank you," the smooth voice said. It took only a moment for the connection to take hold and the computer spoke again. "Welcome to Xanadu's library, Delphine."

Delphine was surprised that this much care had gone into the user interface of these machines. Did people actually sit down here regularly and look through the colony records? She glanced around at the sitting area and noticed a crumpled napkin on the floor next to one of the sofas and a tablet sitting on the end table next to it. Obviously people did if someone left a napkin and a tablet in here. Then it hit her. There were cameras all over Xanadu, probably hundreds of them, and this would surely be the only place someone could monitor them all. This must be where they conducted security checks.

Was it really someone's job to sit in this strange, glowing room and monitor security footage every day? The thought made a chill roll through her and she shook her head. No, she couldn't think about that now. She was here for a specific reason and she needed to get to work. She tapped on the screen and navigated her way to the main directory.

Her jaw dropped when she saw the listing of alphabetically organized directory items. There were at least two hundred files. Every category of information anyone could ever need was listed there, including everything from rover diagnostics and topography maps to mine production statistics and food production projections. When she clicked on any one file, there were hundreds of subfiles and even more subfiles buried within those.

She searched around a bit before she found something interesting—a file labeled Birth Records. Since she had come into here under the pretense of doing research on her sister, she figured she might as well have a look. Maybe she could find her own birth records and see what information they kept on her.

As with the other files, the main file had many subfiles in it—one for each colonist of Xanadu. She went to her own and found multiple documents regarding her conception and birth. The file contained information about the successful egg harvesting treatment done on her mother one year and eleven months before she was born. Fertilization and implantation a few days after that. She was surprised to see that her mother had had two miscarriages before her own embryo finally implanted. Pala had never told her about this and it suddenly made her feel even more sorrow for her mother who she now knew had lost not one, but three children. The file contained every appointment Pala had with medics during the pregnancy and included ultrasounds, heartbeat monitor results, amniotic fluid tests, and fetal growth charts. The final document in the file was her official Xanádu birth certificate showing her name, her mother's name, time and date of birth, and measurements including head circumference, length, and weight.

Next, she found Aura's file and much of her information was similar to Delphine's. Pala had had a successful implantation on the first go that time. This didn't surprise Delphine. She knew the medical team had gotten much better at the in vitro process over time and it was now rare for a procedure not to work.

She navigated through the file until she found Rhayn and Rho. They had a shared file as they were twins. There wasn't much surprising in their file either. Similar ultrasound pictures, although in these, she could make out two babies, ghostly silhouetted against the grainy black background. Their birth wasn't as well documented since their mother, Rhea, had given birth to them in her living compartment due to the hull breach in the medical wing. Pala had helped with the birth and had told Delphine the story of the twins' birth many times.

When Delphine looked through the rest of the birth records, she noticed they were organized by date, with the latest colony births at the top of the list and the earliest at the bottom. She was about to leave the file when the title of a folder stopped her short: Stillbirths and Others. She glanced around the space to make sure Elyn wasn't standing behind her before opening the file.

Inside, there were more subfolders, all marked with four-digit numbers starting at 0001. Delphine used her finger to tap on the first. Inside was a document along with several pictures, all labeled "Female, First-Gen 0001." The document included all the pertinent details of a birth that occurred shortly after the original colonists began in-vitro fertilization on motherhood candidates. The mother, in this case, was a woman named Daisy, one of the original twelve. The child, stillborn after five months of gestation, was the third child born at Xanadu. Delphine felt a shiver run up her arms and she wasn't sure if it was because of the cool air blowing all around her in the temperature-controlled room, or if it was the idea that there existed a folder full of details about babies that didn't make it. She had no desire to look at the pictures, so she closed out the file.

Out of curiosity, she began clicking through the rest of the files. She found, as she went down the line in numerical order, that each file held more of the same—documents with details of the child's birth, reasons for the unsuccessful gestation, and pictures. All were labeled as females with their generation noted and their assigned number.

Until she reached the file labeled 0006. Her eyes grew wide and her mouth dropped open when she saw the name of the document uploaded to this file—Male, Second-Gen 0006.

Male?

She opened the document and saw the child was born sixteen years prior to her own birth. It had actually been born alive, but was fifteen weeks early and succumbed to underdeveloped lungs after just two hours, according to the record. The mother's name was Amara. Delphine drummed her fingers on the desk trying to remember if she'd ever met anyone named Amara, a first-gen, based on the fact that her child was a second-gen. She couldn't place the name to a face, although most of the first-gen was no longer living, so it was highly likely that Amara had passed away before Delphine was born or when she was very young.

Amara's child had been a boy.

All of a sudden, Delphine was happy about the stream of cool air that flowed down on her from the vents in the ceiling. She felt dizzy. A boy born at Xanadu. She had been taught that all implanted embryos were female—all of them. Every person at the colony was female by design and there were no options for male children. It was a basic fact of life that every colonist grew up with—they were a colony of women. She thought about Ligeia's prepared speeches and how she always signed off with the words "Titan girls, have a blessed day." The Titan *girls*.

It took Delphine several minutes to collect herself before moving on to the other files. When she was finished, she had looked through thirty-six total files and found that five of them had been male children, although no male child had been born for at least two decades. The most recent files were all female. They had obviously improved their practices since the early days of the colony. And those were just the ones who wound up in this file. Delphine wondered—if this many male children were stillborn or died as infants, how many healthy ones were born? And what happened to them?

She shook her head, heat rising in her cheeks. They had all been lied to. A lie that had been going on for *years* right under their noses. Who knew about this? The medics would have known. She thought about the various job descriptions of those who worked in the medical wing. There was a specific set of medics who oversaw pregnancies and births. She mentally ran through their names—four in all. And what about the three colonists in charge of reproduction? Surely, they knew.

A dull pain developed in her stomach as her thoughts ran wild. Within the span of a few minutes, she felt as if her world had been tipped over, the questions flowing free, like water spilling from a cup. She closed her eyes and drew in a deep breath to try calming herself.

Her bugs beeped, alerting her of the turn of the hour. It was midafternoon now. She realized she should have set herself a timer when she started as she was sure Elyn would enforce the thirty-minute time limit. Her time in the library was running short. She rubbed her hands together and turned back to the computer.

As she navigated back to the main menu, she did her best to organize her thoughts. Her mind wound back to the discussion she and Rho had in the machine shed two days earlier. Had it only been two days? She couldn't believe everything that had happened over that last forty-eight-hour period. Rho had said she should look into the communication logs from Earth. She ran her finger along the screen, reading each file name as she scrolled. Finally, she came to the file marked Communications and clicked on it.

Inside were about a dozen subfolders. She clicked on one labeled Antenna Status Reports. Inside were what looked like an endless stream of documents each dated. From what Delphine could see, they went all the way back to the original colonists. She opened one and saw that it was a basic diagnostic report detailing the working status of the primary long-range antenna. She was familiar with this antenna array—it stood on the eastern border of the colony complex, just north of the manufacturing and storage wing. She often passed by it when she went out on the surface for a run. The array consisted of twelve antennae of various sizes anchored into the Titanian soil. There was a small service building next to the array where the computer system was housed. In order to retrieve radio signals from Earth, they had to enter the service building and manually import the signals to the primary computer system. Only the council members had access to the communications building and it was Ligeia who took on most of the responsibility for monitoring the radio.

Delphine perused the main communications file before finding a subfolder marked Communication Logs. Inside were hundreds of documents ordered by date and labeled as transcripts. She clicked on the most recent one and saw that it was dated three days prior, meaning this would have been the report Ligeia referenced in the meeting they'd had in the Atrium just two days prior. The transcript read:

> **Incoming (time stamp 0823):** *Xanadu One, Xanadu One. This is ISEF. Please report.*
> **Reply:** ...
> **Incoming signal (time stamp 0825):** *Xanadu One, Xanadu One. This is ISEF. Please report.*
> **Reply:** ...
> **Income Signal (time stamp 0828):** *Xanadu One, Xanadu One. This is ISEF. Please report.*
> **Reply:** ...

Delphine counted thirty-two iterations of the same message at regular intervals spanning three hours, all marked with a blank reply. Why would they not have recorded the return messages? She crossed her arms and stared at the document, trying to make sense of what she was seeing.

She wondered if maybe this was an error—a time when the messages weren't received by the council because of atmospheric interference, or maybe it was an error in calculation by Earth about where the colony would be in its orbit. She opened the next document dated two weeks before the last and found that it was exactly the same. Thirty-two messages, all beckoning the colonists to answer, yet no replies were recorded. The same was true of every document Delphine opened going back over the prior five years. She scrolled as far down as she could and noticed that the communication logs only went back twenty-five years, and all of them, even the oldest ones, showed the same strange pattern of messages. What happened to the communication logs prior to that?

The list of documents seemed to blur in front of her and she felt the beginnings of a headache sneaking into her eyes. She closed her eyes and pressed the palms of her hands against her forehead in an effort to keep the pain at bay.

"Time's up."

Delphine jumped with surprise at the stern voice and quickly swiped out of the communications folder. "You scared me!" she cried, turning around to see Elyn standing directly behind her, arms crossed in front of her chest.

Elyn didn't look amused. "Thirty minutes. Time's up," she repeated.

Delphine cleared her throat and turned back to the computer to log out. "Got it." She stood and smoothed the front of her jumpsuit, trying to calm her pounding heart. Elyn followed close behind her as she made her way down the corridor to the front of the library. Once there, she glanced nervously at the camera above the door. Elyn stepped behind her desk and checked her computer. She paused a moment—no doubt waiting for the camera to scan Delphine's bugs and ensure she hadn't snatched any information. After a few seconds, Elyn nodded and sat down, pressing the button to open the door. Delphine left the library and made sure to get out of sight of the building before she broke into a run.

CHAPTER 18

"Whoa!" Rhayn said, her brown eyes wide.

Delphine finished telling the twins about her experience that day with Ligeia and everything she'd learned while in the library. Out of breath because the words had flowed so fast from her mouth, she'd barely paused to think. Plus, she had run the half kilometer from the library to the living quarters where she now sat in Rhayn and Rho's kitchen.

"Yeah, 'whoa' is right! What the hell is going on here? I can't even comprehend it. Like it's too far above my head to actually absorb. I feel like I'm in some sort of wild dream," Delphine said, elbows propped on the kitchen table, dropping her head in her hands.

"Let me make sure I understand this," Rhayn said, leaning forward, the front legs of her chair squeaking under her weight, "You went to Ligeia's apartment and she showed you a picture of the original colonists on the Sirena, and in the background, there were more than twelve chairs lined up at the table."

"Yes. This was *after* she gave me a big rah-rah speech about the history of the colony and the importance of following the three laws."

"Right. So, she gives you the big speech, and you see the picture. She rushes you out of there and tells you to take the rest of the day off."

Delphine nodded. "Then I went to the library."

"And at the library, you find out that the communication logs on file are incomplete, right?"

"Yes. They only reflect radio signals received from Earth. That's it. There is no record—at least, that I could find—of any of the responses from Xanadu. And the records going back to the days of the original colonists are totally gone. Nothing on file."

Rho cut in. "But you mentioned all of the incoming radio communications are the same. Requests to report. No actual information. Just continued requests to report, right?"

Delphine sat back in her seat and nodded, letting out a long, low sigh. The events of the day had become overwhelming and she was losing steam.

"If the incoming signals are only requests to report, there's no way Xanadu could be sending anything back," Rho said, her eyes narrowed, thoughtful.

"What does that mean?" Rhayn asked.

"It means, based on what Delphine saw in those files, that we aren't communicating with Earth. Think about it." Rho stood and paced the few steps between the kitchen counter and the door to the hallway. "Let's say there were instances where we did send radio signals back—as we've all been told is the case by Ligeia. The incoming signals from Earth wouldn't be requests to report. They would be other things like status updates, monitoring requests, even occasional chitchat. Right?"

Rhayn and Delphine stared at her, neither offering an answer.

"But that's not what was recorded in the file. Only requests to report. So, we can reasonably deduce that there *were no* responses. At least, not to those requests. Maybe there are outgoing communications and they're kept in another file. But from what Delphine says, there are hundreds, maybe thousands, of unanswered communications from Earth."

After several moments of silence, Rhayn, who had begun chewing nervously on her thumbnail, said, "Whoa." Delphine and Rho nodded in agreement, the realization sinking in all at once. The idea that Earth had been sending regular requests to report and none of those requests had been responded to was one of the most disturbing things Delphine had ever heard. All their lives, they had been told that Earth and Xanadu had regular communications. Every colony meeting Ligeia gave an update talking about the great war that waged relentlessly on the home planet. About how they should hold out hope that one day Earth would return to Titan. And it had all been a lie… every last word of it. "Whoa" seemed like the only appropriate response.

Delphine stood suddenly and walked to the kitchen sink, gazing out the faux window behind it, a window capturing video feed from the surface. Night had officially fallen and the only light she could see came from some of the outdoor complex lighting far away from the camera. It cast a strange orange glow over the room.

"What about the male births?" she said, biting her lower lip while still looking out the window. "They've been lying about that too. They've always told us male children were impossible. That the samples that came from Earth could only produce female children. Lies."

She turned around to catch a look pass between Rho, who was leaning against the wall on the far side of the room, and Rhayn, who was still seated at the kitchen table, her boots propped up on the chair Delphine had vacated. The look was fleeting, but it was definitely there. When Delphine had run into the apartment, panting, words spilling out of her mouth about what she'd seen, she'd been in such a rush to get the story out, she hadn't noticed their reactions to this particular part of the story. But now, she saw it. The look was one of knowing. A look of understanding.

"What?" Delphine asked, looking first to Rhayn and then to Rho. "What was that look for?"

Rhayn said nothing and cast her gaze across the room to her sister. Rho sighed and crossed her arms over her chest, shaking her head.

"I think we should tell her," Rhayn said, her eyes never leaving Rho's. "She should know."

Delphine could see the frustration in Rho's face and a strained look came to her eyes. Rho nodded, a slight tilt of her chin, but a nod all the same.

"Sit down, Delphine," Rhayn said, taking her boots off the chair and gesturing toward it. Rho made no move to sit. She remained propped against the wall, her arms crossed tight across her chest, her gaze on the opposite wall, beyond the room where the girls sat.

Delphine obeyed and took the seat. "What the hell is going on?" she asked slowly, unsure she wanted to hear what she was about to hear.

Rhayn leaned forward, placing her elbows on the table and propping her chin up on her interlaced fingers. "You know the story of our birth, right?"

Delphine nodded. "You were born here, in Rhea's living quarters. There was some sort of issue—a hull breach—in the medical wing. And Rhea went into labor during the emergency. Pala helped deliver you while the rest of the colonists worked to fix the issue in medical. She always said it was a surprisingly easy birth considering you are twins."

"Yeah," Rhayn said, "we're twins. *Fraternal twins*. The only pair to ever be born here at Xanadu."

"Yeah, and…" Delphine's voice trailed off.

Rhayn shifted in her seat and cleared her throat. Her mouth was tight as she carefully chose her next words. "Fraternal twins should be impossible here at Xanadu. Eggs are harvested from the maternal candidates, then fertilized, then implanted. The process has been perfected to an almost 100% embryonic survival rate. They never implant *two different* embryos. It just doesn't happen."

"But there have been other sets of twins," Delphine said.

Rhayn nodded. "Yes, identical twins. Those where one embryo is implanted and it splits on its own. But that's not us. We are definitely different."

"Okay, so what do you think happened?"

Rhayn shrugged and leaned back. "Well, we think there was a mistake. And that's what the medical teams assumed. Somehow, the process went wrong and two embryos were implanted. It's possible that one was hidden behind the other… although that's never happened again. But it is possible."

"Okay," Delphine said. "So, there was a mistake. So what? What's the point of this story?"

"The point is, we are not identical. We are an anomaly in the reproduction process of Xanadu. Our birth was never meant to happen. And there's a reason for that…" Rhayn's words trailed off as Rho left her position across the room and came to sit at the table. The three of them now sat face-to-face around the circular table.

Rho cleared her throat and looked at Rhayn, who nodded as if reassuring her twin that she should continue. "I'm not like Rhayn," Rho said. "I was born… different."

"What do you mean 'different'?" Delphine could feel the weight of something big coming toward her. Something bigger than anything else she'd learned in the last twenty-four hours. She was suddenly very uncomfortable with the conversation. She wasn't sure she could handle anything more.

"What I mean is," Rho paused and took Rhayn's hand. Rhayn gave it a squeeze before nodding. "I am actually a boy."

CHAPTER 19

The words seemed to move through the air in slow motion, each one hitting Delphine like a slap on the cheek. *I am actually a boy.* She dropped her head and pressed her palms against her temples feeling the workings of the headache she'd had earlier springing back to life behind her eyes.

"What did you just say?" she asked.

Rho reached across the table and gently touched Delphine's arm. "I'm a boy, Delphine. I was born male and I have been pretending to be female my entire life. I've blended in."

Delphine shook her head, still unable to properly look Rho in the eye. She turned to Rhayn. "You knew about it?"

"Of course. He's my brother. He's my twin brother."

"But… how? How did you keep this from me all these years?"

Rhayn sighed, still holding Rho's hand. "Look, it's not anything to do with you. This is all about keeping Rho safe. There has never been a live male birth allowed to survive here. And it was obviously an error made by the reproductive sciences department. Rhea didn't want to take the chance that her baby would be taken from her. So she and Pala decided to pretend it didn't happen. To say Rhea gave birth to two healthy baby girls."

Delphine jerked her head up to look Rhayn in the eye. "Pala knew about this?"

Rhayn and Rho glanced at each other and nodded. Rhayn said, "Pala has done all of our medical checkups since birth. That's the only reason Rhea was able to get away with it. Because Pala was on her side and worked as a medic in the reproductive sciences department."

The idea that Rho, someone she had known her entire life, someone she had shared some of her best and worst times with, had lied to her the entire time was almost more than she could take. And her own mother knew about it too. The weight of this revelation began to slowly sink in on her soul, washing over it like a cold shower. She needed to get some air.

Delphine stood a little too quickly, the blood rushing from her head, making her swoon. She pushed her chair aside and ran for the door of the apartment. Rhayn jumped up and followed her into the hallway.

"Del!" Rhayn said, grabbing Delphine's shoulder, forcing her to turn around and face her. "Please, calm down. I know this is a lot to handle, but it's essential that you keep your cool. Do you understand?"

Delphine clenched her eyes shut and drew in a long, slow breath, exhaling loudly from her mouth. The air in the hallway felt cooler, less dense. It soothed her and she could feel the fog rising from her mind. When she opened her eyes, Rhayn was peering at her under her heavy, dark eyelashes. She still held firmly to Delphine's shoulder and gave it a quick, reassuring squeeze.

"Will you come back inside?" Rhayn asked before glancing nervously around the hallway. Fortunately, nobody was around, but they both knew there were cameras stationed at regular intervals through the long corridor. Nothing they did or said in this hallway was private.

Delphine took another deep breath and nodded. Rhayn gave her a quick smile and they walked back into the apartment, the door making a faint click as it closed behind them. Rho remained at the kitchen table. He was leaning on his elbows, fingers clasped, eyebrows knitted together. When they walked in, he looked at them and a brief moment of relief passed over his face. Delphine took her seat and crossed her arms over her chest. Rhayn twisted her chair around and straddled it, sitting backward, resting her arms on the backrest.

"I know this is difficult, Delphine," Rho said. "But I assure you, we would never have kept this a secret from you unless we absolutely had to."

Delphine studied Rho's face. She took a moment to really look at him as she'd never looked at him before. It was clear by their matching oval-shaped faces and high cheekbones that Rhayn and Rho were related, but she noticed, for the first time, how different they really were. Where Rhayn's jaw was soft and rounded, Rho's was sharper, with a stronger edge. Rhayn's eyes were large and wide-set on her face, while Rho's were smaller and hooded, giving him a more intense gaze. Rhayn's wavy, dirty blond hair was blunt and choppy, cut just below her chin. Rho's hair was darker, cropped close to his head in the back, longer in the front, with his bangs pushed messily to the side.

Even the way they held their bodies was different, Delphine realized. Rho was lean and tall. He often hovered on the periphery around other colonists, not saying much, hunching or leaning against a wall with his hands casually tucked into the back pockets of his jumpsuit. Rhayn was rounder, curvier, with a warmth about her that put people at ease. She was much more talkative than her twin and often stood with one hip cocked to the side and a hand resting on it. The more Delphine thought about it, the more she realized how obvious it was that Rho was different—not just from his sister, but from them all.

"Who else knows about this?" Delphine asked.

"Just Rhea and Pala," Rho said. "We've made a great effort to keep this a secret. I've done my best to blend in as best I can and keep out of the scrutiny of the council." He sat back in his chair and ran his long fingers through his hair, releasing a big breath. "Actually, it feels good to talk about it. To tell you my secret. It feels good to have it out in the open. Now I can be my real self around you."

A sudden realization hit Delphine and she had to push back the wave of nausea that threatened to escape her stomach. "So, you knew there had been other male births here? And that those children were…" She swallowed, unable to finish her thought.

The twins looked at each other, shame clouding their eyes. A look that confirmed to Delphine that yes, they had known about the male children. They'd known the council was not allowing male children to survive. That's why they went to the trouble to pretend Rho was a female. The thought did nothing to help her roiling stomach. Her jaw clenched. "How could you have known about this all along and done nothing?" Anger rose as blood rushed to her face.

Rho sighed. "Yes, we knew. Not all the details. We had no idea there had been as many of them as you mentioned seeing in that file. But we knew it had happened in the past. That's why Rhea did what she did. To protect me."

Tears sprang from Delphine's eyes and she slammed her fists on the table. "How could you not have said anything? If the rest of the colony knew about what was happening to *children* they would be outraged. The council would be overthrown!"

"Yes," Rhayn said, "the council would be overthrown. And then what? Our world, as we know it, would devolve into chaos."

"We could figure it out," Delphine whispered, her body shaking.

Rho leaned forward and reached for Delphine's fingers which rested on the edge of the table. She quickly snapped them away and crossed her arms tightly across her chest. He slowly pulled his hand back, a look of genuine hurt coming over his face. "You're right, Delphine. We were wrong not to say anything. This isn't right. The way things have been run around here for so many years… it's not right. And I agree, the rest of the colonists should know what's going on around here. I'm just not sure of the best way to go about that."

"He's right," Rhayn said. "There's not going to be an easy way to do… whatever it is we need to do. Frankly, there have to be more colonists who know about the male children. What about the women who gave birth to those children? What about the medics? Many people have sat on this secret for years. How do we force change in a colony of people who have lies hardwired into their programming?"

Delphine hadn't realized it, but her shoulders were pulled almost up to her ears with tension. She allowed them to drop and rolled her neck side to side. "I don't understand why they would do this. Why tell us that only female children can be born at Xanadu? Why engineer *only* female children? What's the goal of it all?"

Rho shrugged. "They were told by Earth that all colonists were to be engineered as female. For the sake of the genetic pool, or whatever. Earth hasn't given them the go-ahead, so they decided that no male children should be allowed to survive."

Rhayn cut in. "But we know now, from what you've found in the library, that they haven't even been talking to Earth! So how can they even know?"

"Maybe the answer is in the space probe," Delphine said, biting her lip. She leaned forward to match the posture of the twins so their foreheads almost touched around the table. "What if there is something in the message from Earth on that probe? Something that will explain what the hell is going on around here?"

Rhayn and Rho looked at each other, some thought passing between them in the way only twins can pull off. They both nodded. "We need to go back and see if we can get the sound to work on that holograph," Rho said. "I may have an idea."

"Okay," Delphine said. "Let's meet there tomorrow morning. We can do it before the work shifts begin—around 0600. Does that work?"

The twins nodded and a smile broke out on Rho's face. "Does this mean you're okay? I mean, with this." He gestured toward himself.

Delphine wasn't sure yet how she felt about it, but she knew that the person sitting in front of her was the same person she'd known her whole life. This information didn't change anything. She smiled. "Yeah, we're okay."

CHAPTER 20

As she walked down the long corridor leading to her own apartment, Delphine took her time, turning every word of her conversation with Rhayn and Rho over in her mind. Examining them, picking them apart. This was one of her more annoying habits: picking apart words and trying to find hidden meaning in them. It meant elevated anxiety levels and the only cure she'd found for that was to go for a run.

The door to her apartment was in view when a message popped up on her ear bugs from Pala.

Are you coming home for dinner?

She sighed and swiped the air in front of her face to clear the holographic image of the words from her view. Yes, unfortunately. She didn't *want* to go home. But she honestly couldn't think of another place to go at the moment. It was well into the dinner hour and most of the colonists were happily tucked away in their apartments, making their own sustenance.

The Atrium would be empty at this time of day as the day workers had already moved through the concourses on their way to the living quarters wing, and the night workers had already started their shifts.

Not that Delphine wanted to be around anyone. But the thought of strolling past her own door and entering the cold Atrium, lit only by a few light bars suspended way up in the ceiling, the oculus an inky black mass looming over the space, made her shiver all over. No, going home would be best. She would have to do it at some point.

The door to the apartment squeaked slightly as she pulled it open, reminding her that she needed to apply some grease to the hinges. Pala stood in the kitchen, staring at the false window behind the sink. As Delphine walked in and dropped her things on the chair in the corner—*Aura's* chair—Pala seemed to snap out of whatever daydream she was lost in and gave her surviving daughter a weak smile.

"I wasn't sure you'd make it," Pala said. "I left the food in the oven in hopes that you would, but it's getting so late, I was about to turn it off."

Delphine sniffed the air and picked up the heavy scent of garlic and basil. She looked through the tiny window on the oven door and saw a tray filled with roasted tomatoes drizzled in oil, each with a single, wide basil leaf on top and a sprinkling of garlic. From the size of them, they must have been the beefsteak heirloom variety grown in Cultivation Tent 2. They were large and thick, and there were at least a dozen slices laid out on the baking sheet, shimmering in the heat from the oven. On the burner, a large pot of rice, also perfumed with garlic steamed in its pot. A small saucepan bubbled lightly next to the rice, a bright yellow curry.

Delphine walked to the oven and opened it, allowing the roasting, saturated air to fill the cold kitchen with warmth. She slipped on an oven glove and pulled the baking sheet out, allowing it to rest on the unused burners of the stove.

"Haven't you eaten?" Delphine asked, closing the oven door and replacing the oven glove on the hook next to the refrigerator. She knew the answer to this question. It was clear from the state of the food dishes that they were as of yet untouched. But she felt as though asking were the appropriate thing to do.

Pala looked at her daughter and leaned her head to one side, clearly contemplating her response to this question. After a moment, she resigned herself to the truth and let out a sigh. "No, I haven't eaten yet." She moved to the cabinet above the stove and pulled out a plate for her and one for Delphine along with two cups. "Water," she said, opening the spout over the sink and filling both cups. "We're out of juice."

Delphine nodded, remembering that rations of grape and apple juice had been short at the last pickup and mentally counting the days until their next ration pickup was due—six more. She accepted the cup of the water and piled her plate high with rice, smothering it in the sauce and adding two of the large roasted tomato slices to the side before taking her usual seat at the kitchen table. Pala filled her own plate, although with half the portions, and followed her daughter. They sat in silence for a few moments, Delphine digging into the pile of rice while Pala examined the food, trying to determine the best way to approach this unwanted meal.

After swallowing her first few mouthfuls of rice, Delphine let out a long, slow sigh.

"What?" Pala asked, an edge of annoyance in her voice.

Delphine considered her mother for a moment. She hadn't even picked up her fork yet as if perhaps she planned to not even make a show of pushing tonight's food around her plate. "I learned something interesting today," she said finally, cutting one of the tomato slices with the edge of her fork. "Actually, I learned lots of interesting things today."

A tired look came over Pala's face at the mention of unwanted news and her eyes dropped back down to her plate. "Oh? And what was that?"

"I learned that Rho is a boy." Delphine calmly picked up her glass and took a big sip of water. The curry sauce was delicious yet quite spicy.

Pala's eyes came alive and darted to her daughter's face, a look of worry pinching her thin eyebrows together. But after a moment, her face relaxed and she sat back in her seat. "Well, I expect it wasn't going to stay a secret forever."

Delphine took another bite of rice, trying to swallow down the anger that rose in her throat. "How could you not have told me about this?"

Pala leaned forward and let out a tired, defeated sigh. She looked Delphine in the eye. "For the safety of everyone involved, that's how. You don't seem to understand how dangerous it was for Rho when he was a baby. How dangerous it is for him now." Despite her tired eyes, her voice had an edge to it. An edge Delphine hadn't heard in a long time.

"I'm your daughter."

"Yes, you're my daughter. And your safety means more to me than anything in the world. The less you knew, the better."

Delphine cleared her throat and set her fork down. "I know Rho isn't the only one." Pala sat back, wincing as if expecting a slap. "And I know why you and Rhea had to pretend he was a girl. I went to the library today and saw the birth logs. I saw how many male births there were on record. I wasn't able to go through the entire file, but I know there have been many more. And I know they were never allowed to live past infancy."

Pala's mouth hung open and she put her hand to her chest. Then she stood suddenly, reached across the table, and grabbed

Delphine's upper arm, her fingers digging into her soft flesh. "Have you lost your mind?"

"Ouch!" Delphine shrieked, instinctively pulling her arm out of her mother's grasp. She rubbed the tender spot where Pala's fingers had squeezed, certain there would be a bruise to come. "What the hell is wrong with you?"

Pala grabbed Delphine's shoulders with more strength than seemed possible for her mother's feeble, bone-thin arms and forced her to make eye contact. It was then that Delphine forgot the pain in her arm and saw the fear tightening her mother's face, her eyes large and liquid with it.

"You must *never* do anything that foolish again! Do you understand me?" Pala said, her voice cracking.

Delphine nodded slowly in an effort to calm her mother. She'd never seen this sort of reaction from Pala and frankly, it scared her.

"Promise me. Say 'I promise,'" Pala said, still holding Delphine's shoulders tight.

"I promise never to go to the library again," Delphine said slowly, enunciating each word.

Pala released a breath and let go of Delphine's shoulders. She nodded and put the back of her hand to her forehead before returning to her seat. Delphine continued to rub the sore spot on her arm, still trying to comprehend what had happened.

"You work in reproductive sciences," Delphine finally said after several moments of silence passed between the two. "How could you sit back and watch this happen? Surely you knew?"

A look of shame crossed Pala's face. "I knew," she confirmed, "but it was well before my time when they were…" She paused, shifting uncomfortably in her seat. "Well, when they were terminated."

"Terminated," Delphine repeated, shaking her head. She couldn't believe she was hearing these words. These were children—babies—they were talking about. Pala talked about them as if they were an unsuccessful hybrid crop that would go straight to mulch.

Pala sighed. "Look, I know it sounds bad. Trust me, I've never had any part of it. It was way before my time. Yes, in the beginning, there were quite a few. But they've perfected the fertilization and implantation process to ensure this type of thing never happens again."

"Except it *did* happen again," Delphine reminded her, thinking of Rho and his dark, wide eyes.

"Yes, it did." Pala massaged her temples with her long, thin fingers. "But it hasn't happened since. I've made sure of that. Rho was an anomaly. Somehow, an extra embryo was implanted. It was an error, but it happened and Rhea and I did what we knew we had to do to keep him safe. We knew what had happened to them in the past and we did everything we could to protect him."

A realization came to Delphine. "So, you knew he was a boy before he was born?"

Pala nodded. "I was the one in charge of Rhea's medical care during her pregnancy. I knew there were twins. And, as with all pregnancies, there were many ultrasounds to ensure the babies were developing properly. We both knew that one of the babies was a boy."

Delphine shook her head. "I don't understand. How were you able to keep that a secret?"

Pala shrugged. "It wasn't too difficult. I made slight edits to the ultrasound videos uploaded into the system to make sure there was nothing noticeable. I made sure the medical charts looked normal. There were three other pregnancies at that time, so the reproductive unit was stretched pretty thin. Nobody looked very close."

"But what about the birth? Surely you knew it would be discovered at the birth."

"Yes, we knew that…" her voice trailed off.

"Oh my," Delphine said, her eyes wide with realization. "The hull breach?"

Pala stood and took her plate of uneaten food to the counter. She gazed at the false window, black against the pale gray kitchen wall. "We knew there was no way Rhea could give birth in the medical lab, that was certain. So, we came up with a plan. The day she went into labor, I went outside and used a saw to create a tiny crack in the outer structure of the medical wing."

Delphine jumped to her feet. "Are you out of your mind? You could have killed everyone in the colony!"

Pala nodded and turned from the window to look back at Delphine. "Yes, it was not so smart. But I tried to make it as small as possible. Just enough to cause the structure alarms to go off. It was a risk, yes, but it was worth it to ensure Rhea could give birth away from the medical wing. It all worked out in the end. The crack was repaired quickly and everyone was safe. Including Rho," she added.

"How did you know they wouldn't catch you doing it? There are cameras everywhere!"

"I scouted out the spot beforehand, so I knew where I could do it without being in view of the cameras. I picked an area of the hull with a storage closet on the other side so nobody would be immediately affected by any air loss or atmosphere seepage. And I made the crack look as though it were a natural part of the aging process of the colony. These things happen all the time. This one just happened to be a bit bigger than others and therefore, they needed to close the medical wing. It gave us the perfect cover."

Delphine crossed her arms and paced the room, shaking her head, trying to wrap her mind around this. The idea that her mother had deliberately breached the colony hull was unthinkable. Impossible. It made her head ache at the mere thought of it.

Pala walked over, gently took hold of Delphine's arm, and turned her, meeting her eyes. "I did it for Rhea. And for the twins. I knew it had been many years since a male child was born and I had no idea how Ligeia would react to it. But I wasn't willing to risk it. Do you understand?"

Delphine watched her mother. She looked even thinner than normal, her cheekbones sharp under her translucent skin. Her eyes sunken and surrounded by dark gray circles. They were pleading with Delphine, *please understand*. Delphine nodded. She actually did understand. Her anger had fizzled with the sight of the fear on her mother's face. She knew the consequences of going against Ligeia and had no desire to expose any of those she held so dear.

Pala's shoulders, which had been hitched up almost to her ears, released and her face loosened. Dropping into the chair behind her, she let out a sigh. She looked drained from their brief conversation. Delphine clasped her hands together in her lap.

"What I don't understand is—why do this? I was always under the impression that male children were impossible here. That all children were created female and that was the end of it. In our studies, we were told this was to create a greater genetic pool for the future of the colony and when the time came and

Earth gave its blessing, we would start to breed male colonists. Why would Ligeia and the council want to destroy babies simply for being male? Why do that?"

Pala considered this for a moment before finally shrugging. "That's just how it's been for so long and we've never received any guidance about changing the way we do things in reproductive sciences."

"It doesn't make sense." Delphine chewed on her thumbnail as she tried to come up with a reason. "If we *could* have men here, why not?"

Pala nodded sadly. "I don't know. And you're right. It doesn't make sense."

"Well, I don't like it." Delphine dropped her fist on the table causing it to rumble and Pala to jump. "I don't like it one bit. Why can't Rho be who he really is? Why can't we allow the offspring to naturally grow into whatever gender they're meant to be. I think we should find out why."

Pala's head snapped to attention. The fear returned to her eyes, full and terrifying. "No! Delphine, no. It's not something we're meant to know. And when we are meant to know, the council will tell us."

"Why do you believe that? There are so many things they're already keeping secret." Delphine shifted forward in her chair to emphasize her point. "While I was at the library, I found the communication logs for the colony. You know what they showed?"

Pala's face grew pale and she shook her head slowly.

"They showed that Xanadu has been receiving regular communications from Earth every few weeks for the last seven decades. And do you want to know what we've been sending back to them?"

Pala sighed and said in a defeated voice, "What?"

"Nothing." Delphine leaned back as she said the word.

Pala sat up a bit straighter, her head tilting to one side. "What do you mean 'nothing'?"

"Nothing," Delphine repeated, putting emphasis on each syllable as if she were speaking to a child. "No return communications at all. No status updates. No requests. Nothing about the 'war'"—she used air quotes—"we've all heard so much about on Earth that's preventing them from coming here. Nothing at all."

"Well…" Pala's voice trailed before she continued, "that just can't be. You must have been looking in the wrong place."

Delphine shrugged. "Maybe. But maybe not. Either way, they have no problem lying to us, so why wouldn't they lie about the communications too? I want to do some more digging and find out why they're doing it."

Again, fear swept over Pala's face and her eyes turned to begging. "No, please. You're the only family I have left. Please!

Promise me you won't go back to the library. Promise me you won't do anything to get yourself in trouble. Please!"

The desperate tremor in her voice was almost too much for Delphine to bear. She sighed out the side of her mouth and a rogue strand of hair flew off her face with the sudden breath. She looked at her mother, tiny, frail, terrified. "Fine," she said numbly. It wasn't necessarily the truth, but it would put her mother at ease, at least for the moment.

Pala turned her tired eyes away from Delphine and stood. "It's been a long night. I think we should both get some sleep."

Delphine nodded. She did need to get her sleep. She had a meeting with the twins in the morning before her work shift and she would need to get up hours before her normal wake time. She stood and took her plate to the sink, washed it, dried it, and put it away before retiring to her bedroom for the night.

CHAPTER 21

Bang!

The sound that emanated from the space probe made Delphine jump. "Careful!" she said to Rho, who lay underneath the probe prying off an access panel. He had been successful and the panel had dropped fast, making a loud noise as it did.

"You think you can do a better job?" Rho asked, his voice muffled under the probe. She noticed he was speaking more around her now that his secret was out, his voice clearly deeper when they were in private versus when he was around other colonists. Looking back on her memories of Rho over the years, Delphine realized his voice had always been slightly off, although she'd never paid attention to it before. Now she could clearly hear the intonation difference and it was almost disturbing, knowing that if any one of the other colonists paid enough attention, they might be able to see Rho for what he really was—a male deep into the ruse of blending in as female.

Delphine let out an exasperated sigh. "Don't be ridiculous." Rho was a machinery repair technician. He was also pretty savvy when it came to computers, making him the obvious choice to work on the probe and try to fix the broken holograph. Delphine's expertise was in chemistry, science, and plants. She was *not* mechanically inclined. Rhayn would have been a better choice than Delphine. She often worked with the equipment in the cultivation tents. Machinery techs were busy and were most often needed to work on life-support equipment, construction machines, and down in the mines. If the tent workers could fix things on their own, they did their best not to involve their busier counterparts, and Rhayn was one of the better tent workers when it came to fixing things. But she didn't have the skills of her brother when it came to space machinery, so she and Delphine had deferred to his expertise.

"I think I found what I need," Rho said after several more minutes digging around inside the probe. He grunted as he pulled something loose and the entire probe shook.

"How can you be sure?" Rhayn asked, biting the edge of her thumbnail.

Delphine and Rhayn stood at what they'd determined to be the front of the probe, where the control panel and holographic projector were. They'd run the holograph recording three more times, trying to get the sound to work, but so far, they'd had no luck. Rho had suggested they upload the message onto a tablet and see if maybe they could get sound that way. He said it looked like the speaker system in the probe had been damaged. But after much searching around the control panel menus, they couldn't figure out how to upload from it. After staring at the probe for what felt like an eternity, Rho had decided it might be best to remove the computer unit from the probe.

"If this probe is anything like other space equipment, there should be a primary computer inside. And even if it is newer technology than what we're used to dealing with, it can't be all that different," he had said with a shrug.

Delphine and Rhayn waited while Rho worked on the access panel underneath the probe. They'd propped up the machine using several spare dozer tracks they'd found in the machine shed to give Rho enough space to scoot under it. After several more moments of Rho grunting and clanging his tools around in the underbelly of the probe, he scooted out and sat up next to it, holding a small gray box in his hand triumphantly.

"That's it?" Rhayn asked, her eyebrow raised skeptically.

"I think so," Rho said, turning the small device over in his hands, inspecting it.

Delphine noticed for the first time how big Rho's hands were. His fingers were long and tapered, yet rough from machinery work. She wondered if she were to put her hand up to his, how much longer his fingers were than her own. The thought of touching his hand suddenly made something inside her warm.

It was as if a tiny flame had been lit inside her chest and she could feel the heat of it start to spread through her heart, following the blood as it flooded her face. She flushed and immediately looked away from her friend, unsure what this sensation was or where it came from.

"What makes you so sure?" Rhayn asked, bending down to get a closer look at the thing in Rho's hand.

Rho twisted the gray box around, showing them a small label. The words on the label weren't on a sticker but had actually been imprinted into the side of the box, which appeared to be made of some sort of metal, an incredibly rare find on Titan. Almost everything they created was made of industrial plastic. Metal could be found in some of the rarer rock formations, but the colonists had figured out ways to live without metal, as the materials to make plastics were much more abundant on Titan. Rho pointed at the label. The printing looked like gibberish to Delphine: a mix of numbers and letters.

"This looks like a serial number," he said. "All parts of a space probe should have serial numbers on them, but a CPU has a longer one, like this. It has a mix of numbers and letters, the same way we label CPUs here at the colony."

"CPU?" Delphine asked.

"Central Processing Unit. It's the control center of the probe. It looks like it has its own battery here"—he pointed to a slim, blue cartridge attached to one side of the box where a tiny red light blinked—"and there isn't any wiring connected to it, so it must use wireless technology to control the various pieces of the probe. In any case, I've looked at all the machinery inside of this thing and I believe this is what we're looking for."

"Great," Delphine said. "Now, how do we use that to read the holograph?"

Rho stood, cradling the CPU next to his body and brushed the dust off his jumpsuit with his free hand. He walked to a workbench near the airlock where he had set a small tablet on the bench when they'd first arrived and pointed at the tablet. "I'm going to connect it wirelessly to this tablet. Hopefully the issue with the holograph is that the sound system on the probe is damaged. If that's the case, then there should be no problem playing it on this tablet instead because the speakers work fine on it."

"And what if it's not the case?" Rhayn asked, still nibbling on her thumbnail.

Rho was quiet for a moment, his forehead crinkling. "Well, let's just hope it is," he said, finally.

He ran his finger over the surface of the tablet, waking it, and allowed it to scan his face to unlock.

Delphine placed her hand on his wrist. "Wait," she said, biting her lip. "What about the colony mainframe? Won't this tablet immediately log onto the mainframe? If it does, then this message will be available to anyone at the colony."

Rho smiled. "I've thought of that. This is my personal tablet. I've engineered it so it doesn't access the mainframe. It actually *can't* connect wirelessly. I've disabled that feature. I could connect it using an actual wired port, I guess, but I've never done that."

Delphine was surprised by this. She'd never heard of anyone doing something like that. "Oh... why?"

Rho glanced at Rhayn and she gave him a knowing look. "Rhayn and I each have one like this. We use them for personal stuff. You know, things we don't want to save in any shared file. I actually have them set up so they can connect to each other, but they are password protected and triple encrypted. We can text between them without having our words go through the mainframe. It's just... safer that way. But I can connect to this CPU the same way, as long as I change the tablet settings to allow it to find the new computer."

Delphine nodded, impressed. Rho turned to the tablet and brushed his long fingers across the screen, moving here and there between programs and menus, updating settings and entering passwords. After a few moments, he pointed at the display and Delphine saw the same serial number stamped on the back of the CPU flash across it. "It's found the signal for this CPU," Rho said. He clicked on the number, the tablet screen flashed, and the word *Connected* popped up. Rho looked at Rhayn, then to

Delphine, before turning back to the tablet. He took a deep breath and said, "Here we go."

They watched as he navigated through the files on the probe's CPU. Most of it didn't make sense to Delphine, but Rho seemed to know where he was going with it. He must have noticed the look of confusion on her face because he said, "I've been tinkering around with the probe over the last couple of days. Coming here whenever I had some free time. So, I've gotten fairly familiar with this operating system. It's unlike anything we've ever used here. But I suppose it would be, considering it came from somewhere about a billion kilometers away from here. You'd think they would code these things in English, but no, it's written using some sort of shorthand. I'm guessing it's done that way because English isn't the only language spoken on Earth." He shrugged.

Delphine thought about this for a moment and it brought her back to her school days, sitting in her child-sized third-gen jumpsuit, listening to the teacher give lessons about Earth. She remembered learning this tidbit about Earth and thinking it so strange, that many of the people living there didn't speak the language of the colony. They had learned that the original twelve colonists spoke English because it was the accepted language of Earth's space program, ISEF. Delphine had asked Pala to explain it to her and she had remarked that Earth was a huge place, much bigger than even all of Titan, and because of those vast distances, people grew up in different ways. She thought about how confusing this had been to her as a child. *Bigger than all of Titan?* She could barely imagine anything bigger than the colony complex at the time. But that was before she'd taken her first walk on the surface to actually see how vast the landscape around them truly was.

"Okay, I think I've found it," Rho said, his voice pulling Delphine out of her thoughts. She looked at the tablet and saw that it was in the process of downloading a file from the probe's CPU. After several seconds, the file pinged indicating it was complete and Rho touched it. The holograph projector on the tablet opened up and almost instantly, the man appeared before them. He was much smaller now, standing only a few centimeters high in Rho's hand, but it was certainly the same man they'd seen speaking to them with silent words through the probe's projector. Only this time, his voice was clear as a bell.

The man clasped his hands in front of his chest and said, "Colonists of Titan. I am Tucker Drew, one of the colonization directors for the International Space Exploration Federation, or ISEF, as you may know it. The current Earth year is 2286 AD, approximately seventy-two years after the original colonists arrived at Titan. This is the exploratory probe Xanadu Thirty-Three picking up where Xanadu Thirty-Two left off. Our mission is to continue to try making contact with the Xanadu colony." As the man spoke, he tilted his head from side to side in a strange cadence, as if he'd timed the movements to coincide with certain words in his pre-planned speech.

"Last known communication occurred in the third month of year 2216. The message included a warning by acting head council member Leah Glenn indicating the presence of an unknown virus among the citizens of the Xanadu colony. Glenn warned that the virus was spreading and several deaths had occurred, but that the medical team was hard at work trying to isolate the virus and create a vaccine to eradicate it. No communication has been made since that time."

"Our satellites indicate that there is still a human presence at the Xanadu colony and ISEF has been trying to reestablish contact. It is our assumption that the communication array is no longer working and that is the reason we have had no communications with the colony. This probe is the thirty-third and closest attempt, with a landing site just outside the dune fields north of the colony."

The man paused and cleared his throat, looking down for a moment before returning his eye contact to the camera. "If you should receive this message, know that you may use the communication equipment on this probe to contact us. Manuals for how to use each of the instruments on board are included in this computer under the program file labeled ManuXC. We have been unable to return to Titan because of the threat of the virus as mentioned by Glenn and, until we can make contact with the citizens of Xanadu and ensure that there is no risk of infection, we will remain at a distance.

"Please, for the sake of every man, woman, and child at Xanadu, utilize the equipment on this probe to make contact with us. We hope to reconnect the worlds of Earth and Titan once again."

The voice cut off and the silence of the machinery shed rushed in so fast, it made Delphine's ears ring. The three of them stared at the now-blank screen of the tablet, their mouths agape, their eyes wide. Nobody said anything. They barely even breathed.

Rhayn was the first to break the silence. She sucked in a long breath and grabbed at the hair on either side of her ears, clenching her eyes shut. "No, no, no, no," she muttered, shaking her head.

"I don't…" Delphine started, but she couldn't finish the sentence. She couldn't seem to string together a whole thought in her mind. What they'd just heard was exploding inside her head like the tiny blasts you could hear through your surf suit when you were close to the mines.

Nobody from Xanadu had been in contact with Earth for seventy years.

Boom!

The people of Earth had made numerous attempts to reach the colonists.

Boom!

They believed there was a deadly virus at the colony because they had been led to believe that by the colonist Leah Glenn.

Boom!

Earth had addressed their message to all the people of Xanadu, including men. They had no idea that the colony was still only female.

Boom!

"Leah Glenn," Rho said, his voice cutting through the dynamite blasts inside Delphine's mind, causing her to jerk her head toward him.

"Leah Glenn," she repeated, realization washing over her.

Rhayn, who had been pacing back and forth in the space between the workbench and the space probe stopped and looked at them. "Leah Glenn," she said, her face frozen, eyes wide.

Rho sighed and Delphine noticed his jaw clench. "Ligeia's mother," he said.

CHAPTER 22

Delphine couldn't control the bouncing of her legs under the table. She bit her bottom lip and listened to the insistent *thump, thump, thump* of her boot on the floor of the machine shed.

Rhayn reached over and placed her hand lightly on Delphine's leg. "Please, stop."

Delphine let out a loud sigh and leaned forward, placing her elbows on the table and lacing her fingers together. She knew it was annoying, the constant leg bouncing, but it felt physically impossible to sit still.

Rhayn nodded in thanks and ran her fingers through her hair. "So, what now?"

The trio sat at a small, round table at the back of the machine shed. Delphine wasn't sure what the table was for, but she guessed it was for the mechanics to take breaks when they were spending long hours repairing and maintaining the machines. The table was covered in a thin layer of gritty orange dust indicating that it hadn't been used in a long time. After they listened to the holographic message, Rho had suggested that they hide the probe under the tarp and sit down for a few minutes before they went back to the colony, an effort to catalogue their thoughts and get their minds in order.

Delphine took a few deep breaths and tried to calm her racing pulse, mentally willing her legs to hold still. "Well," she said, biting her lip again, "we now know for a fact that the elders have been lying to us. Earth believes there are men here. It's clear this colony was never supposed to be an all-female colony."

Rho nodded and leaned forward, his hands on the table only centimeters away from Delphine's. "It's also clear that Ligeia's been lying to us about the communications with Earth." He shook his head in disbelief. "She probably even made up everything she's ever told us about the war on Earth. About why they haven't been back."

"The question now is," Rhayn said, her eyes wide, "was it only Ligeia? Do the other council members know?" She stood up abruptly causing Delphine to jump with nerves. Rhayn began pacing the small floor space next to the table. "Hell, there could be lots of colonists who know. I mean, this might be a gigantic secret that nobody talks about yet everyone secretly knows about."

"Except us," Rho added. "We didn't know about it. And if *we* didn't know, that means *others* don't know about it either."

Delphine nodded. "That means they've kept it a secret for a reason. They don't want us to know. But why? Why hide all of this? Why engineer the colony as all female when they clearly weren't supposed to? Why not communicate with Earth?" The questions kept coming, flowing in waves like the liquid methane that ebbed and flowed in the great lake east of the colony. Delphine rubbed her temples trying to keep her mind from spinning as the questions came relentlessly.

Rhayn continued to pace. She asked again, "So, what now?"

An alert flashed across Delphine's face as her ear bugs alerted her that she was due to work in thirty minutes. "Damn," she said. "I've got to be in the tent soon. I need to get going now or I'll be late for sure."

Rho had been staring at the far wall of the machine shed, his arms crossed tightly across his chest, thinking. He sat up, as if awakened from a dream. "We have to go to Ligeia. We have to get answers to these questions. We can sit here and ponder all we want, but we'll never know for sure unless we go right to the source."

Rhayn stopped pacing and planted her hands on her hips. "How can we do that, Rho? We can't bring any unnecessary attention to you. Going to her is like putting the target square on your back. What if she decides to dig deeper into your records? It wouldn't take a genius to figure out that you've never had a proper medical examination in your adult years." She stepped closer to Rho and knelt beside him, looking up into his eyes. "We can't risk it." There was an element of pleading in her voice that made Delphine's stomach clench with fear.

Rho took her hand and lightly kissed the back of her fingers. "It's not all about me. We, all of us, the colonists, deserve to know what's really going on around here. We can't sit back and allow this to continue. Not now that we know Earth is trying to reach us. To talk to us." He looked up at Delphine then back at his sister. "I'm not afraid for myself. I want to know the answers."

"Me too," Delphine said, pushing herself to standing. "Plus, we have an upper hand. We have the space probe." She gestured toward the back corner of the shed where they'd hidden the probe under the tarp. "We can use it to talk to Earth. We can tell them what's going on here. We can use it to our advantage."

Rhayn's brows knit together. "I don't understand. You mean, we should blackmail her?"

"Why not?" Rho said. "She's been lying to all of us for years. Why not use the probe as a bargaining chip? We can force her hand. She doesn't know where it is or that it can communicate with Earth. We can tell her everything we've uncovered and demand she tell the colony the truth. We'll threaten to tell them ourselves and then tell Earth about what she's done if she doesn't give us the answers we deserve."

Delphine looked Rho in the eye and he met her gaze. For the first time, she noticed how bright his eyes were, a stunning shade of amber. His brow was tight with worry, but his face looked strong, as if chiseled from stone. He was beautiful and for a moment, her breath caught in her throat. "Yes," she said in a whisper. Then she cleared her throat and her voice grew louder. "I agree. We will go to see her tonight after we're done with our shifts. We will tell her everything we know and demand answers. We will threaten to tell Earth what she's done."

"Will that work?" Rhayn asked, the fear rising in her voice, choking off the last word.

Rho nodded and stood. "It *will* work." His voice was strong and steady. It gave Delphine confidence. Calmed her swirling thoughts. Filled her with hope. She nodded and looked at Rhayn, who also nodded. "We agree then. We will meet at our apartment tonight after our shifts are done. We will confront her then."

The girls nodded again and, with trembling hands, Delphine pushed the chair she'd been sitting on under the table and headed for the airlock to suit up.

CHAPTER 23

The longer she stood, staring at the thick, green lettuce patch in front of her, the further away Delphine's mind drifted. She was thinking about the arrangement they'd made in the machinery shed a few short hours earlier. They had all decided to go to their shifts as usual and meet up at the end of the day to confront Ligeia together.

But something wasn't sitting right with Delphine. She didn't like it. Yes, it was the plan they'd agreed on, and it was a good plan on the surface, but as soon as they'd entered the main airlock and passed through the cleaning protocol, she knew it was not going to work. It was the worry on Rhayn's face that did it. Worry was something she rarely saw from her carefree friend and it was an emotion she didn't care to see ever again.

Rhayn was worried, and rightly so, about Rho. He didn't seem to understand the danger he was in if Ligeia, or anyone beholden to Ligeia and the council, found out who he truly was.

Rhayn was right to be worried. If Rho put himself at the center of this, it could unravel years of work by Rhayn and Rhea and Pala to hide his identity. After all, it had been Pala who had delivered the twins and done the necessary work to ensure Rho's medical files showed no trace of his gender.

If something happened to expose the cover-up, Delphine wouldn't be able to live with it. She had started all this when she'd stood up at the meeting a few short days ago. She'd been the one to initiate this search for the truth. If something happened to Rho because of it, she would blame herself forever. It would be like reliving Aura's death all over again. But this time, the pain would be compounded because she'd have Rhayn's pain to deal with as well. Her own mother would be at risk.

No, she couldn't let that happen. A new plan was forming in her mind—a plan that would keep the twins safe. It would keep Rhea and Pala safe as well. She knew what she had to do.

"Are you okay?" The voice came at her so suddenly, she jumped, sending a flow of hydroponic fluid spilling over the edge of the beaker she was using to water the tray of lettuce in front of her.

"What?" Delphine said, shaking her head to clear the daydreams and bring back a sense of reality.

It was Maya, standing just behind her, having walked up the long aisle in the lettuce patch without Delphine noticing her. A large, purple bruise had spread in a circle around Maya's right eye where Delphine had hooked her. Delphine flinched at the sight of it, not quite believing it had been her own fist that had inflicted such a nasty bruise on her fellow colonist. They'd fought only one day earlier. Delphine could hardly believe all that had taken place since the skirmish in the tent. It seemed like it had happened months ago. But the fresh bruise on Maya's eye revealed the truth.

"Are you okay?" Maya repeated, tilting her head to the side, giving Delphine a quizzical look. "You've been standing there like that for the last ten minutes." She pointed at Delphine's right hand which was suspended in midair holding the beaker of fluid poised over one of the lettuce plants. She had obviously meant to pour the fluid into the plant's tray, but had stopped short and gotten so wrapped up in her thoughts, her body had frozen in position.

"I…" Delphine shook her head again, trying to clear the fog and focus on Maya's words. "I… yeah, I'm okay." She set the beaker down and shook her hand to rid it of the spilled hydroponic fluid. "I'm okay," she repeated, giving Maya a slight smile as if to emphasize the point.

Maya continued to look at her with her head cocked to the side. She crossed her arms over her chest. "You're sure? You look," she paused as though thinking of the right word, "distracted."

"Oh, do I? Well, yes. I suppose I am a bit distracted." Delphine bit her lip and gave Maya a shrug. "It's been a long day."

Maya smiled. It was a nice smile. A comforting smile. It seemed to raise the white flag. "Well, it's not even 1000 hours yet. You've still got a lot of day left to go." She walked past Delphine, continuing down the aisle toward the bean plants at the far end, but she stopped after only a few steps and turned back to Delphine. "Look, about yesterday"—she bit her thumbnail— "I'm sorry. About what I said and all. I shouldn't have come at you like that."

Delphine nodded and raised her palms in a show of understanding. "No worries. And I'm sorry about that." She gestured at Maya's swollen eye. Maya reached up and touched the edge of the bruise with her index finger. She smiled and nodded before turning without another word. Delphine watched her walk away and smiled to herself. Maya wasn't the sharpest, but she was a fellow colonist of Xanadu, and she was also a third-gen. They would always have a connection and no amount of bruised eyes or bruised egos could change that.

Delphine turned back to the lettuce tray in front of her and the beaker, now with half its contents spilled out on floor. She glanced down the aisle again and saw Maya turn the corner, her head disappearing behind the row of bean trellises at the end of the row. Peering down the other end of the aisle, she saw nobody in that direction. Thessa and Rhayn weren't in sight either.

She made a decision. Leaving the beaker and all her supplies where they were, she took off down the aisle leading to the exit corridor of Tent 4.

***

Twenty minutes later, Delphine stood in front of Ligeia's apartment, her hand hovering over the access panel. On the long walk over, she'd almost lost her nerve. But the idea of saving the twins from having to make this confrontation propelled her forward. Now, as she stared at the tall gray door in front of her, she couldn't quite make the move to press the button.

This was the point of no return. She knew the moment she rang that bell, her life would be different. Ligeia would know about the probe and about the holographic message hidden inside it. She would know Delphine went to the library without permission and dug up birth records and communications records. Delphine would no longer be able to hide behind a crowd of other colonists, doing her work and ignoring her misgivings.

No, Ligeia would not take to these transgressions well and Delphine knew it. But there was no other alternative in her mind. She needed answers… needed to know what had happened so many years ago, because whatever had transpired with the original colonists, it had shaped the way their colony grew. It had formed the basis for their laws, their society, even their collective gender, and Delphine needed to know why.

Closing her eyes, she took a deep, solid breath in through her nose, held it for a moment, then slowly and calmly let it out through her mouth. She straightened her back and held her head up. She lifted her hand and, pausing only for a second, pressed the button to page Ligeia inside her apartment.

"Yes?" came the pleasant voice from within.

"Ligeia, I need to speak with you." She attempted to make her voice deeper, more coercive. "This is Delphine," she added but immediately felt foolish for it. She glanced up at the camera mounted over the door. Ligeia didn't need her to announce her presence. No doubt she could see her clearly from the video feed.

"Ah, Delphine. Won't you please come in."

The door made a sharp click as the lock disengaged and Delphine pushed the handle down, swinging the door inward as she did. Inside, she was met with the same great room she'd seen only a day earlier on her first visit to the apartment, but she was still taken aback by the sheer size of the voluminous space. It seemed as though the rough cave ceiling loomed even farther over her head than it had before. The walls seemed even farther back.

Delphine took a few steps inside and allowed the door to click shut behind her. She looked around. Ligeia stood at the entrance to the kitchen wearing her traditional first-gen jumpsuit, the red standing out in stark contrast to the solid black countertops and white cabinets of the kitchen.

"It's good to see you again, Delphine," she said, her face pale and glowing, her hair flowing freely around her shoulders instead of tucked up in its usual bun. "Twice in as many days. To what do I owe this honor?"

Delphine flushed. The words took on a mocking tone, although she couldn't be completely sure. One could never tell with Ligeia and her sickly sweet voice. Delphine wasn't fooled though. There was no surprise on Ligeia's face. Her eyes were confident and brazen. "You knew I would come back," Delphine said.

Ligeia held her smile and nodded. "Yes, I did. Come, sit down. Have some lemonade with me." She gestured toward the sofa where Delphine had sat the prior day and turned to retrieve the pitcher from the refrigerator.

"No lemonade, please," Delphine said, taking a seat on the sofa.

"Oh, come now. Don't be like that." Delphine heard the liquid swish as Ligeia poured it into two cups before turning to put the pitcher back into the refrigerator. "I know you enjoyed it when you had it before. Please, have some." She placed one cup on the table in front of Delphine and took the other with her to the adjacent sofa. She crossed her legs and took a long, slow drink, releasing the sip with a sigh. "Now, tell me why you're here."

"I know what's been going on around here."

Ligeia blinked. "What do you mean by that?"

"I mean," Delphine said, swallowing, hoping the involuntary reaction would clear some of the fear she felt clamped in her throat. "I mean, I know about the original colonists. I know that this colony was never supposed to be an all-female colony. And I've seen the birth records. I know there have been male children born here. They had the rotten luck to be born before you had a good grasp on the in vitro process and they were murdered simply for being the incorrect gender!" Heat rose through her. It gave her courage, desperately needed courage. She clenched her fists in her lap.

Delphine wasn't sure how she thought Ligeia would react, but she didn't expect the reaction that came. Ligeia's face was blank for a moment, her eyes wide and wondering. Then she let out a long, low laugh that rose and echoed in the cavernous room. Delphine flinched when Ligeia actually threw her head back, the laugh continuing to escape from her mouth as if it had been trapped inside her for many years. This was their leader. Their guide. She had never indicated she was anything but calm and poised. Yet here she was, laughing like a maniac when confronted with the most terrible accusation.

After several moments, Delphine couldn't stop her outrage. "What are you laughing about? This is an unforgivable thing you've done!"

She did stop laughing, but the smile remained on her face, her eyes wide and wild. Delphine suddenly felt terrified to be in the presence of this woman. "Oh, you've been poking around the colony records, have you?" Ligeia said, her voice rising in pitch on the final two words.

Ligeia drained the last of her lemonade and set the glass on the table. She leaned back on the sofa spreading her arms wide across the backrest. "So harmless little Delphine has been poking around in my records. And what am I supposed to make of that, my dear? What would you like me to say?"

Delphine was shaken. She wasn't sure what she'd expected Ligeia to say. Probably to deny the allegation and threaten her. But she pooled her courage and spoke. "I want you to tell me why. I don't understand why you would murder children in the name of keeping our colony all female. It doesn't make any sense."

Ligeia's face still bore that crazy, wide-eyed look as she swayed her head to one side, staring off toward the kitchen. "What makes you think that women were never meant to rule this colony without the help of men? I think we've done just fine. We've built the greatest colony the human race has ever established in the outer reaches. And we've done it without the help of a single man. No, I think this colony most definitely *was* meant to be an all-female colony. Frankly dear, I don't think I owe you any explanation beyond that."

"I have other evidence too," Delphine said, her throat tight again. "I know you haven't been communicating with Earth. I saw the communication logs as well."

Ligeia continued to smile. Clearly this was not news to her. "Yes, I know what you've seen."

This took Delphine back. "You do?"

Ligeia let out a chuckle. "Of course I do. You think I wasn't alerted to the fact that you'd gone to the library and told Elyn that I gave you permission to be there?" She paused, shaking her head. "You're not nearly as smart as I thought you were then."

"If you knew I was there, why did you allow me to see the records? Why didn't you come immediately and stop me?"

Ligeia shrugged. "Frankly, I was curious as to what you were after. I knew when you saw that picture—the one of the original colonists on the Sirena—that you were *not* going to let the subject die. So, I asked Elyn to track your movements through the records so I could review them. And I told her not to alert you that I knew about it. I was interested to see where you'd look."

"So you knew I found out about the male births and the communications?" Delphine was stunned by this. Ligeia knew, and yet Delphine hadn't been punished or lectured or even confronted about her snooping.

"Yes, I knew." Ligeia's face was twisted into a smirk.

Delphine shook her head, trying to understand what she was hearing. "And you didn't mind? You didn't think I would tell anyone?"

"Did you tell someone?" Ligeia raised an eyebrow. Delphine remained silent, staring down at her lap. "Of course, you did. I'm no fool. And I'm fairly certain I know whom you told. But the thing is—I don't care."

Delphine looked up at her. "I… I don't understand."

Ligeia leaned forward, emphasizing each word as if speaking to a tiny child. "I don't care," she repeated.

"Well, maybe you should care," Delphine said, her voice rising. She was confused and unsure about what to make of these words. This wasn't at all how she'd guessed this conversation would go. "There's no way I can let this go. The colonists *believe* you are communicating with Earth on a regular basis. They think we're receiving direct orders from Earth to continue with our current propagation plan to expand the colony with women and create a larger genetic pool. They won't allow you to get away with this anymore once I tell them."

"Once you tell them?" Ligeia's voice ticked up, offering the repeated phrase as a question. "And what do you think will happen once you tell them, Delphine? Do you think they'll believe you?"

"Why wouldn't they believe me?"

"What proof do you have? I know you didn't take any screenshots. You couldn't have downloaded any files. What makes you so sure those records are even still accessible?" She smiled, content with her rebuttal of Delphine's threat.

Delphine paused, trying to assemble a sentence in her mind. Trying to organize her thoughts so she could get across what she was trying to say. "It's not just the records. I have other evidence."

Ligeia's eyebrow shot up and she cocked her head to the side. "Oh? And what other evidence is that?"

Delphine swallowed, steeling herself. "I found something outside. A space probe. It was sent from Earth—recently. Not decades ago. This was sent within the last few months. It has a holographic message in it. A message from Earth to the colonists of Xanadu. It says they've been trying to reestablish contact for seventy years. It confirms what I found in the communication records. And not only that, I can use the probe to contact Earth. I can use the radio on it to tell them what's been going on here. And I plan to do just that, after I tell the colony what you and the council have done."

For the first time since they sat down, the smile fell from Ligeia's face. Looking straight at Delphine, Ligeia's eyes bore into her face as if trying to get a look inside her mind. Ligeia stood abruptly and walked to the small desk situated at the far end of the room. She produced a tablet, the same one she'd used to show Delphine the picture of the original colonists in her first visit, and walked back to the sofa. She tapped the tablet's face to awaken it and swiftly ran her fingers over the surface, pulling up what she was looking for. Her face was hard and calm. After a moment, she turned the tablet around so Delphine could see the screen.

 What she saw made her blood cool. The image on the screen was a live feed from the machinery shed where the probe was. The camera pointed directly at the spot in the corner of the shed where Delphine and the twins had left the probe that morning covered with an old black tarp. Except there was no probe there now. There was nothing at all in the corner of the shed except drag marks where the probe had been pulled away, leaving trails of surface dust on the floor. As Delphine processed the camera feed, her breath began to flutter, coming out of her lungs in short, light wisps. She could feel her heart pounding through her blood vessels, creating a deafening sound in her ears. She dropped her head into the palm of her hand and closed her eyes, trying to block out the image of that empty corner. Trying to keep herself from fainting.

Ligeia didn't move. She continued to hold up the tablet, moving it closer to Delphine's face. Taunting her with it. "I'm not sure what you mean. I don't see a space probe."

Delphine looked up at her and took several shallow, raspy breaths. "You knew... you knew about the probe. How did you know?"

"Do I look like an idiot? I had you followed after your little stunt in the library. I saw you and your friends go to this shed. I watched you with it this morning. I found it interesting that not one of you stopped to question whether or not there were cameras inside the shed. Well, actually, there wasn't anyone monitoring the shed cameras because there was no reason to. But you led me right to it after your visit to the library. It was your stupid move that gave me the reason to turn to those cameras in the first place." Ligeia finally pulled the tablet back and looked over it herself, a pleased expression on her face.

Of course, there were cameras in the shed! It had never occurred to her or the twins that they would be monitored or even turned on; the shed was so rarely used between harvests. But that was foolish of them. Nausea swept across Delphine's stomach and she swallowed hard.

Ligeia continued, "As you can see by the current image, there is no longer a probe in the machine shed. I've taken care of it. So no, you won't be using the probe to communicate with Earth. Or to prove to any colonist that I have been anything but forthcoming to them as their leader. No, there's nothing here that's any good to you. I've also removed the necessary files from the colony records. And I can imagine that if you made these wild accusations, the colonists would want proof. They won't blindly believe your indictment of me." She set the tablet down and looked at Delphine. "Are you all right? Your face has gone quite pale."

Delphine slowly shook her head. A thin bead of sweat ran down her forehead and she realized there were black spots in her vision. She rocked back and forth, fighting with the tears that threatened to escape her eyes.

Ligeia's face suddenly showed great concern. She moved closer to Delphine. "Oh dear, you're sweating. When was the last time you ate? It won't do you any good to pass out right here on my sofa. Here." She picked up the cup full of lemonade and held it up to Delphine. "Drink some of this. It will help."

She didn't want to take it but realized it had been almost twenty hours since she'd eaten anything. A wave of dizziness passed over her and, with trembling fingers, she took the cup from Ligeia. She took a long, slow gulp. This time, the juice was much more sour than it had been the day before. It caused her face to pucker and her cheeks to spasm. She set the cup down after swallowing the last of the bitter liquid.

Ligeia smiled. "That's a good girl. My Titan girls are so good sometimes." Her voice was wistful now, almost like a child's. "Perhaps you'd like to lie down?"

Delphine shook her head. She wanted to get out of there. She couldn't handle being in that vast room anymore. The walls, she realized, were spinning around her. With all her might, she pushed herself up off the sofa. She had to get out. But her legs didn't seem to want to cooperate. As soon as she stood, they collapsed beneath her and she dropped heavily back onto the sofa. Her eyes were cloudy. She realized that she couldn't feel her limbs anymore as she fell backward, her head landing on the sofa. The last thing she saw before she passed out was Ligeia, standing over her, holding the empty cup of lemonade and smiling.

CHAPTER 24

In her dream, Aura came to her. This, in itself, wasn't abnormal. She often dreamed of her sister. But in this dream, something about her was different.

They were standing shoulder to shoulder outside on the surface of Titan, each in their surf suits, staring at the colony in the distance. It was daytime in the dream, and she could feel the glow of the clouded atmosphere all around her. She turned to look at her sister, who turned back to her, as if a mirror of her own self. Aura smiled and raised her hand, waving hello to Delphine. Delphine smiled back. Her sister looked so beautiful inside the surf suit. She wasn't as young as the day Delphine had last seen her. The vision of Aura had grown older in Delphine's mind. She would be seventeen years old now and the older version of Aura that stood next to her now easily encompassed a colonist of seventeen years.

They both turned to look back at the colony. It was far away, at least half a kilometer by Delphine's best guess. But the atmosphere was clearer today than on other days. There wasn't any haze in the air and she could easily make out the balloon-like cultivation tents protruding from the ground. She could see the jut of the mining complex off to her left. And she could vaguely make out the shores of Baikal Lacus as it dropped off the edge of the horizon into nothing.

"What are we doing here?" Delphine said.

Aura tipped her head to one side, a sly smile on her face, and a giggle escaped her lips. She opened her mouth to speak, but before any words came out, a shadow passed over them. They both looked up to see a vast, bulky shape hovering in the atmosphere above them. Delphine couldn't make out the exact shape—it was too high up and the edges were blurred by the atmosphere. But whatever it was, it was huge, big enough to cast a shadow over the two girls.

"What is it?" Delphine said, still looking at the great thing in the sky. She turned to Aura and the look on her sister's face made her gasp. Aura was terrified.

She grabbed Delphine's shoulders and Delphine could feel the warmth where Aura's gloves rested on her thick surf suit. Aura looked at her, eyes wide. "You have to wake up," she said.

Delphine crinkled her nose. What was she talking about?

Aura shook her head forcefully, looking up at the dark shadow and then back at Delphine. "You have to wake up!" she repeated, her voice trembling.

Delphine continued to look at her, trying to figure out what was going on. Somewhere deep in her mind, she knew this was a dream, but she didn't understand what Aura was so worried about. She couldn't figure out *why* she needed to wake up. Why couldn't they simply enjoy this time together?

Aura shook Delphine's shoulders hard, hard enough that Delphine let out a little gasp from the sudden pressure. This time, she screamed. "Wake up *now!*"

Delphine's eyes flew open, the words echoing in her head. Even though her eyes were now open, she couldn't see anything. She blinked several times to try to clear them. Slowly, a picture of her surroundings took shape.

She was lying on her side, her back resting against something that felt like a cushion. Ahead of her, she saw the inner door of an airlock. There were foldable seats on either side of the airlock but they were all folded up as if they had no occupants. It took a few moments for Delphine to recognize her surroundings. She'd been here before—many times. She was inside a rover.

From where she was positioned, she could tell she was lying across the three larger seats that lined the side wall of the rover. These seats were where crew members sat when riding out to a work site and they butted against each other, making a long bench that ran the entire length of the wall. They didn't fold up like the seats on the opposite wall as those were there only for overflow seating and were always locked in their upright positions when not in use.

Delphine blinked again and realized the rover was moving. She could feel the steady hum of the engines and the occasional bump as it rolled over the rocky Titanian surface. Based on how the rover moved, the machine must have been driving over one of the well-established roads that looped around the colony. If it were outside the colony grounds, the ride would be much rougher.

She twisted her head to see the front of the rover where the captain and cocaptain seats were, but from where she lay, she couldn't see the rover driver over the top of the captain's chair. When she tried to push herself up so she could identify the driver, she realized she couldn't move. She attempted to wiggle her fingers and found that she couldn't even feel them. Looking down at her body, she realized her hands were bound behind her back and her body from the neck down felt like dead weight.

Panic rose inside her and she took a few deep breaths in an attempt to calm herself. She looked around for something she could focus on and settled for the access panel to the airlock which blinked a bright green *Ready* in the dim lighting of the rover interior. As she stared at the green light, she clenched her teeth and tried to force her fingers to move. After a few moments, she stopped and took a few more deep breaths before trying again. Still, nothing happened. Sweat formed on her forehead and the back of her neck. Again, the panic threatened to overtake her.

To stop from freaking out, she closed her eyes and tried to remember what had happened before she woke up in the rover. She had been at work, where she'd talked to Maya and felt grateful that all seemed to have been forgiven between the two. She had decided to leave and go to Ligeia's apartment without Rhayn and Rho. It was coming back to her in waves. She remembered walking into the apartment and confronting Ligeia. She recalled that high, terrifying laugh Ligeia had let out when she'd stated what she knew.

Her memories became fuzzy. She knew they were sitting on the sofas across from each other and she remembered Ligeia getting up and bringing a tablet back to the sofa. What had she shown her? Delphine squeezed her eyes tighter and forced herself to remember.

Suddenly, the memory flooded back. The probe. Ligeia had shown her the machine shed where the probe had been hidden. She had destroyed the probe.

And then there had been the lemonade. Delphine remembered being faint, feeling as though she might pass out. Ligeia's sweet voice. *Drink some of this. It will help.*

The lemonade.

That was the end of Delphine's memories and now she lay incapacitated inside one of the rovers going who-knows-where. Turning her head again, she caught the edge of a red first-gen jumpsuit on the person occupying the captain's seat.

At that moment, Ligeia turned. Her eyes met Delphine's and a smile spread across her face. Her red hair, which had been loose when they were in the apartment, was now swept back in a tight bun. Her eyes were wide and glinted with that strange expression Delphine had seen in the apartment. She looked… unhinged.

"Ah, you're awake," Ligeia said and another cold, dark laugh escaped her lips.

CHAPTER 25

Rhayn stared at the tiny faux window over the sink in the kitchen. It was set to show the feed from an outside camera, one facing east of the colony where the lake was. But it was black, the Titanian night dense. This particular camera had a motion sensor light, so it only popped on when someone walked near it. And given its location facing the lake, very few colonists ever tripped it. So it sat dark. The only thing Rhayn could see was the reflection of her own image against the blackness.

    She sighed and turned to look at her brother who was hunched over at the table, literally twiddling his thumbs. Rhayn pulled up the time on her ear bugs and saw it had been forty-two minutes since she had left the cultivation tent—without Delphine.

    When she'd finished her shift and made her way to the locker room in the tent to change out of her work coveralls, she had been a bit on edge about their impending meeting with

Ligeia. But she wasn't overly worked up about it. She rarely let anything bother her.

That was, until she realized that Delphine was not in the locker room and failed to show up after their shift. Rhayn had waited there a good ten minutes before going back out into the tent to try to find her friend. She'd run into Maya who told her she saw Delphine earlier in the day. She said Delphine seemed fine and she'd been working with the beans. When Rhayn went to that section, she found Thessa there inventorying the plant stock.

"Do you know where Delphine went?" Rhayn had asked.

Thessa shrugged and pointed to the locker room. "I assume she went to the locker room to change."

"No, she's not in the locker room. And I can't seem to find her," Rhayn said.

"She didn't mention anything to me," Thessa said, turning her eyes back to her work.

Rhayn crossed her arms over her chest. "She would have said something to you if she were going to leave her shift early, wouldn't she?"

Thessa nodded and pointed at a tray of newly sprouted bean plants, moving her finger back and forth as she counted the number of spouts.

Rhayn cleared her throat in an attempt to get Thessa to pay attention to their conversation. "Have you spoken to her today?"

Thessa finished her count and entered the number into her notes, then turned to Rhayn and sighed. "No, Rhayn, I haven't spoken to her today. But I've been doing this inventory count all day and I was in Tent Three for quite some time helping them with theirs. So it's possible I missed her." She put her hand on Rhayn's shoulder, patting her lightly in a comforting manner. Rhayn simply stared at it.

"What time did she clock out?" Rhayn asked.

Thessa tapped on her ear bugs and Rhayn watched as she scrolled through time cards. "Hmm," Thessa said after several moments, raising a single eyebrow. "Looks like she didn't clock out at all. She's still clocked in, actually." Thessa shrugged. "Maybe she forgot. She's done that before. I'm sure there's an explanation. Perhaps she took off a bit early."

Rhayn had nodded, smiled, and left the tent before heading to her apartment. She had sent Delphine a message asking her where she was. That was twelve messages ago.

Now, as she sat with Rho, she had a feeling something wasn't right. She checked her ear bugs again. Forty-four minutes since she'd left the tent. "What should we do?" she asked him.

Rho's head snapped up as if she'd pulled him out of some deep thought. "So Thessa didn't hear from her all day?"

Rhayn nodded and turned back to the dark window. "Maya saw her but didn't seem to think there was anything wrong. I was hauling harvested crops to the storage buildings all day, so I didn't see her either."

Rho stood from the table and ran a hand through his hair. "We had a plan to meet here right after work. She wouldn't have skipped out on us."

"No," Rhayn agreed.

"And she hasn't answered any of your messages? I sent her one about five minutes ago that she hasn't answered."

"No, she hasn't answered any of my messages."

"Okay," Rho said, sighing and turning to the door. "Let's go look for her."

***

Pala answered the door slowly. Her graying hair hung limp at her shoulders and Rhayn realized for the first time how thin Pala had gotten. Her green jumpsuit draped around her shoulders, the sleeves so long she'd had to roll them up around the wrists. Her eyes were sunken into the pits of her skull and the lids lay heavy and dull.

She looked surprised to see the twins standing at her door, but not surprised enough to lift her drooping shoulders. "Rhayn, Rho, what can I do for you?"

"Do you know where Delphine is?" Rhayn asked, biting her lower lip.

This seemed to perk Pala up as she raised her chin and eyed the twins up and down. "No. Didn't you just come from your shift in the tent? Wasn't she with you?"

Rho shook his head. "When Rhayn left the tent, Delphine was nowhere to be found. We were all supposed to meet at our apartment after work, but she never showed up. We were hoping maybe you knew where she was."

Pala turned and headed into the kitchen, allowing the door to swing open. Rhayn flinched as the hinges squealed. They needed grease.

The twins came in, although they didn't sit. Rhayn continued to bite her lip while Rho closed the door behind him and leaned against the doorframe. Pala wrapped her arms around herself and her gaze darted between Rhayn's and Rho's faces. "Well, she's not here. I've been here all day and I haven't seen her. Maybe she went outside…" Her voice trailed off as she must have realized this was impossible, for in the corner of the kitchen, Delphine's surf suit lay slung over the extra kitchen chair. Her boots and life pack were tucked underneath the chair.

Rho glanced at Rhayn, giving her that quizzical look he had been so good at since he was a child. The look that told Rhayn he was working things out in his mind. "She wouldn't have gone without us, would she?"

Rhayn bit her lip again, unsure of how to answer. Of course, it was a possibility. But they'd had a plan and Delphine had agreed to it. Rhayn couldn't think of a reason why Delphine would have deviated from the plan.

"Gone where?" Pala asked, moving a step closer to the kitchen table.

Rho sighed. "To see Ligeia."

Pala stared at him for a moment before sinking into the chair and resting her elbows on the table. "To see Ligeia," she repeated, shaking her head. "And what were the three of you planning to say to our leader?"

Rhayn moved toward the table and took the seat directly opposite Pala. She gestured for Rho to do the same. After he sat, Rhayn went through everything they'd discovered. Delphine had told her about what she'd learned in the library, but she hadn't mentioned the space probe to Pala. When Rhayn told her about it and the holographic message, Pala sank back in her chair and rolled her head back, staring at the ceiling. "Oh my God," she repeated several times.

"We decided the only way to get Ligeia to listen to us and to actually admit to the truth was to threaten her with the space probe," Rho said, filling in when Rhayn finished. "We can communicate with Earth using its equipment. Ligeia will have to tell the truth. She'll have to step down. We were planning to go to her tonight after we got done with our shifts. But Delphine never showed up."

"She went on her own," Pala said, shaking her head. "I know it. There's no other explanation."

"But why would she do that?" Rho asked, his jaw clenched.

"Because of you," Rhayn said, looking at her brother.

"Me? Why me?"

"You're the one with the most to lose. You are the one who might be exposed. She probably went there knowing it would keep *you* from having to be involved." Rhayn shook her head and sighed. "I can't *believe* I didn't think about this before. She saw how nervous I was about doing this and she must have decided to protect us both."

Pala stood suddenly, her eyes sharp. The lethargic look she'd had when they arrived was gone, replaced with what Rhayn could only describe as sheer determination. "We have to go to Ligeia's apartment. We can't sit here and wait. Ligeia will not bow down without a fight and we can't allow Delphine to fight that battle on her own."

Rho stood and nodded. "Let's go."

CHAPTER 26

"I'm glad you're awake, dear. I've been growing nightshade for years—I use it to help me sleep, you know—but I've never given it to someone else and I've certainly never used it in this quantity." Ligeia turned back to face the front of the rover briefly as she tapped the control screens. From what Delphine could see, she was setting a course and putting the rover on autopilot.

After she completed the set of commands, Ligeia stood and moved to the back of the rover where Delphine lay. She unfolded one of the seats across from Delphine and sat, crossing one leg over the other.

"I apologize for the nightshade, but you know, I had to do it. There's no way you would have come with me willingly."

"Nightshade?" Delphine had never heard of such a thing.

"Yes, well, *atropa belladonna* is the proper name for it. But I've always called it nightshade. It's how my mother referred to it." A faint smile crossed Ligeia's face and she stared off as if conjuring some distant memory.

"I've never heard of it. It's not grown in the main tents." Delphine wasn't sure what was going on, but Ligeia had just confessed to drugging her, so she was relatively sure that the woman who now sat across from her had lost her mind. She quickly decided that keeping Ligeia calm and talking would be her best bet until she could think of some way to get herself out of this. Again, she tried to wiggle her finger but found the movement impossible.

"Oh no!" Ligeia chuckled. "No, we couldn't have that! It's much too dangerous to be near the rest of the colonists. No, I grow it in my personal garden in the council members' tent. My apartment connects right to it, so I can stroll around in there whenever I want. The nightshade grows right next to the lemons, actually." Again, she smiled.

"I can't move. What does it do?" Delphine asked tentatively. She focused on pushing the command to wiggle her fingers through her mind, willing it to travel all the way from her brain to her hands. To her surprise, she was actually able to make the tip of her index finger move. It was a fraction of a centimeter, but it was something.

"It's a sedative. When used in small quantities, it makes a great sleep aid. And, as you might guess, I have such a terrible weight of burden on my shoulders keeping this colony active and thriving. Sleep is not something that comes easy to those of us with great worries." As she spoke, Ligeia ran the backs of her fingers across her forehead for dramatic effect. Had Delphine not been terrified for her life, she would have rolled her eyes.

"But I can't move," Delphine repeated. "Why can't I move?" Again, she tried to wiggle her fingers and found the gesture easier this time, her synapses firing faster.

Ligeia nodded and cupped her hands together over her knee. "Yes, paralysis is one of the unfortunate side effects of nightshade. In greater quantities, that is. Like I said, I've never used it in such a way, so I'm really unsure how long the paralysis will last."

"So, it's not permanent?" Delphine asked. Now she could move several of her fingers. As her nerves came alive, the feeling of pins sticking into her skin was worsening and the pain was making her sweat. A drop slowly slid down the side of her face and landed on the seat where her head rested.

"Oh, no. Definitely not permanent. Although it can be fatal if too much is used. But I made sure not to overdo it." She chuckled as if they were having a perfectly normal conversation. As if they were talking about the proper measurement of spices for making roasted yams rather than a poisonous tincture.

"Why did you drug me?" She pinched her thumb to the tip of her middle finger, making an O shape, and repeated the movement several times.

"Ahh, yes." Ligeia clapped her hands together with a rapid smack. Delphine would have jumped had she been able to move. "Of course, you want to know why. Where should I begin?" Ligeia paused, contemplating. After several moments, Delphine wondered if she was meant to answer the question. But then, Ligeia spoke. "Yes, well, I suppose with all that you've uncovered, it doesn't do any good to continue lying about it. Perhaps it's best to start from the beginning."

"S-s-sure, the beginning sounds good." Delphine kept her voice calm. She could now feel her fingers and her hands almost down to the wrists and the pain of the pins in her skin was making her head spin with dizziness. But the sensation was lessening in her fingers and moving down to her arms, which she figured was a good sign.

"The beginning then," Ligeia agreed. "It starts on the Sirena."

There was a loud beep from rover's console and Ligeia stood to inspect it. As she turned her back, Delphine shifted her weight to give her more space behind her to wiggle her hands. She now had feeling in her wrists and the pinpricks from the reawakening nerves were making their way up her arms. Her wrists were bound with what felt like string and the binding was snug, but she thought maybe she could free one of her hands if she could slip a finger through binding.

Ligeia, apparently unconcerned with whatever reading had caused the rover's computer to beep, swiped the display clear and returned to her seat. "The Sirena was a magnificent vessel," she said. "My mother, Leah, told me many stories about their journey on it. She was so fond of that ship—it had been her life's work, the mission to come to Titan. She was a researcher. They conducted hundreds of experiments during their trip, many of them in preparation for colonization, and she was in charge of the science department. Second-in-command for the entire ship. Each person on the crew was chosen for a specific reason and my mother's role was one of the most essential."

Delphine thought about this for a moment. The picture she had seen in Ligeia's apartment came back into her mind and she remembered the table in the background. "What about the chairs?" she asked quickly, before she could stop herself.

"The chairs?" Ligeia raised an eyebrow.

"The chairs in that picture you showed me of the original twelve colonists. There were fifteen chairs in the background. There were more than twelve on the Sirena, weren't there?"

Ligeia smiled. "Ah, yes. That picture. It's probably what jump-started your desire to expose my secrets. You are a smart girl—I'll give you that. And you are correct. There were more than twelve on the Sirena. Fifteen, to be exact."

"They weren't all female, were they?" She could now wiggle both of her arms and her shoulders began to come to life.

A solemn look came over Ligeia's face and she lifted her chin and straightened her back as if this were the part of the story that would justify her actions. "No, they weren't all female. There were three men and twelve women on board the Sirena."

"The colony was never meant to be only female, was it?"

Ligeia didn't answer at first. She stood and turned to the airlock door behind her, running her fingers over the cool pane of the window where one could look into the airlock. The rover made a sudden jolt as it barreled over a particularly rough patch of terrain. Delphine could tell by the movements of the craft that they were now far from the colony and no longer on any of the established rover paths. Ligeia remained there, staring into the window for what felt like a long time. Delphine's heart beat faster with worry and she could hear the blood flowing through her ears. It made her remember that her bugs were no longer clamped to the implants behind her ears. She wondered where Ligeia had put them. If she'd kept them in the rover, then maybe someone could track her.

After several long, painful moments of silence, Ligeia finally turned around. "I apologize, but speaking about the men on the Sirena is difficult for me." She emphasized the word *men* as if there were something dirty about it. "What they did… it just makes me so angry." Delphine noticed the flex in her cheek as she ground her jaw. So this was the real issue behind all this nonsense.

"As I said, there were three men. In fact, one of them was the ship's captain. His name was Rowan. Of course, they would put one of the men in charge." She shook her head, a disgusted look on her face. "They had these twelve brilliant women. Top of their fields, each of them. Chosen for their specific talents, genetic traits, and lifetime achievements. Yet they thought they needed a man to lead them." She rolled her eyes and laughed, a high sarcastic peal.

Delphine saw the shade of the skin on Ligeia's neck had risen from pale peach to intense pink as she became more animated. "Why only three men? I mean, why not an equal number of men and women?" she asked, hoping it would cool her captor down.

The redirection seemed to work. Ligeia visibly relaxed as she took her seat again. "We've always told the colonists that there were twelve women sent to Titan to create a wider genetic pool. And that isn't a lie. Women are a necessary part of the procreation process. The men were not actually sent because of the genetic pool at all. That's why they also sent along thousands of cryogenically frozen male DNA samples, because they knew that was the one truly effective way to create a sustainable colony that didn't have overlapping genetic traits. But, as my mother described it to me, it would have been unheard of to send a crew without men. That's not how their society worked. And so, three men were chosen to accompany the women, with one, Rowan, wearing the badge of captain." She grimaced for a moment.

"According to my mother," she continued, "Rowan was the strongest of the crew. He spent his free time exercising and lifting weights in the limited gravity provided by the centrifugal force of the spinning part of the ship. He was a commanding presence, both physically and emotionally. And she fell in love with him."

This caught Delphine off guard and she couldn't help allowing a shocked "Oh!" to escape from her lips. She wasn't sure where she thought this story was headed, but she wasn't expecting that.

Ligeia smiled and crossed her legs, folding her hands in her lap. "Yes, I know that's surprising. My mother was in love with Rowan, the captain of the Sirena. They carried out an affair during that long journey. She told me those were some of her happiest days when the Sirena was en route to Titan. She was at the pinnacle of her life's work and she had found love." Ligeia shifted in her seat and her mouth fell from a smile to a tight frown. "Or so she thought."

Delphine swallowed hard but didn't say anything. She *wanted* to know how this story ended.

"One night, about two months into their trip, Rowan summoned my mother to his living quarters. She went, of course, expecting a tryst with the strong, kind man she loved. But sadly, that is not what happened to her that night." Ligeia straightened her back and stared at Delphine, whose eyes were wide. "Something came over him, she said. He wasn't himself. She said it felt as if something evil had taken over his mind. He asked her to do something she did not want to do, and when she refused, he became enraged."

Ligeia's eyes were wide and cold. Tears slowly rolled along her cheeks as she spoke her next words, choking over them. "He assaulted her... in the most vile way possible." She closed her eyes and held a tight fist up to her mouth, breathing deep to calm herself. She wiped the tears from her cheeks and cleared her throat before looking at Delphine again. "My mother thought he was going to kill her. He wrapped his hands around her neck and she told me she could see the hate in his eyes as he tried to squeeze the life out of her." Ligeia touched her neck and swallowed hard. "But my mother was no pushover. She grabbed a boot from under the bed. These were no ordinary boots, you see. They were magnetic boots, part of their space suits, and they used them when outside the hull. Very heavy when in the artificial gravity of the Sirena and lined from heel to toe in thick metal. She stared at Rowan, her vision starting to blur as he choked her and she swung that boot, making solid contact with the side of his head."

"Oh my God," Delphine whispered.

Ligeia smiled a small, wry smile. "She thought she'd simply knocked him out. It wasn't until she'd recovered from the strangling that she realized Rowan was not knocked out. He was dead. And she had killed him."

Delphine took a breath and watched Ligeia carefully. Her eyes were wide and her breathing had grown more ragged and rushed as she told the story. She had that look on her face—the same look Delphine had seen in her apartment—as if she were moments away from going completely unhinged. What should she do? What did Ligeia expect her to say? She went with a compassionate response. "But that was self-defense. Surely, they knew she had no other option, right?"

"Absolutely!" Ligeia's eyes grew wider. "It was *absolutely* self-defense! Anyone with half a brain could see that. But"—Ligeia stood and walked to the front of the rover, glancing through the windshield at the dark Titan landscape—"that's not how it went on the Sirena all those years ago. They didn't have a bit of sympathy for my mother. The two remaining men, in particular, wanted to *arrest* her!"

"That's ridiculous!" Delphine said with as much disgust in her voice as she could muster. She needed to play along with Ligeia. She needed her to keep talking. Delphine continued to work on the bindings, but she wasn't making much headway. Now that she had all the feeling back in her wrists, she realized they were tied much tighter than she'd originally thought.

Fortunately, her feet and legs were starting to awaken as the nightshade worked its way out of her body. Unlike her wrists, her ankles were not bound. She wondered if she might be able to muster up the strength to kick Ligeia. She tried to lift one leg but her hip and thigh were still too weak and she groaned with the effort.

Ligeia continued to stand with her back to Delphine. After a few silent moments, she reached down to the console and tapped it to pull up the map. Delphine couldn't make out the terrain and she was about to ask where they were going when Ligeia spoke again. "They wanted to *arrest* her! Can you believe that?" She swung around so suddenly that Delphine froze. Ligeia's eyes still held that wild, terrifying look. "She was an innocent victim and yet they wanted to put *her* in a cell for the remainder of their trip. They even debated about sending her back on the Sirena after the payload and crew members were delivered to the surface. They *said*"—Ligeia rolled her eyes and began to pace back and forth in front of Delphine—"there was no evidence of an attack. The medical officer claimed that she could find no bruising on my mother's neck or body to indicate an attack had been made."

Delphine watched as Ligeia paced, her brow furrowed, staring at the floor as she walked the short distance from the front to the back of the rover. No evidence? How could there be no evidence? Unless there was no attack at all. Delphine swallowed hard at the prospect that Ligeia's mother could have made up her story to cover her tracks. But she kept silent with these thoughts.

Ligeia stopped and put her hands on her hips. She was looking in Delphine's direction but not really at her. It was almost as if she were contemplating something herself. But this lasted only a few moments before she turned and began her slow pace again. "But that's all nonsense, of course. My mother *was* attacked by that man. This didn't stop them from locking her up though. The rest of the crew members came together one night to decide what to do. They hadn't radioed the development to Earth yet as they weren't sure how to handle the situation. She told me that they sat at the communal table and discussed for hours, her trying to plead her case and the others providing evidence."

She shook her head in disgust before continuing. "It was the two other men on the crew who were most in favor of locking her up and telling Earth about what had happened. The women on board weren't so sure. They believed my mother. But they were also cowards, unable to stand up to the men. It was decided that my mother would be relegated to her living quarters for the remainder of the trip."

"She wasn't able to leave her room?" Delphine continued to wiggle at her bindings. She managed to slip her index finger in between her skin and the cord. She felt the large, raw divot where the cord had bitten into her skin and she yanked at it, hoping it would snap free. It didn't.

"Originally, that was the plan. But my mother was a strong woman, Delphine. She wasn't going to sit around and watch while they ruined her life's work because of a situation where she was the victim. After all, their plan was to send her back to Earth. She wouldn't have been able to live without the colony. It was her dream! Her purpose!" Ligeia's hands waved around in big, looping gestures as she told the story. "No, she couldn't allow that to happen. She took the matter into her own hands and ensured that the other two men on board were... taken care of." A slight smile spread across her lips.

"Taken care of?" Delphine asked, although she wasn't at all sure she wanted to hear the meaning behind those words.

"Yes," Ligeia said, tilting her head to the side. If Delphine had to guess, she almost looked *proud*. "You see, she knew the two men were scheduled to go on a spacewalk to do maintenance on the hull of the Sirena within the next few days. She snuck out of her room with the excuse that she was going to organize her experiments so that someone else could take them over while she was confined to her cabin."

She paused for a moment then went on. "She tampered with the space suits by uploading a computer program that would tweak the air mixtures on a timed basis. It was not all that complicated, she told me. She had actually been on the team that had designed the space suits and she understood how to get around the suit alarms by creating the timed atmospheric effect.

The gas ratios on the air mixtures would be normal at the beginning of the spacewalk but would change slowly as the program ran its course." Ligeia threw her head back with a wicked chuckle. "They had no idea what hit them, those silly men! Partway through their maintenance run, their air started to taste funny. They mentioned it over their comm links, but nobody thought much of it. Until the men both complained of faintness, shortness of breath. Their vision started to blur and they could feel weakness in their muscles."

She grinned, her eyes sparkling. "The program my mother ran worked like a charm and because it was running through the space suit's own computers, no alarms went off. It wasn't until one of the other crew members manually pulled up the air mixture levels that they saw how far off they were. By then, it was too late. The men were much too far away from the airlock to allow time for any other crew members to suit up, and since they didn't know the cause of the suit malfunction, they couldn't be sure it wasn't something that would happen to the other space suits. So nobody went out to save them."

"Didn't they suspect your mother though? I mean, surely they knew she was part of the suit research team." Delphine could feel the tops of her legs tingling. She lifted one limb and found it a bit easier to lift then it had been a few minutes before. Maybe she *could* get up the strength to kick.

Ligeia shrugged and again turned to look at the rover console, pulling up the map again. "It's possible they had their suspicions. But none of the crew were as expert in the workings of the space suit as my mother. There was no proof. They didn't have security cameras on board the Sirena so there was no way to prove if she'd been inside the suit room. So they ruled the deaths an accident. My mother was the next in line to take command of the Sirena, and so she did."

"But they had decided that she should be kept on house arrest in her living quarters. Why did they abandon that?" Delphine knew she was walking a thin line by questioning Ligeia's story, but she had the feeling she wasn't getting the full picture of what really took place on the Sirena.

Ligeia turned and flashed a broad smile. "My mother could be *very* persuasive. There were no more questions about the incident with Rowan after that. The crew of the Sirena were not stupid. They knew my mother was a natural leader and they believed she had been abused by Rowan. The death of their male crewmates was an unfortunate accident."

"But, what about Earth? Surely ISEF would have asked questions about what happened to the men."

"It's true, that was an issue. But my mother handled it. She told Earth that there had been an accident with all three men during the maintenance run. Then, she took over all communications with Earth. Some of the crew members were still shaky about the story and she knew, as the new commander of the Sirena, that it would be much easier if she did all the talking. And that was how it went from then on. Earth communications were under her control and nobody else was allowed access to the radios. This was passed on to me. And now, I plan to pass it on to Lara, my daughter, and the newest member of our prestigious council of five."

Ligeia continued to smile and her chest puffed outward as if swelling with pride for her family. Delphine felt sick. She finally understood. This was why Ligeia so desperately needed her daughter to be on the council of elders. The family secrets had to be passed down, and they needed to stay in the family.

The rover bobbed suddenly as it navigated over a large rock and the movement brought Delphine back to her present reality. Ligeia turned to look at the map again and said, "Ah, we're almost there."

"Where are we going?"

Ligeia took the captain's seat and began looking through the screens on the console. Over her shoulder, she said, "We're going somewhere very special, my dear. And if you look over there"—she pointed at the window—"you'll see exactly what I'm talking about."

Delphine lifted her head, straining her neck as far as she could to see out the window. At first, she couldn't see anything, only the bright bluish light cast twenty meters in front of the rover and what appeared to be an endless Titanian boulder field. But after a few short moments, something started to come into view. She felt the deceleration as the rover's autopilot slowed its pace.

When it finally came to a stop, the rover lights illuminated a vessel. A very big vessel. At least five times the size of the rover. In the distance, Delphine could see there were more of these large vessels. They looked unlike anything she'd ever seen, their skins made of metal and glinting in the rover light. They appeared to be spacecraft. On the side nearest the rover were letters and numbers written in tall, block letters: SIRENA DS-001

Ligeia gave the rover orders to align its airlock with that of the spaceship and stood, staring through the window. She turned to look at Delphine and let out a chuckle when she saw the puzzled look on Delphine's face. "That, my dear, is one of the Sirena drop shuttles. There are three of them, as you can see." She gestured out the window. "These are the shuttles the original colonists used to bring their supplies from the Sirena to the surface. They are remarkable spacecraft. Also partially designed by my mother."

Delphine shook her head, more confused than ever. "I don't understand. Why are we here?"

Ligeia turned to her and smiled. "You'll see."

CHAPTER 27

The long hallway at the back of the living quarters complex was wider than the hallways leading to the rest of the colony's apartments. The air felt cooler here, almost as if it were cleaner. Rhayn took in a deep breath of the crisp air and wondered if they had their own air filtration system. So the council members who lived in these larger apartments wouldn't even have to breathe the same air as their fellow colonists.

Rho led the march with Rhayn a few short steps behind him. Pala brought up the rear of their group and Rhayn was surprised at how well she kept up with them. They were practically running through the corridors. It didn't take the trio long to reach the door at the end of the hallway, a tall gray door at least twice the width of a normal apartment door. An access panel blinked a muted purple indicating the door was locked.

For a moment, they all stared at the access panel, but Pala quickly broke her stance and slapped it hard with the tips of her fingers. Her lips were pursed and she had a look of determination on her face that Rhayn had never seen on Pala before. The purple light flickered several times as it paged the apartment's owner, but after several seconds, it flashed red—there was no answer. Pala tried again, pressing the panel even harder this time. It gave the same reaction.

Rhayn tried. She shrugged at the others. Maybe it would help if someone else did it. It was possible the panel read fingerprints. But to no avail, the door remained locked.

Rho stood behind the two women, staring intently at the panel. He stroked the edge of his jaw with his fingertips. Rhayn could see the dark shadow of his beard coming in and she realized it had been a long day. He was normally very careful not to allow his facial hair to come through, but they hadn't been home in over sixteen hours.

"Is there anything you can do?" Rhayn asked, nodding at Rho.

He narrowed his eyes and reached for the access panel. "I think there may be a way…" He brought up the main menu of the panel. All door access panels in the colony were programmed to read the signal broadcast by a colonist's ear bugs. When anyone pressed a door panel, it would open based on that person's security clearance and how it was programmed. This door was obviously not programmed to allow the regular colonists to enter without Ligeia's permission. So, Rhayn was curious when Rho pulled up the manual entry screen showing a full keyboard. All doors also had a code that could open the door manually if a colonist's ear bugs were disabled or if they had special permission to allow them into an area of the colony beyond their security clearance. Rho began typing in a series of letters and numbers, and after a few moments, the access panel flashed green and the door made a soft click as it unlocked.

"Whoa!" Rhayn said, genuinely impressed with her brother.

Rho winked at her. "It's a general access code. Only the technicians know it. It can be used to open most doors in the colony. Frankly, I'm surprised it worked. I would have thought Ligeia would have disabled that for her personal apartment." He shrugged. "But perhaps she wasn't aware of it."

Pala gave the door a push and it opened easily, revealing darkness beyond. The trio walked into the room and Rho slowly closed the door behind them. It took Rhayn a moment to allow her eyes to adjust to the darkness, but she could make out the faint outline of a sofa directly in front of them.

"Lights?" Pala asked.

Rho spoke a command into his ear bugs and the lights in the room glowed to life, dim at first, gradually becoming brighter. "Looks like the interior programming for the apartment utilities work with anyone's ear bugs. I guess they figure anyone who is allowed entry to the apartment should be allowed access."

The three of them took in the space around them. Rhayn's eyes drifted up along the raw cave walls that surrounded them on three sides of the great room and settled on the oculus at the top. "Wow," she said softly. "I had no idea that was here." She pointed at it and the other two looked up.

Pala sighed. "I knew it was there. I've seen it before when I was out on the surface. It's hidden behind a rocky embankment on the western border of the colony. Nobody much comes this way, so I imagine most people aren't aware of its existence. But I found it once when I was out scavenging as a kid. My mother explained that it was part of the council members' apartment complex. I never realized Ligeia had it all to herself."

Rho walked around the perimeter of the room, running his fingers over the peach-colored walls that reminded Rhayn of the walls in the Atrium. "This is the edge of the natural cave," he said. He reached the kitchen, what looked like a block of a room cut into the cave wall, and pointed at something. "Look at this." Sitting on top of the black countertop was a half-full pitcher of liquid. He bent down and sniffed it, his face puckering at the scent. "Smells like lemons. Lemonade maybe?"

Rhayn examined the clear pitcher. The liquid was milky and the same shade as urine. She sniffed it too and quickly drew back. It was much too strong for her liking. She couldn't imagine drinking it.

"Over here," Pala said, gesturing for the twins to come to the middle of the room where two large sofas sat face-to-face with a small table sandwiched between them. She was pointing at a cup lying on the ground next to the table.

There was a stain on the rug underneath it where it appeared the cup's contents had spilled. Rhayn bent down, sniffed, and recognized a muted version of the same sour smell that had been given off from the pitcher. "Same stuff," she said.

As they looked around the room, they noticed more odd things. Two of the cushions from the sofa closest to the door had been pulled out and put back slightly askew. The small table was sitting at a strange angle with one edge almost touching the sofa farthest from the door. At one end of the great room, opposite the kitchen, there was a small desk and the chair was sitting next it, tipped on its side. A tablet sat precariously on top of the desk, half of it hanging over the edge, threatening to fall with the slightest tap.

"Let's look around the rest of the apartment," Rho said.

Rhayn and Pala nodded and they split up. Rhayn walked down a small hallway into what looked like the main bedroom. It was also large, bigger than her family's entire apartment. A huge bed sat in the middle of the room draped in luxurious red fabrics. A wide, gray rug spread out from the bed, running almost to the walls. This room wasn't part of the natural rock cave. Its walls were square and covered in insulated panels. It was much warmer in this room too.

Rhayn touched the bedding, wondering where Ligeia had gotten such fabric. She must have had it specially made because Rhayn had never seen or felt anything like it before. On either side of the bed were two small tables with lamps atop them. Next to the bed was a door to a bathroom. Rhayn walked inside and commanded her ear bugs to turn up the lights.

The bathroom was as large as Rhayn's own bedroom. It had the usual: toilet, sink, shower. But dominating the center of the room was a huge bathtub. Rhayn shook her head. Apparently, water rations did not apply to Ligeia.

Nothing about the two rooms seemed out of place and Rhayn made her way down the small hallway and back to the great room. Rho and Pala followed shortly.

"There's a tunnel leading to her private cultivation tent that way," Rho said, pointing to an opening in the cave wall. "There's nobody in there and I didn't see anything out of place." He rolled his eyes. "But she has her own lemon trees."

"I found two small bedrooms and a bathroom," Pala said. "But no sign of anyone."

"Are we even sure Delphine is here?" Rhayn asked. "Is there any way you can track her ear bugs?" She looked at Rho.

Rho thought for a moment and pulled up something on his own ear bugs. "I might be able to. Let me check something."

He spent a few moments flicking through shared files before he pulled something up. "We have a directory of all colonists in the maintenance files. I think there's a way to link up directly to their bugs and track them that way. Let me try." After several more seconds of looking around, he smiled. "Got her."

"Where?" Pala asked, wringing her hands together.

Rho shook his head, the smile fading from his face. "The tracker says her ear bugs are right here. In this apartment." He gestured around them.

"How can that be?" Rhayn asked. "We've looked all around it and there's nobody here."

Rho looked at the floor and rested his hands on his hips. "I don't know."

"Well, she can't have just disappeared into thin air," Pala said. She turned from the twins and started walking around the perimeter of the great room. "We must be missing something."

Rhayn crossed her arms at her chest and bit down on her lower lip. Rho walked toward the kitchen and ran his fingers over the countertop. He began opening cabinets and drawers.

Suddenly, Rhayn heard Pala gasp and say, "Oh my God!"

The twins ran to her and saw that she was pointing at something on the floor in front of a ventilation grate. Rho reached down and picked up the object. As soon as he did, Rhayn knew exactly what it was.

"Delphine's ear bug," Rho said. They could tell it was hers based on the color of the small device. It was purple, the color worn by all third-gens.

Rhayn looked down at the floor where Rho had found the bug and noticed something interesting about the vent on the wall. It wasn't like any vent she'd ever seen. It was grated, but there was a faint light on behind the grate. She bent down to examine it further. Rho joined her and gave her a look, showing that he saw the same thing.

"What?" Pala said.

"This grate," Rhayn said. "Something is lit up behind it."

"And it shouldn't be here," Rho added.

"What do you mean it shouldn't be there?" Pala said.

Rho touched the edge of the pale gray grate and ran his fingers across it. "This is the natural cave wall. There shouldn't be anything behind it. If they had put ventilation pipes in it, the cave wall wouldn't still be here. It would be insulated wall covering like everywhere else in the colony."

"So," Pala said, sighing with frustration, "what does that mean?"

Rho continued to run his fingers over the grate. He swiped up and down along the grooved ventilation holes, then over the top of the grate, and finally, around the edges when—click. All three of them jumped back at the sharp sound as the latch released and the grate swung open. Behind the grate was an access panel, similar to the one at the main door.

Rho touched it, and without warning, a narrow rectangular door appeared in the wall and slowly swung outward.

CHAPTER 28

They stood back, watching the now-opened door, their mouths hanging open.

"That's a hell of a camouflage job!" Rho said, his eyes wide. He moved toward it and opened it wider, revealing a narrow, dark hallway beyond. He turned and looked at Rhayn and Pala. "Who's first?"

Pala didn't hesitate; she walked past him and into the darkness beyond. With a shrug, Rho followed her. Rhayn, still amazed by how well hidden that door had been, brought up the rear. The hallway was more like a tunnel. It was barely wider than Rhayn's shoulders and she had to duck slightly not to hit her head against the rock wall above. She ran her fingers along the walls as she walked and it was the same texture as the rock walls in the great room they'd just left, although these walls weren't as smooth, indicating this tunnel hadn't been here as long as the apartment.

Pala turned on the flashlight feature in her bugs and Rhayn could see that the tunnel went on for a long time. The air got thinner the longer they went and before long, Rhayn found herself out of breath. They continued to walk and Rhayn was sure they'd gone a hundred meters into the Titanian underground when they came to a door with a flashing green access panel. Pala pressed it and the door opened into a large room.

As the trio walked into the room, Rho spoke a command to his bugs and the lights in the room came to life. They saw that they were in an airlock. A very large one. It wasn't meant to be used by colonists using surf suits but rather, for rovers. There were two rovers parked in front of them and a third rover spot was empty. On the other side of the rovers was a large, sliding airlock door that opened in the middle. Rhayn walked up to the door and looked out one of its four oblong windows. Outside, there was only blackness, but Rhayn could tell the door opened to the surface and the frozen Titanian night beyond. They were no longer underground.

"I'll be damned!" Rho said, also peeking through the large windows. "They have their own rovers! I had no idea this was here."

Pala gestured toward two more tunnels sealed off by their own doors leading out of the room. "This must be for council member use. Looks like Ligeia's tunnel isn't the only one leading to this airlock."

The three walked around the room, taking in what they saw before they all stopped right in front of the missing rover spot. Particles of surface sand littered the floor on the inside of the door. They looked at each other and then back at the empty spot.

"She's taken Delphine somewhere in a rover," Pala said, her voice low and quivering.

Rhayn banged her hand against one of the remaining rovers. "Let's go get her."

Rho nodded and went to the small airlock in the rover's side, touching the access panel and opening the outer door. He stepped in and gestured for the other two to go inside. It was a tight fit for all three of them to enter the rover through the small airlock, which was generally meant to be used one person at a time, but they weren't interested in waiting for the airlock to cycle three times for them. They squished together and Rhayn typed the correct commands into the inner door.

"Seems to be the same airlock system as the rest of the rovers," she said.

It took the airlock about a minute to cycle before the inner door opened. Although the rover was technically inside an airlock already, it still required the occupants to cycle in and out through the airlock system. It was a safety feature built into every rover to ensure someone couldn't open both the inner and outer doors while outside the colony's atmosphere.

When the door opened, the three spilled out into the interior of the rover and looked around. As with the airlock, everything inside looked the same as any rover they'd ever been in. There was a bench of three seats opposite the airlock, a small closet to their left that held a spare surf suit and an emergency toilet, and the captain's chair and cockpit on the right.

"I'll drive," Pala said, taking the captain's seat.

Neither of the twins argued. Pala, being the oldest, had logged many more hours driving rovers than either of them had. They took two of the bench seats behind her. She touched the control panel screen and the front of the rover came to life with a subtle glow. In seconds, she entered her commands, and they waited several minutes while the airlock outside the rover worked to stabilize the pressure between Titan's atmosphere and its own. When it was done, the large door at the front of the chamber split down the middle, each side sliding out of the way. Pala wasted no time and put the rover into drive, maneuvering it out of the airlock, turning the vehicle so they could see the airlock doors. She typed in the commands for them to close and they watched through the long-range headlights of the rover as the giant doors sealed shut. Then Pala turned the rover 180 degrees to face away from the airlock, illuminating the terrain around them.

Rho stood and looked over Pala's shoulder at the control panel. "Is it in good shape? I mean, do you think it's safe?"

Pala nodded. "Everything appears to be in good condition. Great actually. I ran a diagnostic check and everything checked out. They must keep them maintained. Plus, there's a full tank of methane." She pointed at the fuel gauge on the upper left side of the console.

"Great," Rhayn said, coming up behind Rho and gazing out the front window. "Now how do we know where to go?"

But before the question had escaped her lips, she knew the answer and so did the others. In front of the rover in the bright, bluish glow of the headlights, heading straight north, were two perfect rover tracks running parallel to each other into the Titanian night. The tracks were fresh and there was very little wind so the odds of following them a long way were good.

Pala nodded and commanded the rover forward to follow the tracks.

***

Rhayn paced around the tiny interior of the rover, chewing on her lip. They had been following the tracks of the first rover for what felt like forever. In reality, it had only been about forty minutes, but it still made her uneasy.

For the first ten minutes of the trip, they had driven on the relatively flat and well-traveled area around the colony. But they had long since left the established roverways behind and were headed straight north, into the dune fields. The terrain was much rougher out here and it wasn't an area that colonists visited often. Rhayn had actually never been this far away from the colony and the farther they went, the more nervous she got. Why had Ligeia taken Delphine out into this desolate field of endless boulders and rolling dunes? Rhayn had no idea what the geography of the moon looked like this far north. Hell, they could be headed right to one of the thousands of methane lakes that dotted Titan's surface.

Rho seemed to be getting as nervous as Rhayn. He stood behind Pala who was doing an excellent job navigating the rover on the rough ground, staring at the surface map showing on the console. He shook his head. "I just don't understand this. We're in the middle of nowhere. Why would she have come all this way out here?"

The truth was, they had suspicions about what had gone on between Delphine and Ligeia and in none of the possible circumstances was it a good sign that they were traveling out into the middle of nowhere. But nobody voiced this. Rhayn continued to pace and chew her lip. Pala kept her gaze fixed on the controls and glanced occasionally out the front windshield. Rho simply stared.

After several more minutes when Rhayn felt like she couldn't take another moment of the ride, the rover's surface radar beeped.

"Is it a lake?" Rho asked, looking at Pala.

She shook her head. "Doesn't look like it. But won't know for sure until we get a visual. If it is, it's a small one."

The rover continued to move forward, albeit at a slower pace due to a particularly rough patch of boulders. The headlights continued to illuminate only the pale ground ahead of them and the parallel rover tracks they were following.

It took only a few more minutes before the object the radar had detected became visible in the hazy atmosphere. All three were now huddled around the console staring out the windshield. The closer they got to it, the stranger the object looked.

"Is it… a spacecraft?" Rhayn asked, squinting to try to decipher the thing in front of her.

"It can't be," Pala said. "It's huge."

Rho shook his head. "No, I think Rhayn's right. It looks like it's a spacecraft. Some sort of freighter or something. Look over there." He pointed to the left of the object in front of them and Rhayn could see off in the distance, another craft, apparently the same as the first, just a little farther away.

"Multiple spacecraft?" Pala said, watching as they slowly drove closer to the vessel. Rhayn gasped suddenly causing Pala to jump.

"What is it?" Rho asked.

Rhayn pointed at the front of the spacecraft. "Look! There's the other rover!"

"It looks like it's docked," Rho said and looked at Pala. "Can you drive us around this thing? Maybe there's another airlock on the back side where we can dock too."

Pala nodded and steered the rover to the left. The spacecraft was long and box-shaped. Rhayn read the letters SIRENA DS-001 printed along the side. The craft was huge, at least thirty meters long and ten meters tall. It was shiny, the outer skin made from metal, and as Pala steered the rover closer to it, the craft loomed in the front window, eventually eclipsing the entire view. There were four large engine bells, two halfway down the side of the ship and two at the end. The bells were turned so they pointed down, perpendicular to the length of the ship.

"It looks like those engines turn," Rhayn said, pointing at the one closest to their rover. It was almost as tall as the rover itself. "Look at those hinges on the side."

Rho nodded. "I bet they would turn them based on what they needed to do. If they were turned toward the back, they could provide forward thrust. Turned how they are, they would help decelerate while landing."

They reached what looked like the front of the vessel. It wasn't boxy like the sides, rather it was curved to form a flattened cone. To Rhayn, it seemed almost like a giant, curved window poking out of the front of the ship. The inside of the vessel was dark, but she could see consoles and navigational equipment through the window as the rover's lights passed over it. It seemed almost like a cockpit. They rounded the front and saw that the other side of the vessel was much like the first, long and boxy. Unlike the other side where the rover was docked, this side had three large, square doors.

Rho pointed at the three doors. "That looks like where they must have loaded cargo. It must have been a shuttle to bring equipment and supplies to the surface from the Sirena."

"Look down there," Pala said, pointing to the space between the two engine bells at the back of the spacecraft where there was a small hatch about the size of a person in a spacesuit. "There's a pull-down ladder under it. That has to be an airlock entry. Right?"

"Maybe," Rho said, standing up straight and moving toward the back of the rover. "There's only one way to find out."

"Wait," Rhayn said, putting her hand on her brother's shoulder. He turned to look at her. "You're not seriously thinking of going out there are you?"

"Do you have a better plan?"

"We don't even know what that thing is! You can't just go out there!" Rhayn's voice had jumped an octave and her voice quivered.

Rho sighed and crossed his arms over his chest. "We can't get into the other rover. It's docked to this thing. The only way to get to the other rover is to get into that spacecraft. So, that's what I'm going to do." He pushed her hand off his shoulder and turned to the closet in the back of the rover.

"I'm going with you then," Rhayn said, her hands balled into fists at her side.

"No, you're not." Rho was calm and the fact that he denied her made her furious.

"Am too!"

Rho opened the closet door wide and pointed inside. "There's only one surf suit. So no, you won't be going with me."

Pala joined them at the back of the rover. "I will go. She's my daughter."

Rho put his hands on Pala's shoulders and Rhayn could see the vast size difference in the two. Pala looked tiny and breakable. Rho was tall and lean and had at least twenty kilograms on her. The idea of Pala heading off into the night to wrestle her daughter away from Ligeia seemed almost laughable.

"I will go," Rho said. "Besides, I have the most mechanical knowledge of any of us. It might come in handy navigating around inside there."

Pala looked into his eyes before allowing her shoulders to fall. She nodded weakly and pulled him in for a long hug. "Thank you," she whispered into his chest.

Rhayn cleared her throat. "I still don't agree with this."

Rho smiled and started pulling the surf suit over his clothes. "Your opinion is noted, dear sister."

"Argh!" Rhayn stamped her foot causing a loud *bang* to echo throughout the small rover. "I hate it when you say that." But she had to admit, Rho had a point. He was the most qualified to use the airlock and whatever other mechanisms he might have to use inside the ship. He was also the strongest of them. It still frustrated her though and she crossed her arms over her chest and dropped down hard into one of the rover's back seats.

Pala helped him pull the suit up over his shoulders and fasten the lifepack to his back. Before he put the faceplate on, he walked over to Rhayn and kissed the top of her head. She squeezed her eyes shut.

"I'm not planning to be gone long. You stay here and don't move the rover. I'll keep in contact on the radio and tell you everything I see. When I come back, I'll have Delphine with me and we can get the hell out of here."

Pala nodded. Rhayn looked away. Rho put the faceplate on and strapped a tool belt he dug up from inside the closet around his waist. He ran a diagnostic check ensuring the suit was working properly and stepped into the airlock.

CHAPTER 29

Delphine felt dizzy as the rover moved back and forth to align with the shuttle's airlock. She had realized not long after they arrived that the nightshade was having a greater effect on her than simply causing paralysis. Her stomach rolled with nausea and her mind felt foggy.

After it docked, Ligeia hooked her arms under Delphine's armpits and dragged her into the rover's airlock. The movement caused Delphine to scream in pain. Despite the numbing effect of the nightshade, her weak limbs were not fully awake and the pins and needles ran up and down her skin. Once inside, Ligeia commanded the airlock to cycle so it could match the pressure of the adjoining vessel. Delphine wondered about the atmosphere in the much older ship. Obviously, it was holding pressure or the airlock wouldn't have allowed the air to cycle through, but if it hadn't been used in over seven decades, the air mixture easily could have been off. Even a slight deviation in oxygen or nitrogen levels would make the air toxic. She voiced this concern, but her captor didn't seem worried because she ignored the question.

Once inside, Ligeia easily hoisted Delphine's body over her shoulder and carried her prisoner through the shuttle's adjoining airlock and into the ship. There, Ligeia set her down on the floor, her back resting against the interior wall. It took several minutes for the shooting pains in Delphine's body to dull and she again fought back nausea.

Ligeia touched a control panel on the wall next to the airlock door and two long rows of light bars sprang to life above her. It took a moment for Delphine's eyes to adjust to the sudden and unexpected change from pitch black to bright light and when they did, her mouth dropped. The room was huge and by Delphine's best guess, it took up almost the entire space inside the shuttle. It was clearly a payload bay used to store equipment and materials for the journey through the atmosphere.

On the far side of the payload bay were three large loading doors that slid up into the ceiling when opened. The ceiling was ten meters above her, with lights so bright she couldn't quite look at it.

Delphine licked her lips. The air tasted strange, stale, and she picked up the faint smell of grease and ammonia. But it didn't feel toxic. She took in a deep breath and craned her neck to inspect the space further. The size of the space reminded her of the Atrium. In one corner stood a bunch of plastic storage boxes stacked neatly in rows. By her estimation, there were at least thirty boxes there.

The floor was dirty, covered with a fine layer of orange Titanian dust that had been disturbed in the corner where the boxes stood and in a path leading from the airlock to a hatch at the front of the ship. Based on what she'd seen from the outside of the ship's layout, that hatch led to the cockpit and front quarters of the ship. There was another hatch at the back of the payload bay, perhaps leading to an engine room or some other storage area. Of course, it made sense that these hatches were in place to guard certain areas of the ship from atmospheric decompression while the payload bay doors were opened.

Delphine realized she was wearing only her third-gen jumpsuit and she shivered as the cold from the floor and the wall behind her back easily seeped through the thin material. Ligeia continued to type commands into the control panel and from somewhere deep in the ship, Delphine heard a rumble.

"The heat," Ligeia said, turning back to the panel.

Delphine thought about this for a moment. "You've been here before, haven't you?"

Ligeia smiled and turned the control panel off. She walked to where Delphine was sitting and tapped her temple with her index finger. "You're a smart girl. Yes, I actually come out here often. Whenever I need to get away or when I'm bored."

"Why?" Of all the strange things Delphine had seen Ligeia do over the past few days, this was by far the strangest. Why come out to the middle of nowhere to visit these old shuttles?

Ligeia's head fell back and she let out a loud, high laugh. It made Delphine flinch. "That is a good question! Yes, why?" She turned to look at the empty space around her, a wild smile crossing her face as she spread her arms out wide and started to spin in circles, laughing more. Delphine pressed her back against the wall harder as if the wall might absorb her and protect her from this madness. After several long moments, Ligeia stopped spinning and closed her eyes before taking in a deep breath.

"It is a good question," she repeated, looking at Delphine. "I come here because this place reminds me of my mother. You see, she flew this vessel. She was the pilot." She pointed at the floor. "This was *her* shuttle. Did you know that the original colonists lived on these shuttles for many months while they built the infrastructure for Xanadu? This was where they first became settlers on Titan. Right here in this spacecraft!"

Delphine swallowed. "Why were they so far away from the colony? Why didn't they dismantle them to be used for materials?"

"Oh, they were dismantled!" Ligeia said, running her hand along the wall as she slowly walked the perimeter of the payload bay. "The other two shuttles—DS 002 and DS 003 were dismantled for the most part. The pieces lying out here are what was left after they took what they needed. But my mother could never bring herself to strip this one. She was the leader, after all. And this ship was special to her. After they were done with the shuttles, they hauled them out here to be rid of them. But they left this one intact." She turned to Delphine and winked. "Just in case."

"Just in case, what?" Delphine asked, timidly.

"In case," she said, continuing to run her fingers along the wall as she walked, "they needed to go back to the Sirena."

"Wait," Delphine shook her head. Something about this story wasn't right. "The Sirena left. After they were done unloading their materials, the Sirena went back to Earth. *You* said that yourself. You gave me that speech about how the Sirena leaving meant the original colonists were here to stay. This was their new home, you said."

Ligeia chuckled. "I lied."

It shouldn't have been a surprise that Ligeia would lie. But the blatant admission struck Delphine as if it were a barb to her chest. "What do you mean?"

Ligeia had now completed her loop around the interior wall of the loading bay and was back in front of Delphine. She leaned down, resting her elbow on her knee, and looked Delphine straight in the eyes. "I lied," she repeated, smiling. "The Sirena is still up there. Still in orbit around Titan."

Delphine's eyes grew wide and her mouth dropped. "But… but how is that possible?" she stammered.

"It's possible because of my mother. And after she passed away, because of me. And, when the time is right, my daughter Lara will take over."

"I… I don't understand." The words were coming out of her mouth in slow bursts. She shook her head, not able to believe what she was hearing.

"This ship," Ligeia said, gesturing around her, "has a direct link to the Sirena. It's able to communicate with the onboard computer and we are essentially able to fly the Sirena from it. This was a safety precaution built into the operating system so that when the Sirena's crew was on the surface unloading supplies, they could command the ship without having to leave someone behind. Since that time, my mother, and now I, made regular trips here to monitor the Sirena. It has a nuclear ion engine and its own nuclear reactor with enough fuel to last it five thousand years. Over the years, we've given it commands to make regular engine thrusts to ensure it stayed in a stable orbit. We've run remote maintenance diagnostics on it. Kept things going. It's really not difficult." Ligeia shrugged.

It took Delphine a few moments to process it. The Sirena had been in orbit this *entire* time, over seventy years, and nobody at the colony—other than Ligeia—knew about it, with the possible exception of Lara. She had a direct link to the Sirena with this abandoned shuttle, and she had been visiting it regularly for years to check on the status of the Sirena. It was almost like tiny explosions, each new revelation going off in her head. The nausea she'd felt earlier came back at her hard and her stomach clenched as she forced back the urge to throw up.

"Look, Delphine," Ligeia said, dropping down to sit next to her with her back against the wall. "My mother had a vision for this colony. After what she endured at the hands of Rowan on the Sirena, she knew what had to be done. You asked me earlier if Xanadu was meant to be an all-female colony all along. The answer to that is no, it was not." She turned to face Delphine and took hold of her hands. "However, after the incident with Rowan, my mother knew that the colony structure would not work if there were men in charge of it. They would turn out to be rotten, just like Rowan."

"What about the other eleven women? What did they think?"

Ligeia smiled. "My mother could be very persuasive, and with the right amount of cajoling, anyone can become convinced. She had a vision of us, the Titan girls, creating the perfect oasis on an imperfect planet—and that's exactly what we've done! Xanadu is not only surviving, we are thriving! All because my mother made a decision. It wasn't an easy decision, but I believe it was the right one. I love Xanadu and its colonists. I wouldn't jeopardize what we've built for *anything*."

The last word escaped her lips with a hiss and Delphine felt the force of the threat hit her full-on. This was wrong, all wrong. Leah and the original colonists had made a decision about the future of the colony based on one terrible experience. She wondered about the three laws of Xanadu. Perhaps they hadn't come from Earth at all, but rather, from the mind of Leah, their original leader. The whole basis of their existence on Titan was built on a pillar of lies and murder at the hands of one woman who became so powerful, the rest of them would not stand up to her.

She closed her eyes and leaned her head against the wall, trying to keep the dizziness at bay. After several deep breaths of the stale shuttle air, she asked, "What now? Why are we here, Ligeia?"

"Ah, yes. Here we are, back at the beginning, asking why." Ligeia stood and crossed her hands over her chest. "We are here, Delphine, because I've decided it is finally time for the Sirena to leave Titan's orbit."

"I don't understand. You're going to direct it to fly back to Earth?"

Ligeia shook her head and a slow smile spread across her lips. "No, *you* are going to fly it there."

Delphine's breath caught in her throat causing her to choke, her coughs deep and raspy. "Wh-What?" she said when she had recovered enough breath to speak.

"*You* are going to fly the Sirena back to Earth," Ligeia repeated. "This shuttle will take you directly to her. It's what you wanted, right? You said it at the election—you want change. Well, I'm giving it to you."

"I still don't understand. Why would you…" She shook her head as her voice failed her.

"I debated about what to do with you, Delphine. As angry as I was with your behavior at the election and in the library, I knew murder wasn't a good solution. It would raise so many questions. There was always a possibility that your remains would be found, especially since I couldn't take your body too far outside the safe travel zone around the colony. As the colony expands, more and more people will venture farther out. No, I couldn't do that. I decided, in the end, that you know more than I'd like you to know and I cannot allow you to resume your life back at Xanadu as if nothing happened. As I said, I will not jeopardize all that my mother and I built here for anything or anyone. This was the best option."

"Why is sending me up to the Sirena the best option?"

A pensive look crossed Ligeia's face. "When I saw that you and your friends had found the probe, I knew it would only be a matter of time before Earth really did send another ship back here. Without the Sirena, they would have to build a ship from scratch. You see, my mother disabled the remote pilot capabilities on the Sirena so that only this shuttle could pilot it and Earth could not call it back on its own. There have been many probes sent, but the one you found was closer to the colony than any other before it."

She threw her hands up over her head. "I simply cannot allow Earth to bring another ship here. They will destroy *everything* I've worked for. You can take the shuttle to the Sirena and pilot it to Earth." She pointed to the corner of the payload bay where the boxes stood. "I've gathered enough supplies on the shuttle to last you through your trip and all of the shuttle systems are still in good working order. Once you make it to Earth, you can tell them the colony on Titan failed. You can say there was a resurgence of the virus that originally wiped out many of the colonists and, this time, it was almost one hundred percent fatal, but that you survived somehow and made it to the shuttle and finally, back to the Sirena."

The story Ligeia spun was both well-planned and utterly insane.

"There's no way they'll believe that," Delphine said, her voice shaking as panic gripped her.

"That is where you come in. You must make them believe. For the sake of your mother and your beloved friends and the rest of the colonists. You must make them believe that Xanadu is no more! It's the only way we can continue to grow our beautiful colony. It's the only way the Titan girls can survive!"

Delphine sucked in a deep breath and tried to make her brain work faster. Tried to think of something, *anything*, she could say to dissuade this delusional woman, when suddenly, a loud noise came from the rear of the shuttle. They both turned and heard the unmistakable hissing sound of an airlock cycling.

"Noooo!" Ligeia's scream was so loud, it bounced off the walls and pounded Delphine's ears causing her head to throb. Before she could speak, Ligeia grabbed her by the armpits and hoisted her up, throwing her body over her shoulder. Delphine winced from the sudden pain of being moved. She opened her mouth but couldn't form words as Ligeia ran toward a small hatch at the front of the ship.

CHAPTER 30

With each step Ligeia took, pain shot up and down Delphine's back. She wanted to pound her fists on Ligeia's back to get her to stop, but given her intense pain with every move, she couldn't summon the strength. She tried to scream out to whomever was coming through the airlock, but she could only make a weak gasping sound as her lungs struggled to take in air.

Before she knew it, they were at the hatch and Ligeia was typing a code into the access panel. The hatch swung open and Ligeia pushed through it, slamming the hatch closed behind them. Once inside, she dropped Delphine on the floor. Hard. Knifelike pain dug into her spine. Ligeia entered another code on the access panel inside the hatch and Delphine heard several loud clicks as the locks on the door engaged. Then she spun around and looked at Delphine.

"Oh dear," Ligeia said, cocking her head to one side. Her voice was high and her eyes were wild. "Did that hurt? I apologize for having to move you so quickly, but it looks like someone has followed us." She made a tsk tsk sound and shook her head. "Probably one of those nosy friends of yours. What are their names? The twins—Rhayn and Rho! Well, it's okay. It puts a minor crimp in the plan. But I can work with it."

She turned away from Delphine and went to the front of the cockpit. There was a large domed window jutting out into space in front of the captain's chair. Ligeia sat and began touching the screens surrounding the chair. Slowly, they glowed to life, revealing the various flight programs necessary to fly the shuttle. It was apparent by the ease with which her fingers moved that Ligeia had certainly done this before.

"Have you flown this thing before?" Delphine asked, wincing from the force of the words.

Ligeia turned, surprised by the question. "Me? Heavens no! I've turned it on for routine maintenance before, but never to fly. It's large enough that it could be picked up by the colony radar if it were to go airborne. No, I couldn't risk that."

Delphine nodded. As deranged as she was, Ligeia wasn't an idiot.

As Ligeia continued to run her fingers over the various screens, typing in commands and opening up the various systems on the shuttle, Delphine heard a low rumble from the back of the ship. The rumble got louder and the entire ship began to vibrate and before long, she wondered if the ship could handle the forces of whatever was going on behind her.

"Fuel pumps!" Ligeia yelled over the roar. "There's a methane lake just over that crest." She pointed to something outside the window although Delphine couldn't see anything from her position on the floor behind the captain's chair. "Well, it's more of a *pond* really, but it'll do. I hooked up a hose from the shuttle to the methane and it's filling the tanks now. Working like a charm!" She laughed a high, wild laugh. Moments later, the noise died down to a distant hum, which Delphine assumed might be the engines warming up.

"What are you doing?" she yelled as loud as her lungs would allow. "You can't take off! There's someone else on board!"

"I certainly can! And I will!"

"But that's not part of your plan!" Delphine knew she was reaching, but she needed to keep Ligeia talking. If she could stall Ligeia from taking off for even a few minutes, it might save her. "This is wrong! You aren't supposed to go. What will the colonists do without you?"

Ligeia paused for a moment, her hand hovering above the control panel, clearly thinking about this problem. Only for a moment, though. She resumed her commands. "I will fly you up there and bring the shuttle back down. It's okay. No harm done. Just a minor setback."

Delphine ground her teeth together, willing herself to think of something. Anything!

Suddenly, there was a loud thud at the hatch. Whoever had come through the airlock had made it to the cockpit. Delphine turned to the side, trying to bring herself onto her hands and knees so she could attempt standing to see who was there through the small porthole window. But Ligeia beat her to it and when she saw Delphine trying to stand, she pushed her down. Delphine landed hard on her shoulder, grimacing and curling into a fetal position.

"Argh!" Ligeia screamed and ran back to the control panel. She spoke into a tiny microphone sticking out of the desk in front of her. "Don't you dare try to come in here!" The sound of her voice reverberated out of the intercom speaker mounted above Delphine's head, looping on a slight delay from the actual sound of Ligeia screaming into the microphone. "I'm decompressing the payload bay. I know you have a surf suit on, but neither of us do! If you open that hatch, we'll lose atmosphere in here and die!"

As she said this, she pulled up what looked like the atmospheric regulator on the screen and gave the commands for the ship to start decompression of the payload bay. Delphine knew once that started, there was no hope. The hatch would *not* open if the payload bay was triggered to decompress. Even if her savior knew the code to enter the hatch, it would be no use.

Three things happened almost simultaneously. To Delphine, who watched helplessly from the floor, it felt like they happened in slow motion. An alarm screeched from somewhere just outside the cockpit. A moment later, an explosion roared on the other side of the hatch, blasting it from its hinges. Delphine felt intense pain run through her left leg. Someone in a surf suit emerged from the smoke of the explosion and Ligeia screamed and lunged at them.

The pain in her leg and the tickling sensation of smoke curling up her nose were the last things Delphine remembered before she passed out.

CHAPTER 31

Aura came to her side. This time, she was not wearing a surf suit and instead had on her purple jumpsuit. They were not outside, but in the room they'd shared as children in their mother's apartment.

Delphine looked at her sister and smiled. Aura took her hands and squeezed them. She was smiling too and her gray eyes twinkled. Delphine felt calm and safe. She wanted to wrap Aura in a tight hug, but as she lifted her arms, Aura stopped her.

"Wake up, Delphine," she said, her voice low and soft.

Delphine was confused. Was she dreaming?

"Wake up," Aura repeated in the same soft, sweet voice.

Delphine frowned and shook her head. She didn't want to wake up. Not now. Not while Aura was there.

"Wake up!" This time, Aura's voice was not soft or sweet. It sounded anxious and tight. It was a voice she recognized but couldn't quite place. Someone was shaking her. She could feel hands on her shoulders. She could hear more voices behind her.

"Delphine! Wake up!"

Her eyes popped open and she saw Rho hovering above her. Relief passed over his face and she felt his hands leave her shoulders.

"She's awake!" he said, turning to speak to someone behind him.

Rhayn and Pala appeared. Rhayn shouted, "Yes!" and slapped her brother on the back. Pala grabbed Delphine's hand and held it up to her cheek.

Delphine took in a deep breath and looked around. She was in the rover, lying across the bench seats. What happened at the shuttle? Her mind felt foggy and sluggish. She closed her eyes and forced herself to remember.

Ligeia standing in front of her, inside the payload bay.

The sound of the airlock cycling.

The pain of the sudden movements when Ligeia picked her up and ran to the cockpit.

The explosion.

The person in the surf suit walking through the blasted door.

Ligeia lunging for them.

The pain and the smell of smoke.

Suddenly, panic rose inside her and her eyes popped open. She tried to sit and was confronted by shooting pain in her left leg as she moved and let out a scream of surprise at how vivid it felt.

"Whoa!" Rho said, putting his hand on her shoulder. "Don't move. Your left leg is broken. We've splinted it, but we don't have many supplies in the rover, so you'll need to take it easy. Let me help you sit up." He put his arm behind her back and lifted her body to a seated position. The movements were slow and gentle. Rhayn wadded up two blankets from the rover's emergency supplies and wedged them behind Delphine's back to support her.

"What happened?" Delphine asked, wincing from the pain in her leg.

It was then that she saw Ligeia sitting across from Delphine next to the airlock. Rope encircled her body, tethering her to the chair and a piece of gray tape covered her mouth. Her hair was wild around her head and her eyes were large, either from fright or anger, Delphine couldn't tell. Perhaps a mixture of both. A tiny drip of dried blood ran out of her nose and she had a large bruise on her cheek. She strained against the restraints when Delphine looked at her and started mumbling furiously into the tape.

"Calm down!" Rho said to Ligeia, turning his glare her way. She immediately complied, shrinking back into the chair and letting out a low growl from the back of her throat. Delphine cocked her head to the side, genuinely surprised—Ligeia was *afraid* of Rho. She looked back at Rho and he smiled.

"She's a little freaked out," Rhayn said, patting Rho's shoulder. "My brother really showed her what was up!"

At the mention of the word "brother" Ligeia flinched, shrinking farther into her seat as if that might protect her from this mysterious male figure.

Rho held up his hands in surrender. "Hey, she figured it out on her own. I would have been more than happy to tell her, but she's smarter than she looks."

"What happened?" Delphine repeated. "The shuttle… and the explosion…" She shook her head, not sure she could trust her own memories. They seemed like the type of thing she would dream.

Rho scratched his temple and put his hands on his hips. "Yeah, there's a lot to fill you in on. We realized when you didn't show after your shift that something was up. So we got Pala and went to Ligeia's apartment. We figured that was where you'd gone."

Pala, who had been sitting by Delphine holding her hand, said, "A *very* unwise decision."

Delphine blushed. "Yeah, I suppose it was. I was trying to protect the twins."

"We understand," Rho said. "But Pala is right. It was not smart to go there on your own. When we got there, I tracked your ear bugs and saw that they were in the apartment, but nobody was answering when we paged." He shrugged and smiled. "So we broke in."

"Rho hacked her door using a cheat code! It was so cool!" Rhayn smiled at her brother, her face beaming with pride.

"Yeah, well..." Rho blushed. "Anyway, when we got inside, we found your ear bugs on the ground and discovered a false wall in the great room. It opened up a tunnel that led to an airlock with rovers docked at it. We saw one of them was missing, so we took one of the others and followed the tracks." He walked over to Ligeia and put his hand on her shoulder. She cringed away from him. "She led us right to you."

"But what happened in the shuttle?" Delphine asked. "I remember an explosion and an alarm going off. It was so loud."

Rho nodded and went to Delphine, sitting next to her. "There was only one surf suit in the rover, so only one of us could go. I won." He smiled and glanced at Pala. Rhayn shrugged. "Anyway, I went through the rear airlock of the shuttle and saw Ligeia dragging you into the cockpit. She actually tried to decompress the payload bay to keep me out. That was the alarm you heard, warning that decompression was about to start. I knew I only had a few seconds."

"But the explosion... how did you cause an explosion?"

"There were several rounds of rock blasts in the tool belt on the surf suit. This rover was originally part of the mining fleet until the council members commandeered it for their personal use. It was lucky really. Most surf suits don't have tool belts, especially mining belts with blasts in them, but this one did. When I left to find you, I took the tool belt with me, just in case. Turns out, it came in handy. I used one of the blasts to open the door before the ship decompressed. Once the door was open, the ship's safety mechanism took effect and it automatically ceased decompression. The only problem was that it was a pretty big explosion and it caused the hatch to fly off its hinges."

"That's when he found you," Pala said, tears in her eyes. "It was clear you'd been drugged and the door broke your leg when it flew backward. He didn't realize you were right behind it. We're lucky it didn't do more damage."

"And then Ligeia attacked him!" Rhayn cut in. "Rho took her down!" She turned to Ligeia and gave her big grin. Ligeia growled in response.

"I didn't want to have to fight her," Rho said, "but she gave me no choice. She lunged at me and I managed to push her off me. I think once she realized her plan wasn't going to happen, she made a run for the other rover. I stopped her though."

"You did more than stop her!" Rhayn said, her eyes wide with excitement. "You tackled her to the ground!"

Rho blushed again, clearly uncomfortable with his sister's rendition of events. "Yeah, well, I did what I had to do to get her to stop fighting me. Once she was restrained, I loaded you and Ligeia into the rover and we undocked from the shuttle. Then we docked with this rover so we could all ride back together. I figured it best so there would be more eyes on our 'leader,'" he said, making air quotes. "Now we're on our way back to the colony."

"I've already radioed the colony," Pala said, squeezing Delphine's fingers. "I've told them all about how Ligeia drugged and kidnapped you." She turned her gaze to Ligeia and a stony look crossed her face. "She'll have much to answer for when we get back."

"But there's so much more!" Delphine said, her voice sounded groggy and more like a croak after her ordeal. She started from the beginning and told the trio everything she'd learned. How Ligeia had poisoned her with nightshade. About Leah and the murder of the astronauts on the Sirena. How the Sirena was still in orbit and Leah and Ligeia had been communicating with it for years. The lies told to Earth about what happened on the Sirena. Ligeia's plan to send Delphine back to Earth so they would stop trying to interfere with the colony. That the colony was never meant to be an all-female colony. How Leah had manipulated and coerced the original colonists.

When she'd finished her story, she felt the energy flow out of her like water down a shower drain. The words had tumbled out of her so fast, she was out of breath, and the pain in her leg was getting worse. Pala helped Delphine lie back on the bench seat and removed a first aid pack from a small compartment in the rover's wall. She dug through the pack and pulled out a tiny case holding two tablets. Delphine recognized them as a common, plant-based sleeping aid used by many of the colonists. Pala placed the tablets on Delphine's tongue and she felt the fizzy sensation as they melted into nothing inside her mouth.

"Rest now, daughter," she said, kissing the back of Delphine's hand.

Relief flooded over her as she closed her eyes. She had done it. Survived the whole harrowing ordeal. Unearthed the truth of what was going on behind the scenes in her colony and helped stop the madwoman at the helm of the ship. She breathed deep, allowing the calming breath to ease the tension in her muscles. Change would come to the colony now. Things would be different.

She felt the medication taking effect, removing the dull ache from her leg and making her thoughts peaceful and wobbly. Smiling, she allowed sleep to overtake her and anxiously awaited her dreams, where she would see Aura again.

CHAPTER 32

"Are you ready to do this?" Rho asked, winking at Delphine.

"I think so," she said, nervous flutters of energy dancing around in her stomach as she typed the predetermined message into the computer screen.

It had been fourteen days since she, Pala, and the twins had returned to the colony with a restrained Ligeia in tow after their ordeal at the shuttle. Delphine had been on a strict healing schedule in the medical wing since they got back. Fortunately, the break in her leg was only a small fracture and would heal completely in a few weeks. She was now up and moving around with her leg in a cast.

The effects of the nightshade were hard to shake. It took several days for her body to rid itself of the substance. The medics told her she was lucky it hadn't killed her based on the amount of the chemical they found in her bloodwork. The plants Ligeia had grown in the private council cultivation tent were immediately destroyed and the tent was opened up to the rest of the colonists, allowing them first-time access to such treats as lemons, passion fruit, and watermelon.

As soon as Delphine was well enough to attend, the colonists held a meeting in the Atrium to discuss next steps. Delphine recounted her experience and everything Ligeia had admitted to. The colonists were particularly unsettled by the discussion of what had happened to the male children born early in the colony's history.

Restrained and stripped of her council robes, Ligeia was there to watch, as were the rest of the council members. Chin jutted upward in defiance, Ligeia sat tall and proud, never daring to glance at Delphine as she told her story. Ligeia was allowed a rebuttal but refused to speak and the meeting moved on.

Rho had saved the holograph from the space probe on his tablet and played it for the colonists. One of the second-gens actually fainted when the holographic man appeared in front of them. The truth about how Ligeia and her mother had not communicated with Earth for over seven decades was a tough pill to swallow for many of the colonists. Rhayn had to step in front of several angry colonists asking for Ligeia's head.

They decided that Ligeia and the rest of the council members, who had most certainly known about the deceit, as well as Ligeia's daughter, Lara, would each have a trial, deliberated on by a jury of twelve colonists chosen at random. The jury would decide the fate of their disgraced rulers based on the evidence presented to them.

At the meeting, the colonists had decided to hold another election, this time, allowing many people to run, replacing the council of five with a ruling council of twelve elected members. They were to have representatives from each of the generations, as well as representatives from all the work programs, including miners, medics, mechanics, and cultivation workers. After the realization that Leah had made up the three laws of Xanadu and tricked her fellow colonists into believing they had come from Earth, it was decided that the etchings of the laws on the great wall of the Atrium would be removed.

Many of the colonists had dropped by the medical wing to visit Delphine and encourage her to run for one of the new council member spots. She was still undecided.

Rho's gender was no longer a secret and Delphine could see an obvious change in her dear friend. He no longer stood to the side, eyes focused on the floor, trying not to be noticed. He stood tall, proud of his identity, and he was much more outgoing. Rhayn was so proud of her brother and never missed an opportunity to retell the story of how he had stopped Ligeia from sending Delphine into space and single-handedly detained her in her wild state of mind.

In fact, he had become famous among the colonists overnight. Before this ordeal, many of the women on Titan had never considered what life would be like if the colony weren't all female. Now that they had Rho to show them that male colonists were not to be feared, they often followed him around, asking questions and watching his reactions.

"It actually makes me really uncomfortable," he'd confessed to Delphine one day when he came to visit her in the medical wing.

The all-female birthing policy would be abandoned as well and going forward, there would be no more gender typing of embryos for procreation. Rhea, the twins' mother, actually cried when the colonists decided on this. Rhayn told Delphine that Rhea had been worried for so long about Rho's identity that it had become hard for her to function. Now, she could finally relax knowing her son would not be in any danger at Xanadu.

It was also decided that communications with Earth should resume as soon as possible. Now that Ligeia no longer had control of the communications array at the colony, they were free to send radio signals to Earth. At the meeting, one of the colonists, a second-gen named Aeria, suggested that Delphine be the one to compose the first message.

She had been humbled by the nomination but unsure if she was up to the task. The twins offered to help and it was voted on by the colonists that Delphine, Rhayn, and Rho would create and send the first message to Earth in over seven decades.

As Delphine stared at the console in front of her, her nerves mounted. She and the twins had spent hours debating what they should say. Would they send a long message detailing the entire story? Or would a short message be more appropriate? Something to confirm they were still there, still alive, and ready to talk again?

They had opted for the latter and had come up with something short and sweet. Now, the three were standing at the control console inside the communications building on the north side of the colony complex. They had run diagnostic checks on the antenna array and found everything was in good working order. They had typed their message into the computer and the only thing left to do was press send.

"You should do it," Rhayn said, gesturing at Delphine. "You should be the one to send it."

Delphine shook her head. "I don't know. I'm nervous."

"Why are you nervous?" Rho asked.

"It's just that..." Delphine shrugged. "Once we do this. Once we communicate with Earth again, we can't take it back. You know? Once we send this, they will *know* we are here. They will want more information. They will ask us all the questions. And they may even come back here. Maybe Ligeia was right... maybe we don't want Earth to return."

Rho tilted his head to the side, considering this. "The thing is," he said at last, "we'll never know if we don't do it."

"That's right," Rhayn agreed. "We can't be afraid of change, Delphine. We came from Earth. They are our people. We were never meant to be cut off from them. It's time we reconnect that bond. Who knows? It might be amazing!"

Delphine smiled, always impressed with Rhayn's ability to brighten any situation. "Okay," she said and moved to send the message.

"Wait," Rho said, gently touching her wrist to stop her. "We typed in the message, but we didn't sign it off."

"Sign it off?" Rhayn asked.

"Sure," Rho said. "Every radio message has a sign-off so the recipient knows who sent it and that the full message was received."

"Okay," Delphine said, pursing her lips as she thought. "What about this?"

She pulled up the message draft and added one more line to it.

"It's perfect!" Rhayn said, clapping her hands.

Rho nodded and smiled. "Yes, it's perfect."

The trio took one last look at their carefully crafted message, capped off by Delphine's sign-off:

Friends on Earth, we are the Titan Girls of Xanadu, signing off.

Delphine took a deep breath, smiled, and hit send.

Acknowledgments

To my husband, Tim, who is my most vocal supporter and the easiest-to-please beta reader out there. I am grateful for everything you do for my writing career and for our family.

To Jack and Lilly, who amaze me daily with your charm and wit. I like to think you got some of your brainpower from me.

To my editor, Nikki, who truly does help me build better stories.

To all my friends and family members all over the world. Thank you for your support and love during this crazy writing journey.

To my readers, social media followers, and newsletter subscribers. Thank you. I am truly grateful for you.

Made in the USA
Middletown, DE
20 July 2022

69651964R00203